ALMOST THERE

A TWISTED TALE

ALMOST THERE

A TWISTED TALE

What if Tiana made a deal with the Shadow Man?

FARRAH ROCHON

DISNEP · HYPERION

Los Angeles • New York

For Jasmine Gabrielle,
my very favorite friend of Tiana's.
You'll always be the best princess.

—*F.R.*

Prologue
Tiana

New Orleans, 1912

"Daddy! Daddy!"

The little girl ran as fast as her wobbly five-year-old legs could carry her, irrepressible joy shining in her dark brown eyes. Her pigtails bounced gaily, the ribbons tied around them precariously close to flying away with the brisk breeze blowing in from the pond.

James stooped down to one knee, his arms open wide, waiting for his little ray of sunshine to rush into his embrace.

"Come on, baby girl. I got you." He scooped her up and spun her around. The hem of the green-and-yellow dress his wife, Eudora, had made for their daughter, Tiana, fluttered as they twirled around.

"You wanna dance with your daddy?" James asked as he set her on his hip and playfully pinched her chubby cheek.

"Yeah, Daddy. Let's dance!"

He and his sweet girl rocked back and forth to the drumbeat of the band playing in the center of Congo Square.

Their family had gathered for the annual neighborhood picnic to celebrate the arrival of Mardi Gras, the biggest party on the face of the earth—and the most jubilant time of the year here in their hometown of New Orleans.

Blankets of every color and fabric adorned the square, each representing a family that had come to contribute to this beloved ritual. The air was fragrant with the aroma of home-cooked creole food, and the chatter of neighbors catching up with old friends competed with the music from the brass band.

"No, Daddy. I wanna dance like you do with Mama," Tiana said.

James threw his head back and laughed. "And just how do I dance with your mama?"

"Like this." She slid down his legs and placed her tiny

feet on the tops of his much bigger ones. Then she reached for his hands. "Here, hold mine," she said.

James's hands swallowed hers as he wrapped them around her fingers.

"Is this right?" he asked.

"Yep." Her pigtails bobbed with her emphatic nod. "Now we move like this!"

She swayed her hips from side to side, her dress rocking like a bell. She stared up at him with a cheerful, gappy smile. Her two front teeth had fallen out just a few days ago.

James looked over at Eudora, trying to catch her attention so that she could see her daughter in action. But his wife was busy laying out the feast he'd cooked that morning and entertaining the friends and family who were steadily dropping by to offer their congratulations on the new house he and Eudora had just purchased in the Ninth Ward.

It wasn't the fanciest place, but it was a lot better than the one-room apartment they'd lived in for the past five years. There was a yard with enough room for a garden in the back, and a porch that James couldn't wait to spend time on. A good, sturdy house that a man could be proud to raise a family in.

He looked down at his baby girl, imagining the years of

happy memories to come in their new home, and his heart swelled with joy.

"What's going on here?" Eudora asked as she sidled up to them.

"I'm dancing with Daddy the way he dances with you!" Tiana beamed.

"Is that so?" his wife asked.

"Yeah! Does this make me a grown-up?" Tiana asked.

"Don't you worry about growing up anytime soon." James chuckled. "I like my baby girl just as she is right now."

Tiana pulled her hands away from his and jumped off his feet. She rushed over to her mother and shoved her toward James.

"Now you do it!" Tiana ordered. "Come on, Mama and Daddy. Dance."

James held a hand out to his wife. "You heard the child," he said.

Shaking her head at their daughter's antics, Eudora placed her hand in his. She tugged Tiana close to her side, and together, the three of them rocked to the music.

Gratitude filled his chest, wedging into every corner and crevice. He had never asked for a perfect life, but somehow he'd been blessed with one anyway.

* * *

New Orleans, 1917

Tiana struck a match on the edge of the table and used it to light the wicks of the half-melted tapered candles she'd found in the drawer of the kitchen bureau. She'd wrapped tinfoil around the bases to catch the dripping wax, but now she wasn't so sure about that. It took away from the romantic ambience she was trying to create.

"Can we come in now?" her mother called from behind their bedroom door.

"Not yet," Tiana said. "Give me just a minute."

She ran over to the stove and flipped over the beignets she'd set to frying a few minutes earlier, then used the stepping stool to retrieve a plate from the cupboard. Give her a few more years and she wouldn't need this stool to reach the upper cabinets. Like her daddy always joked, she was sprouting up like a weed in his vegetable garden.

Tiana scooped up the hot beignets, added a little sugar on top, and took them over to the kitchen table. She filled a mason jar with water, then added the flowers that she'd picked on her walk home from school. She set it on the table in between the two candles.

"Perfect," Tiana whispered. "Okay, y'all come out now!" she called. Her entire body vibrated with excitement as she waited to see their faces.

"Happy anniversary!" Tiana screamed when her mama and daddy entered the kitchen.

"Well, looka here! Did you make beignets, baby girl?"

"I sure did," Tiana said, proudly lifting her chin in the air.

"These look better than any I've had down in the French Quarter," her daddy said. "Between my gumbo and this girl's beignets, I say we can open ourselves up a restaurant one of these days. What you think, Eudora?"

"I think I want to eat my beignets before they get cold," her mother replied.

They all sat at the table and gorged on the fried doughnut squares until there were none left. Once they were done, her daddy sat back in his chair and rubbed his flat stomach.

"That was some fine beignets, Tiana. You really do have talent in that kitchen."

"Thank you, Daddy!" Tiana's smile grew so wide that her cheeks started to hurt.

James reached across the table and took Eudora by the hand. "How about an anniversary dance?"

They pushed their chairs back from the table and strolled to the center of the kitchen, between the stove and her mother's sewing machine. Her daddy gathered her mama in his arms, and Mama laid her head against his broad chest as they began to sway.

"How are y'all gonna dance with no music?" Tiana asked. She set her elbow on the table and rested her chin in her upturned palm. "Of course, if we had a gramophone, I could play music for y'all to dance to."

"We don't need no expensive gramophone to hear music," her daddy said. "In this family, we make our own music."

He started to hum a tune that made her mother blush like a schoolgirl.

Tiana put both elbows up on the table and smiled as she watched her parents rock slowly from side to side, their eyes closed and both singing softly, in their own world.

New Orleans, 1921

"Tiana, are you still in that kitchen?"

"Umm . . . maybe," Tiana called over her shoulder. She blew at the steam rising up from the spoonful of gumbo she'd just taken from the pot and quickly slurped it up.

Her mouth twisted in a bemused frown as she tried to dissect the flavors hitting her tongue.

"I taste the cayenne and the roux. And the smoke flavor from the neck bones is there. What am I missing?" Tiana murmured.

"Little girl!"

Tiana jumped and turned at her mother's call.

Eudora carried a bolt of fabric from her storage room in the rear of the house and dropped it next to her sewing machine. She plopped a hand on her hip and regarded her daughter with a stern, pointed look.

"There is nothing more to do with that gumbo other than to let it cook," she said. "Now go finish up your school-work so you can be done by dinner."

"I will, Mama," Tiana said. "I just need to figure this out. I don't know why I didn't have Daddy write down his recipes before he left. I'm gonna have him do just that the minute he gets back home."

"I think your daddy will have other things on his mind when he finally comes back home," her mother said. "Besides, he never writes down a recipe. It's always just a little bit of this and a little bit of that."

Eudora walked over to the stove and gestured to the spoon Tiana held. "Let me have a taste."

Tiana scooped up a helping of the brown liquid and held it up to her mother's lips. After taking a sip, Eudora pointed to the cabinet that held the spices.

"Sprinkle in a bit of that ground sassafras," she instructed.

Tiana did as she was told, then stirred up the gumbo. She took a taste, then smiled at her mama.

"Your daddy's not the only one who knows how to cook, you know? He just likes doing it more than I do." Eudora took the spoon from Tiana's hand and bumped her with her hip. "Now go on and finish that homework."

A half hour later, Tiana and her mother sat at their small kitchen table, enjoying her daddy's signature dish. Even though gumbo was more of a Sunday meal, Tiana had decided to make it on this random Tuesday. She just wanted to feel closer to her daddy.

He'd been away for over five months now, fighting a war in a far-off place that Tiana had only read about in her schoolbooks.

"It's a good thing I made a big pot of gumbo," Tiana said. "Because I'm going for seconds."

"Well, if you're getting seconds, so am I," her mother said with a laugh.

Just as Tiana pushed away from the table, there was a knock at the door.

"You get the gumbo, I'll get the door," Eudora said.

Tiana carried their empty bowls into the kitchen and heaped another helping of gumbo into each of them. With one bowl in each hand, she turned back toward the table.

She stopped short at the sight of her mother standing in the doorway.

Two uniformed men stood on their front porch, their

caps in their hands and solemn frowns on their faces. She heard her mother gasp, then let out a God-awful scream Tiana knew she would hear in her nightmares for years to come. Her mother crumpled to the ground.

And the bowls of gumbo shattered at Tiana's feet.

1

Tiana

Lafayette Cemetery, New Orleans
1926
Mardi Gras

The jubilant sounds of Mardi Gras resonated throughout New Orleans as vibrant, colorful floats wound their way along the wide avenues of the city. Flambeau carriers hoisted their torches high, lighting up the deep purple sky and making way for the costumed revelers who danced in the street.

But within the dark, secluded recesses of Lafayette Cemetery, it was eerily quiet.

Tiana's tiny green body trembled as she raced down a narrow alleyway, the cemetery's crumbly stone catacombs lined up like sentries on either side of her. Her heart pounded against her chest, the *thump thump thump* ringing more loudly in her ears with each inch of the pavement she traversed. She had no idea where she was going; she just knew she had to get away from the shadows that were hot on her heels.

Tiana clutched the amulet her friend Ray had shoved into her hands moments before, treating it with the same care as her daddy's Distinguished Service Cross from the army.

Oh, if only her daddy could see her right now. What would he think? How would she explain this mess she'd gotten herself into? Wishing on an evening star for her restaurant and getting mixed up in some nefarious dealings. Falling for a prince. Becoming friends with a gator and a firefly along the way.

And now running through the cemetery like the fires of hell were at her feet, fleeing from something she barely understood herself.

Her conscience pleaded with her to go back and make sure her firefly friend was okay, but her instincts told her she couldn't. Not yet. She had to hide. And she had to keep this amulet out of the Shadow Man's clutches until she figured out what was going on.

Tiana sprinted around a corner and galloped toward a menacing stone facade. Just as she reached it, an other-worldly shadow appeared out of nowhere.

Terror robbed her of her ability to think. To breathe. All she could do was quake in fear as the terrifying blob loomed overhead, its spindly fingers reaching for her.

This was it. She was caught.

But she never gave up on anything without a fight.

Holding the amulet as far away as her tiny arms could stretch, she glared at the shadow and issued a warning.

"Back off, or I'm gonna break this thing into a million pieces!"

"Don't!"

Tiana went still. She recognized that voice.

Facilier.

The Vodou practitioner was known for prowling about the French Quarter, reading palms and hustling poor unwitting souls with his card tricks. Everyone in New Orleans called him the Shadow Man due to his dabbling in dark magic—and other shady dealings, no doubt.

"Where are you, Shadow Man?"

"You have something that belongs to me," Facilier said as he emerged from the darkness. "And I want it back."

"No." Tiana clutched the amulet against her chest. "Ray said to keep this away from you no matter what. He wouldn't have told me to do so without good reason." She straightened her shoulders and silently prayed her voice wouldn't quiver when she spoke. "I'm not giving you a thing."

His lips curled in an evil snarl. But then his expression changed, an air of nonchalance replacing his impatience. He buffed his nails on his lapel and observed her with blithe disregard.

"I'm a businessman, after all. I understand how this game is played." His brow arched in inquiry. "What do you say to a trade?"

"I'm not interested in anything you have to offer. I won't—"

A blast of wind caught Tiana unawares, followed by a cloud of glittery purple dust that swirled around her. An odd sensation shot through her like a bolt of lightning, nearly bringing her to her wobbly knees.

She blinked. Hard.

"Wha—what's happening?"

She stretched out her arms—her *human* arms—and wiggled her fingers. She was human again!

Tiana peered down in stunned delight at the sparkling white silk draping her body. The rhinestone- and pearl-studded gown she now wore was unlike anything she'd ever owned.

When she lifted her head, she gasped at her

surroundings. Tiana twirled around in a slow circle, mes-merized by the glitz and glamour of a place she had only seen in her nightly dreams.

The old sugar mill she'd had her heart set on buying for years was no longer decrepit and falling apart. The floors gleamed underneath her feet, shining so bright they nearly blinded her. Brilliant crystal chandeliers hung high above her head, illuminating a massive dining room that was crowded with patrons. Men in suit jackets and women wearing their Sunday best sat at cloth-covered tables adorned with extravagant centerpieces and sparkling china. Everyone seemed to be having a grand time, enjoying rich, fragrant dishes that smelled like the food Tiana used to cook with her daddy.

"Where am I?" she whispered.

"You know where you are. You've been dreaming about owning this restaurant for years. And it can all be yours, Tiana."

"But . . . but how?"

"Why don't you hand me that talisman," Facilier said. "And I'll fill you in on all the details."

Tiana stared at her hand in perplexed awe as it extended the pendant toward Facilier of its own accord, as if she had no control over it. With a jolt, she snapped herself out of the daze and yanked the pendant away.

"No," she said. She shook her head, ridding herself of the vestiges of whatever trance Facilier had put her in. She had to remember to keep her guard up around this one.

His fevered gaze remained on the amulet, amplifying the alarm bells ringing in Tiana's head. She had no idea what this pendant held, but the Shadow Man wanted it something fierce. Which meant he could never have it.

"I'm not giving you anything," she reiterated.

"Not even in exchange for your restaurant?"

"I . . . I can still get my restaurant. I just have to keep working for it."

"But why continue to toil when my friends on the other side can get you your restaurant just like that?" He snapped his fingers. "All I have to do is ask them on your behalf. Come on, Tiana. You're almost there. Let's make this deal, and I'll get you across the finish line."

"No!" she said more forcefully. He still towered over her, even though she was now human, but Tiana refused to be intimidated. "I don't need to rely on help from the likes of you, Shadow Man. And I don't want anybody to *give* me my restaurant. I'm gonna *earn* it, just like my daddy taught me."

At the mention of her daddy, Facilier's eyes lit up. He opened his palm and blew another cloud of iridescent dust into her face.

Tiana's head jerked back as she was once again plunged into a dream world. It took her a moment to find her bearings as she tried to navigate the foggy edges of her mind. She stood just inside the doorway of a state-of-the-art kitchen, like the ones she'd seen in magazines. Her mouth watered at the delicious aroma wafting up from the large copper pots that occupied the gas stove. Waiters in sharp tuxedos flittered about the space, grabbing plates filled with artfully arranged food and carrying them out the door.

She took a tentative step forward. With that one step, her body began to move about the kitchen, not walking, but gliding, as if on a cloud. Through the sea of cooks and waitstaff, Tiana noticed a figure that looked eerily familiar. The man stood at a stove at the far end of the kitchen. He stirred a big cooking spoon around a gumbo pot she instantly recognized. She couldn't make out the face, but she would have known those broad shoulders and muscled arms anywhere.

"Daddy?" Tiana gasped.

"That's right," the Shadow Man whispered. "It's your dear old daddy."

"What is he . . . ? How . . . ?"

This couldn't be real. It had to be a figment of her imagination.

The figure turned, and Tiana let out a sharp breath. It *was* him.

Joy burst inside her chest as she took off running, her arms stretched out wide in front of her. Everyone else in the kitchen disappeared. It was just she and her beloved father. It had been so, *so* long since she'd seen him, other than in the countless dreams she'd had over the years.

But just as she got near to him, he vanished.

"Daddy, no!" she shouted.

"Ah, ah, ah." The Shadow Man's loathsome voice rang out in her ears, once again knocking her out of her daze.

Tiana glared at him as he stood before her with that sinister smirk on his face. He wasn't playing fair, toying with her emotions in such a cruel way. But then again, what did she expect from a no-good hustler like Facilier?

"What do you say to my deal now, Tiana? You can work hard, scrimp and save; maybe you'll get your restaurant in another fifty years. But there is *nothing* you can do that can bring your daddy back to life. You need *me* for that." The Shadow Man shook his head. "Tragic what happened to him. James was a good man. He didn't want to leave his family the way he did."

"You keep his name out of your mouth," Tiana hissed.

Facilier shrugged his bony shoulders as he casually searched for nonexistent dirt underneath his fingernails. "Suit yourself. It's a shame that you would turn down the chance to see your daddy again. Makes one wonder if you ever loved him at all."

"Don't you dare!" Tiana yelled. "He was everything to me."

"Then why won't you take me up on my offer?" Facilier said. "All I have to do is ask my friends on the other side for a little assistance, and you and your daddy will be making gumbo again. Think about your mama, and what it would mean to have her husband back."

Tiana closed her eyes and conjured an image of her mama and daddy dancing in the middle of the kitchen of their small but comfortable home in the Ninth Ward. The love beaming from them warmed her like rays from the bright summer sun.

"That's . . . it's impossible," she said. "He's gone."

"What's impossible to you is child's play for my friends on the other side. They have powers you can never under-stand. The favor will carry a small price, of course, but that's to be expected. It will be hardly anything, if I'm being honest."

Her eyes blinked open.

"I don't believe you," Tiana said. "My daddy has been gone for years. How can they just bring him back?"

"Don't worry your pretty little head about the

particulars. That's a problem for me and my friends on the other side to solve. Just trust me, Tiana."

Trust him? Her eyes flared, his ridiculous statement bringing her back to earth. After all he'd put her and her friends through . . .

"You're the last person I'd ever trust." She held the amulet high above her head, preparing to smash it to the ground.

But Facilier was quick. He stretched out his hand, releasing a bloodcurdling scream.

2

Facilier

"Just . . . just wait a second there, Tiana," Facilier implored after he'd collected himself. He forced out a chuckle. "Be careful with that. It's an heirloom."

He tried to project an air of cool indifference despite the rampant desperation pulsing through his veins. That amulet was the key to everything. As long as it held a sample of Prince Naveen's blood, its designated wearer could take on the prince's appearance. Without it, Facilier's ploy to gain control of Eli LaBouff's fortune through his lovestruck daughter, Charlotte, would crumble.

But even more important, *he* would have to pay the

high price his friends on the other side had attached to it.

Tiana held his very life in her hands.

Facilier clutched his fists at his sides, wishing he could wrap his hands around that gutless Lawrence's neck. Striking up an alliance with the prince's incompetent valet had been more than just a miscalculation on his part—it could prove to be a deadly mistake.

Lawrence had allowed Facilier's treasured talisman to fall into Tiana's hands, and because of that, he now found himself in a position of weakness, having to make a bargain with this slip of a girl.

He should have known Tiana wouldn't take the easy way out when it came to her restaurant. She would never take pride in something she hadn't earned. People like her suffered under the foolish notion that their hard work made them better—made them more deserving than those who were smart enough to take advantage of life's shortcuts.

People like him.

Even after turning down his offer to get her that restaurant, Facilier had been certain that dangling the prospect of seeing her father again would do the trick. Bringing James back was a tall order and would come at a high price, possibly more than he'd ever had to pay to his friends on the other side, but he had been willing to do it. He was willing to do just about anything to secure that talisman.

And Tiana had thrown his offer back in his face.

He hadn't wanted to resort to this, but she left him no other choice. If he couldn't sweet-talk her into returning his property, intimidation was his only recourse.

"Before you turn down my proposition, there is still the matter of your little froggy prince to discuss," Facilier said.

"Naveen?" Her eyes widened.

It was exactly the reaction he'd hoped for. He had a feeling that she'd fallen in love with that prince.

It would be her downfall.

"Where is he?" Tiana asked. "Where's Naveen?"

"Don't you worry about where he is. You need to think about *what* he is. You might be willing to give up *your* dreams, but will you give up his in the process?" Facilier continued. "If you want your precious Naveen to ever become human again, you'd better give me what's mine."

"You're lying." Tiana shook her head. "All Naveen has to do to turn human again is kiss a princess, and Charlotte LaBouff is a princess, because her daddy is the king of Mardi Gras."

"Come now, Tiana." Facilier tsked. "You're smarter than that. You know Miss LaBouff isn't a real princess. And neither are you. If Naveen doesn't kiss himself a *real* princess by midnight, he will live forever as a frog."

"No." Tiana gasped.

"Yes." He detected the tiniest signal that she was starting to waver, and pounced. "But you can save him, Tiana. You can get everything you ever wanted. You and your prince can—"

He stopped.

What was he thinking?

Naveen was his ticket to Eli LaBouff, the most powerful man in New Orleans. Now that the scheme he'd crafted with Lawrence had fallen apart, Facilier needed the real Naveen to continue a courtship with LaBouff's daughter. An eventual marriage between those two was still his best shot at gaining control over LaBouff's money.

He should have focused on the prince from the very beginning instead of partnering with that spineless Lawrence. That devil-may-care attitude of his made Naveen an easy one to manipulate. As long as he could keep getting a drop of Naveen's blood every so often, he could control him.

But that would never happen if Naveen and Tiana were together.

"*Almost* everything you ever wanted, I should say. Here's my offer," Facilier started. "You hand me that talisman. In return, I'll bring your daddy back, *and* I'll make your little prince human again." He held up a finger. "There's just one thing. Once the spell is broken, Naveen won't remember a single thing about any of this. And if you want him to *remain* a human, the little dalliance between you two can be no more."

"Are you saying—"

"I'm saying that you must forfeit the love of your sweet Prince Naveen in return for him being human again."

She gasped. "But . . . but that's not fair."

"Life isn't fair," Facilier snapped.

Where was the fairness in what he now faced? He would have to strike yet another bargain with his friends on the other side in order to deliver everything he'd promised her. The price would undoubtedly be high, putting him in even deeper debt to them.

And what was *she* sacrificing? Her little infatuation with that dunderheaded prince?

He was doing her a favor. According to Lawrence, Naveen was useless. A broke, lazy burden on his parents. He would only hold Tiana back. Without Naveen weighing her down—and with the help of her father, once Facilier bargained for James's return—Tiana would have her restaurant in no time at all.

Compare that to what he was getting out of this deal. Nothing.

But wait a minute. Maybe there *was* more in it for him.

Facilier thought about the small vial in his jacket pocket that contained a tincture he'd whipped up for some of his more stubborn clientele. It made those who consumed it more malleable to his wishes, at least for a little while. If he could convince Tiana to add a bit of it to her gumbo, he could manipulate all who ate it into giving him whatever valuables they had in their possession.

Facilier's lips curled up in a smile as something else occurred to him. Tiana and LaBouff's daughter, Charlotte, were thick as thieves. It stood to reason that Eli LaBouff would become a loyal patron of any restaurant Tiana eventually opened. If he could get even a drop of this tincture into LaBouff himself . . . it could be another avenue to get to the sugar baron should his plan with Naveen fall through. Another way to fill his coffers. A fail-safe.

The possibilities were too delicious to contemplate.

But first he had to convince Tiana.

"Before we go any further, I'll need to consult my friends on the other side," Facilier said. "You understand, don't you?"

He closed his eyes, leaving a short sliver open so that he could keep Tiana in his sights. Then he began to speak gibberish, yammering like a baby. He would make the bargain with his friends on the other side once he returned to his shop, but Tiana had to believe he was making the deal for her daddy here and now. He put on a stellar show, if he did say so himself.

"Ah. Ah, yes," Facilier said.

"What are they saying?" Tiana asked.

He held up a finger, silencing her.

"Oh. Oh, of course. Yes, that's very reasonable," Facilier murmured. "That shouldn't be a problem at all."

He added more gibberish for good measure, then made a production of releasing himself from his trance. He belonged on a vaudeville stage with that performance.

Facilier settled his gaze on Tiana once again. "My friends on the other side have named their price. You are very lucky, Tiana. It's hardly anything at all."

He produced the vial from his pocket.

"In return for making your froggy prince human again, and for bringing your dear father, James, back to life, all you have to do is add a small drop of this potion to your gumbo once you inevitably open your restaurant. After all your *hard work* helps you to do so."

Tiana was instantly suspicious. "What's in it?"

"Well . . ." He needed to think fast. "Well, you . . . you know better than anyone that gumbo was your father's signature dish. I had some of James's gumbo a time or two myself." He rubbed his stomach. "Delicious stuff."

"What does that have to do with whatever is in that little bottle there?"

"This contains the magic that will keep your daddy

alive. What better way to do that than through his gumbo? You see, Tiana, that's just how my friends on the other side operate. It's poetic in a way, isn't it?"

"How do I even know you were talking to these friends of yours a minute ago?" she asked. "Why should I trust you at all, Shadow Man?"

This was exactly why *he* couldn't trust *her* around Naveen. She was too smart for her own good.

"Because we can both benefit from this, Tiana. You have something I want, and I can provide things that you want."

"How do I know whatever you have in that vial won't kill anyone who drinks it?"

Facilier chuckled. "If that's what my friends wanted to do, they could have done that a long time ago." He tipped the vial to his lips, pretending to take a sip. "It's harmless," he said.

"What is it supposed to do exactly?"

Facilier held up his hands. "I don't question my friends, Tiana, and neither should you. Their magic is a thousand times more powerful than mine. If they say that a tiny drop of this in your gumbo will keep your father alive, then you need to trust them." Sensing the need for extra insurance, Facilier added, "And don't forget about Naveen. You're saving him, along with all the people you love. You can make sure no harm comes to any of them, Tiana."

Her eyes widened with alarm. "What do you mean by that? *All* the people I love?"

"Accidents happen all the time." Facilier hunched his shoulders.

"Are you threatening me?" she asked, her voice once again strident with staunch defiance.

"I'm *warning* you," he snapped. "Things will get very, *very* ugly if you choose to ignore such a generous offer." He could tell she was starting to waver. He waved a hand, and one by one, phantom versions of Tiana's loved ones appeared in the air: her mother, that maddening prince, the LaBouff girl, the neighbors she had grown up with. And one by one, the figures crumbled, lying lifeless on the invisible floor. Tiana gasped as the apparitions disappeared. Facilier moved in closer. "So, do we have a deal?"

"You're not giving me much of a choice, are you? Either I make this deal with you, or innocent people will be hurt."

"We all have choices to make, Tiana. The question is whether or not we're prepared to face the consequences of those choices."

She defiantly thrust her chin in the air and held her shoulders back, but Facilier saw through her bravado. He was back in control. She might have held his life in her hands, but she didn't know that. That was his ace—Tiana's not knowing just how much power that talisman possessed.

"What's it gonna be, Tiana?"

She glared at him with burning anger in her eyes, but Facilier knew he'd backed her into a corner.

"If I have to give up Naveen, there are several things I want in return," Tiana said.

Even when she had no way out, she still drove a hard bargain. In a way, he could admire that. It was too bad she was such a goody two-shoes. With her gumption, Tiana could help him take over this entire city.

"What is it you want?" he asked.

"You have to promise that my family will be safe. I don't want any harm coming to them." She hesitated for a moment, then said, "And you have to help my two friends Louis and Ray. Louis wants to be human so he can play with a jazz band in the music halls here in N'awlins. Either your friends make that happen, or no deal.

"And Ray . . . well, I would feel better knowing that he's close by, where I can keep an eye on him. That he's safe—"

Facilier interrupted her. "I'm afraid that won't be necessary." He almost felt sorry for Tiana as her forehead dipped in a confused frown. Almost.

"What do you mean?" she asked.

"Remember what I said about our choices having consequences?" He arched one brow. "Well, your little firefly sealed his fate when he stole my talisman."

Her face fell as understanding dawned. Tiana clutched her hands to her chest. "Oh, Ray," she cried.

"But the gator?" Facilier continued with a shrug. "I'll have a talk with my friends, but I'm pretty sure I can make that happen."

"You can assure me that whatever is in that vial won't harm anyone? That it's simply the magic that will keep my daddy alive and keep my family safe?"

"There's nothing simple about this magic, except for your part in this, of course. You just remember to put a drop of it in your gumbo, and no harm will come to anyone. And you and your dear father will be cooking once again." Facilier squeezed his hands at his sides as he leaned forward, his excitement on the verge of overwhelming. "So, Tiana, do we have a deal?"

She pressed her lips together.

"For dear old dad?" he continued.

For a moment, a streak of true terror rushed through him at the reluctance he saw in her eyes.

But then Tiana stuck out the hand that held his talisman. "Deal."

3

Tiana

The Ninth Ward, New Orleans
Thursday, February 1927
Five days before Mardi Gras

Tiana couldn't think of a better way to wake up than to the aroma of salty bacon wafting through the air. She sucked in a deep breath and blew it out with a sigh.

The promise of a hearty breakfast of buttery grits, fluffy eggs, and thick, crispy bacon beckoned, but she remained tucked underneath her covers with her eyes closed. She basked in the feel of the warm sun caressing her face as it shone bright through her windows. The jaybirds flittering about outside chirped songs of cheer, a happy soundtrack for what was sure to be a stellar day.

"Tiana, baby. Come to breakfast."

Tiana's eyes popped opened and a smile as wide as the Mississippi River stretched across her face.

"I'm on my way, Daddy," she called.

It had been nearly a year since the Shadow Man made good on his promise to bring her daddy back to them. The sound of that deep baritone echoing throughout the house never failed to send grateful chills skittering along her skin.

She sat up in bed and threw the well-worn quilt off her legs. Stretching her hands high above her head, Tiana rocked her neck back and forth, working out the kinks. Maybe she should put new pillows on her shopping list the next time she and Mama visited Krauss Department Store.

Or maybe not. These pillows had served her just fine for years.

She had bigger plans in store for the profit she made from the humble restaurant she and her daddy had opened three months ago. Every cent she earned went back into her savings. Eventually, she would earn enough to buy a larger building to house the grand restaurant she had always dreamed of opening.

Not that she wasn't grateful for the supper club; it was a proper stepping stone. And it really was a feat that she and her father had been able to get the cozy little spot and open up so quickly. But Tiana had her sights on something bigger, and no one was getting in her way this time.

Buoyed by the thought of her future, she hopped up from the bed and ran over to her bureau. She pulled out a yellow-and-white gingham dress along with a matching yellow ribbon to tie back her hair. Once done, she left her room in search of that bacon she'd been smelling.

"Well, look who decided to make an appearance. Good morning," her mother said from where she sat behind a worn wooden table, working the hand crank on her Singer sewing machine.

"Good morning, Mama." Tiana walked up behind her and clamped her hands on her mother's shoulders. She leaned forward and planted a loud kiss on her cheek. "Is there any breakfast left? Please tell me there is."

Eudora nodded toward the stove, where a plate covered with tinfoil sat next to the dented copper teakettle that had taken up permanent residence on the stove now that her daddy's big gumbo pot was at the restaurant. Tiana walked over to it, lifted the tinfoil, and snatched a strip of bacon.

"Where's Daddy?" she asked.

"Out in the garden."

"Oh, shoot! I almost forgot," Tiana said. She grabbed another slice of bacon, then covered the plate back up.

"Aren't you gonna sit and eat?" her mother asked.

"I can't. I promised Daddy I would help pick some peppers and tomatoes for tonight. I'm working on a new recipe for my jambalaya, and I want to give it a test run before we open for supper." She looked at her mother with a raised brow. "You willing to play guinea pig later today?"

"Don't I always?" Eudora answered with a laugh. "Promise me you'll eat something more substantial soon, Tiana. You're too skinny."

"I promise," Tiana called as she lifted a black cloche from the hat rack near the door and secured it over her hair, sighing a little. The promises she made these days were so blissfully uncomplicated. It sort of made her wonder when the other shoe would drop.

Standing up straighter, Tiana walked outside, automatically shielding her eyes from the unforgiving sun. She dropped her hand when she realized it wasn't necessary. The sun still shone, but it was muted by a murky haze that hung in the air.

It was peculiar, to say the least. So close to the river, it wasn't all that strange to see a mist roll off the Mississippi early in the morning, but the fog typically lifted after a couple of hours.

She looked up at the sky, wondering if maybe a storm was coming.

Tiana snatched up one of the wicker baskets next to Daddy's rocker, then descended the back porch steps and made her way to the small garden behind the house. She paused for a moment as she came upon him, his large frame bent over a row of black soil.

Her heart expanded within her chest as a mixture of gratitude, wonderment, and profound love merged together, threatening to overwhelm her.

She still could not believe her daddy was here.

Despite her skepticism, it turned out that she *could* trust Dr. Facilier, at least when it came to holding up his end of their bargain. The day after Mardi Gras last year, her daddy had walked through their front door as if returning from a typical day's work. Her mother had greeted him as usual, with a hug and kiss on his cheek, not missing a beat.

Tiana smiled softly at the memory of running up to him and wrapping her arms around his large shoulders as she cried uncontrollably, unable to suppress her joy. Both her mama and daddy had stared at her as if she'd lost her ever-loving mind. But then they'd all burst out laughing, and that was that. Her family had been made whole again.

Tiana had decided then and there not to question whatever mystical forces Facilier had called upon in order to bring about her daddy's return. He was here and she was grateful for it. And she would never *ever* take the time she had with him for granted.

"How's it going, Daddy?" Tiana greeted as she sidled up to where he knelt between the rows of freshly tilled earth.

He looked over his shoulder and smiled that wide, handsome smile of his. "Mornin', baby girl. You had your breakfast?"

"I ate a little. I didn't wanna take too much time away from helping you harvest."

He opened his massive palm, revealing a collection of small green seeds. "I decided to get these limas in the ground. Gotta get them planted before that summer heat arrives. It won't be long now."

"Well, you stick to your lima beans and I'll start picking the peppers and tomatoes for my new signature jambalaya. I think I've finally got the recipe just the way I want it. It's gonna be a hit."

"Everything you make in that kitchen is spectacular. But, Tiana, you know you don't have to spend so much of your time there. Have some fun. Join your friends for a night out every once in a while. You planning on attending any Mardi Gras parties?"

Tiana did her best to hide her exasperation. She couldn't understand why her parents were so determined to see her flouncing about this city with her friends. As if she could afford to waste time on such frivolity. If the previous year had taught her anything, it was that you never knew when things might change. Better to focus on the things you could control, and the people you loved the most.

"I don't have time for parties and Mardi Gras balls, Daddy. I have a restaurant to run. And besides, we have to get ready for our own festivities."

He looked up over his shoulder again. "You remember what the J stands for in T&J's Supper Club, don't you? You're not the only one responsible for everything."

"I know." They were bona fide business partners, just as she'd always imagined. "But what kind of co-owner would I be if I skipped out on my duties to go frolicking around N'awlins?" She clamped her hand on his shoulder and gave it a squeeze. "This restaurant is *our* dream, which means we *both* have an obligation to it."

Her daddy patted her hand. His callused fingers were a testament to a life defined by long hours of hard work.

"I can handle things on my own every now and then, baby girl. Especially if it gives you the chance to paint the town red with your friends. Promise me you'll think about it."

"I'll think about it," Tiana said smoothly. "But now, I need to pick some tomatoes."

She balanced the basket on her hip as she strolled along the row of evenly spaced tomato vines. As she mulled over which looked ripest, her mind wandered to a place she seldom allowed it to go these days: a place where she was the kind of girl who attended parties and balls and soirees with her friends.

Not that she'd ever been all that much of a party girl. The last party she'd attended had been her best friend Charlotte LaBouff's Mardi Gras ball the year before, and even then she'd been there to serve up some of her famous beignets to the guests. The ball where she'd met Naveen . . .

Don't, Tiana chastised her errant imagination.

She knew better than to even think about him. She'd spent the better part of a year doing her best to avoid Naveen altogether. Unfortunately, that had become more difficult lately. He'd taken to joining Charlotte down at the supper club, which meant Tiana now spent even more of her time hiding away in the kitchen, too afraid to go out into the dining area to chat with her guests in case she ran into him.

You just have to come up with more creative ways to avoid him.

She released a mournful sigh. She'd known giving up Naveen would be the most difficult part of the deal she'd made with the Shadow Man, but ever since he'd started frequenting her restaurant, denying how she really felt about him had become downright unbearable.

If there was a bright spot in all of this, it was that Charlotte had given up her pursuit of him. Now she and the prince shared an unlikely friendship that Tiana would have found charming if she could ever see past her own heartbreak.

She swallowed past the knot of emotion clogging her throat.

This was for Naveen's own good—for the sake of his very life. She would gradually come to terms with the fact that they could never be together. Hopefully.

Banishing all thoughts of Naveen from her mind, Tiana got back to work. Once she was satisfied with the tomatoes she'd amassed, she turned to the vibrant green bell peppers, plucking several from the stalk and adding them to her basket.

Tiana walked over to where James now tended the cucumbers. "I'm gonna head down to the restaurant and get started." She leaned over and planted a kiss on his cheek. "I'll see you there, Daddy." She turned to leave, but before she could take a step, her daddy grabbed her hand. When she looked back at him, Tiana suffered a flash of alarm at the odd look on his face. "Is something wrong? Are you feeling okay?"

A gentle smile drew across his lips. "There's nothing

wrong, baby girl. In fact, everything is just right. I only wanted to tell you how proud I am of you and what you've done with the supper club. You made my dream come true, Tiana."

A cluster of gratefulness, affection, and unabashed joy blossomed within Tiana's chest. She set the basket on the ground and threw herself into her father's arms.

"Thank you, Daddy. It's my dream, too. And there is no one else I'd rather share it with." She held on to him for several more moments before finally finding the strength to pull away.

"All right now," Tiana said. "We can't spend all day blubbering along."

"You're right," James said. "You get to that restaurant and cook up that pot of jambalaya. I'll be along as soon as I get cleaned up."

Tiana picked up her vegetable basket and began to hurry out of the garden, then turned around and threw herself into her daddy's arms again.

"What's that for?" James asked.

"I'm just so happy you're here."

4

Tiana

As she traveled along the cobblestone sidewalk on her way to the St. Claude Avenue streetcar stop, Tiana's spirit was invigorated by the charge that suffused the hazy air. It was rich and vibrant and teeming with the unmistakable energy of Mardi Gras. There was something about that time of the year that grabbed hold of the city and wouldn't let go.

Even though the big day was still several days away, the festivities leading up to Fat Tuesday had already begun. Elaborate balls with men dressed in tuxedos and women in magnificent ball gowns would be held nightly at all the fancy hotels downtown. There would be plenty more gatherings for those who weren't lucky enough to attend the balls, whether small house parties or live music venues. On Saturday there'd be the annual neighborhood picnic in Congo Square, not too far from her restaurant, and then gatherings to commemorate Shrove Monday.

As tempting as it was to get caught up in all the Mardi Gras revelry, Tiana was more interested in using the citywide celebration to bring attention to T&J's Supper Club. She'd kick things off later that evening with live music and a special menu, and the next day, they'd have a special guest for entertainment to draw more folks in.

Excitement coursed through her veins like the electricity zipping through those newly installed wires overhead. She mentally ran through the new dishes for that evening, including the new jambalaya, which would be daringly made with pasta instead of the traditional rice.

It was a risk to make such a drastic change to one of New Orleans's most beloved dishes, but if she managed to pull this off, T&J's would be the talk of the town! She wouldn't be surprised if people came in from as far as Biloxi, or even Jackson, Mississippi, to try her new recipe.

She hoped Mr. Salvaggio had delivered her order of spaghetti. His small macaroni factory in the French Quarter made the best pasta in the city. And, more important, Mr. Salvaggio didn't mind bartering. A pound of pasta in exchange for a dozen of her beignets.

Tiana stopped short.

She whipped around, searching for the dark silhouette she was sure she'd seen out of the corner of her eye.

Nothing.

She did her best to shake off the eerie feeling that crept up her spine. She was being foolish again. Or maybe she should pay a visit to that new doctor on Canal Street, whose sole focus was on eye diseases. There must be something to account for the strange shadows she'd sensed slithering alongside her lately.

Unless they had to do with another doctor . . .

Shivering slightly, Tiana continued toward the streetcar stop, a smile emerging as she came upon the welcome sight of Ms. Margery Johnson sitting on the wooden bench. Ms. Margery was known all throughout the Ninth Ward for her baked goods. Before the war, Daddy had often surprised them with one of Ms. Margery's apple pies or sweet vanilla cakes as the grand finale to their Sunday dinner. After he was gone, she and Mama still ordered a cake from Ms. Margery on each of their birthdays, including her father's. It had been one way to keep his memory alive.

"Good morning, Ms. Margery," Tiana greeted.

"Well, hello, Tiana," the woman replied, her kind smile lighting up her face.

Tiana took a seat on the bench and settled the bag with her vegetables in her lap. "You're looking mighty fine today," she said. "You on your way to the market for baking supplies?"

The older woman's forehead furrowed. "Why, Tiana, I haven't made any baked goods in years, not since my Edwin left for the war."

Tiana's head flinched back slightly. "But . . ."

Ms. Margery's son had gone around the same time her daddy had. And the older woman had received word that her son had become a casualty not long after Tiana and her mother received their similar devastating news.

How could she claim she hadn't baked anything in all those years when she'd made Tiana's favorite caramel cake for her birthday last year? Ms. Margery was not all that much older than her own mama, far too young to start losing her memory to old age.

"Are you sure about that, Ms. Margery?" Tiana asked cautiously.

The woman nodded. "The last thing I baked was a batch of sweet rolls the morning Edwin left for the service.

They were his favorite." She glanced at Tiana, a sad smile tilting up the corners of her mouth. "But I sure do miss baking."

An odd sensation prickled at the back of Tiana's mind. A week earlier, while Tiana was out shopping with her mother for materials for new curtains, Mr. Smith at the fabric shop had greeted them as if he hadn't seen them in ages. And then she'd had a similar encounter with the butcher, Mr. Phillips, when she'd visited his butcher shop a few days ago. Even though she'd gone in just a week before, he'd prattled on about things that happened years ago.

"Maybe you should take it up again," Tiana told her. "I reckon there's a lot of people who want your sweets for their Mardi Gras parties."

The streetcar rolled up to their stop, and Tiana helped Ms. Margery up the steps. She paid her nickel fare and took a seat in the rear, grateful there was one open near the window.

There was something magical about New Orleans when seen from the vantage point of a rolling streetcar, and the view distracted her from the odd encounter. Despite the thin haze that hung in the air, she could still make out the colorful shotgun houses of her Ninth Ward neighborhood. The humble structures soon gave way to an array of storefronts along Rampart Street. From Dix's Barbershop and King's Shoe Shine Parlor to Polmer Tailoring and Pelican Billiard Hall, Tiana was fascinated by the hustle and bustle along the busy promenade.

As the streetcar neared Ursulines Avenue, she reached above her head and tugged on the cable that hung just above the window, letting the driver know she wanted to get off at the next stop. The streetcar came to a halt and the driver cranked the brass handle on the wheel lever as he opened the door for her.

When she alighted from the streetcar, she spotted a familiar face.

"Hello there, Ms. Rose," Tiana greeted.

She'd first encountered Ms. Rose at her flower stand in the French Market several months earlier, during one of her weekly trips to buy supplies for the restaurant. The woman seemed to have an innate ability to coax her flowers into producing the most stunning blooms. Even in the dead of winter, her stand abounded with vibrant sprays in every color under the sun.

She'd called Tiana over that first day and offered her a bunch of fragrant lilacs, free of charge. The next time she visited, Ms. Rose had added peonies to the bunch and surprised Tiana with a lovely painting of a courtyard like the ones scattered throughout the French Quarter. Tiana tried to pay her, but Ms. Rose refused to take her money. And she continued to give her gifts every time she visited.

"Fancy seeing you outside of the French Market," Tiana said. "What brings you to Tremé?"

"Just visiting a friend," Ms. Rose said with a gentle smile. "She has been feeling under the weather, so I brought her flowers to brighten her day. It's a common practice among my people back home in Haiti." She held up a finger. "I'm happy I ran into you." She reached into the burlap sack that she kept draped over her shoulder and retrieved a large spray of lavender and bunches of marigold.

"To decorate your supper club," Ms. Rose said. "They are the colors of Mardi Gras: purple for justice, gold for power, and the green leaves represent faith."

"These are beautiful," Tiana said as she took the flowers. Their coloring was so vivid they looked otherworldly. "Thank you so much. Ms. Rose, I do wish you would let me pay you for these."

"Never." She shook her head. "A gift does not require payment."

"Why don't you let me make you some beignets?"

The older woman put a hand to her stomach and shook her head. "I've gotta watch my figure," she said with a laugh, although her figure remained a mystery since she was always dressed in layers of clothing. Even now that winter was melting into spring, Ms. Rose still wore a heavy purple cloak and a flower-print scarf tied around her head.

"Well, I should be heading back to my flower stall," she said.

"No wise sayings today?" Tiana asked. Ms. Rose loved sharing nuggets of wisdom she said were passed down from her mother.

The woman's brow lifted. "Actually, I do have one for you: *Ti bwa ou pa wè, se li ki pete je ou.* The twig you don't see is the one that puts out your eye."

Tiana peered at the flowers Ms. Rose had handed her. "Are there twigs in here?"

"Be cautious," the woman said. "It means to always be aware of your surroundings." She smiled and patted Tiana on the arm. "Take care." Then she continued along Rampart Street.

Tiana gathered her flowers and the vegetables she'd brought from her daddy's garden and continued toward the supper club. A familiar feeling of pride bubbled up inside her as the green facade of the building came into view.

It might not be the palatial restaurant of her dreams, but it was everything she needed for the moment.

For the first six months after her daddy returned, she'd continued working at her waitressing jobs. She still had the money she'd saved up to purchase that old sugar mill that the Fenner brothers had sold to another buyer behind her back—making the infuriating claim that someone of her "background" was unfit to run a restaurant. And she had diligently set aside every extra penny she earned, trusting that one day the opportunity she'd been waiting for would come along.

It was fate that had brought her to the neighborhood of Tremé last fall, just as the weather was changing. And it was fate that had nudged her into taking a shortcut to Krauss Department Store, where she'd been on her way to buy a new coat. She'd happened upon this building just as the banker was sticking a For Sale sign in the window.

Tiana had made him an offer on the spot and had raced to the bank to withdraw half of the down payment to show him that her money was good. Daddy had accompanied her to that same bank the next day, adding his severance pay from the army to cover the other half of the down payment so she could keep saving for whatever came next.

Tiana hadn't been able to contain her smile when she'd walked into Duke's Cafe and given Buford her two weeks' notice. She'd spent the next couple of months alongside her daddy renovating their new restaurant, and three months ago had welcomed their first guests—her mama, Charlotte, and Mr. Eli LaBouff—to dine at T&J's Supper Club.

Tiana pulled a copper key from her pocketbook and opened the door.

She took a moment to bask in the joy she felt whenever she entered this place. After setting her bags on the table nearest the door, she zipped around the dining room, removing the red carnations she'd received from Ms. Rose a few days earlier from the simple blue vases at the center of each table.

It struck Tiana as odd that the carnations had wilted so much overnight. She could have sworn each of these flowers had been healthy and fragrant when she'd wiped down the tabletops before locking up the restaurant yesterday. She replaced the modest carnations with arrangements of lavender and marigold.

"Wow!" Tiana plopped her hands on her hips, regarding the dining room with a smile. Ms. Rose was right; the flowers instantly made the place more festive.

Done with the front of the house, she grabbed the bag of vegetables and started for the kitchen. But before she made it to the swinging door, the sun that had managed to break through the haze shone directly on a scuffed spot on the floor, just underneath one of the paintings Ms. Rose had given her.

"Oh, no, you don't," Tiana said. She continued into the kitchen, set the bag down, and picked up an old rag. She headed straight for the mark and buffed it out of the floor. There would be none of that in her restaurant, thank you very much.

She stood and straightened the slightly crooked picture frame that held Ms. Rose's painting. Tiana was sure the flower monger had never set foot in this restaurant, yet the four pieces of artwork she'd gifted to T&J's matched the decor perfectly. Each featured a subject that was uniquely New Orleans and complemented the stunning mural her daddy had commissioned by an artist from the neighborhood.

The mural, which depicted the rich Cajun and creole cuisine they served, covered the entire back wall, just behind the wooden dais where Louis and his band played jazz music for the crowd.

Tiana frowned. Had she reminded Louis about the music for tonight?

"Hey, Tiana!"

She spun around. "Just the man I wanted to see." Louis smiled that big, almost frightening smile of his. "What are you grinning about?"

"You said just the *man* you wanted to see. I still get a kick out of hearing that. Me. A man." He fiddled with his waistband. "Truth be told, I'm still getting used to it. Who knew pants could be so . . . confining."

"Please, keep them on," Tiana said quickly.

"I know, I know," Louis replied. "So, why did you want to see me?"

Tiana stepped closer to the stage. "I was wondering if we should go over the song list for tonight."

"You don't need to worry yourself with that." He tapped the side of his head. "I've got it all up here. In fact, I came over to get the sheet music I left. Me and the guys are practicing over at Gerald's place."

"Great," Tiana replied. "I'm thinking if word gets out that things are rocking at T&J's Supper Club tonight, then people will decide that this is *the* place to celebrate their entire Mardi Gras weekend. And when they hear that Rudy Davis and the Allstars will be here—wait, Rudy Davis *is* still coming tomorrow night, right?"

"They'll be here," Louis said.

"There's just so much riding on this, Louis," she said, straightening a nearby tablecloth. "I'm counting on the money we bring in during the next five days to pay off a large portion of the loan on the building. I *have* to make sure Mardi Gras is a success. Nothing can go wrong."

"Nothing will go wrong." Louis headed over and patted her on the shoulder. "I know you've had to deal with a lot this past year, but this is one thing you don't have to worry about. In fact, I asked Rudy if he and the band could come back next week. I've been thinking about home a lot lately. Maybe it's time for a visit."

She paused, hearing the wistfulness in his voice and feeling a twinge of guilt. She hadn't considered that Louis would feel homesick, but why wouldn't he? He'd been away from his family for an entire year.

Tiana just wasn't sure how Louis would be received back in the swamp now.

She turned to look up at him and put a gentle hand on his arm. "Umm . . . sure. Why don't we talk about it after Mardi Gras?"

"Yeah, good point. Let's focus on this coming weekend and making it the best that T&J's has ever had. I know you can do it, Tiana. You've worked too hard not to."

Louis was the only other person who knew about her deal with Facilier, but even Louis didn't know the entire story. He wasn't privy to all the details in the agreement that had made his dream a reality—the bits about her father, for example, and the concoction she added to the gumbo.

And yet, their shared history had made him into something of a confidant this past year. At times, Tiana felt as if he was the only person she could turn to, the only one who would understand when she found herself faltering.

"Thanks for being here, Louis," Tiana said. "For listening."

He hunched his broad shoulders. "It's what I'm here for. Well, that and making your customers shake their rears." He did a little dance, then took off for the stage. "I need to get back to the guys. We're gonna sound better than ever tonight. You mark my words, Tiana!"

"I believe you," she said with a laugh. "I'll see you in a few hours."

The music taken care of, Tiana decided to focus on more pressing issues, like perfecting the jambalaya.

Just as she reentered the kitchen, there was a loud knock on the back door that led out to the alley behind the restaurant.

"I'll be right there," Tiana called. Relief rushed through her when she opened the door and found Mr. Salvaggio staring back at her. He wore his signature page-boy hat.

"Salve!" Tiana exclaimed in the greeting they always shared. "You are a life-saver, Mr. Salvaggio."

"And you remain my favorite customer, Ms. Tiana," the kind-faced Italian man said. He followed her inside, carrying a paper bag in each hand. "Here is your extra order of spaghetti, and here is biscotti that my beautiful wife made for you. You must enjoy with a nice hot cup of coffee." He kissed his fingers. *"Perfecto."*

"That sounds marvelous," Tiana said. "If you give me just a few minutes, I'll fry up your beignets. You know they're best when they're hot out of the oil."

She retrieved the already-prepared beignet dough from their brand-new electric icebox and settled in to listen to one of Mr. Salvaggio's stories. It had become a standing routine whenever he made a delivery. He would share memories from his childhood in Sicily while she made his beignets. Tiana wasn't sure she believed some of the tales Mr. Salvaggio spun, but they always made for a good laugh.

She packed up his beignets and bade him goodbye. As he left through the back door, Mr. Salvaggio made Tiana promise that she would stop for a moment to enjoy the cookies his wife had sent over.

Friendships like his were an unexpected bonus to owning her restaurant. The vendors she worked with viewed her with respect, as an equal. It was a far cry from the treatment she'd received from the Fenner brothers.

Tiana's blood boiled like a hot pot of gumbo whenever her thoughts turned to that old sugar mill. Seeing all her hard work and sacrifice tossed aside like yesterday's trash had left her feeling powerless.

And wishing on evening stars.

Her eyes fell shut as a fresh wave of torment washed over her. But she opened them just as quickly. She didn't have time for wallowing. In a few hours this restaurant would be full of hungry customers.

Besides, none of that other stuff mattered anymore. She was doing just fine without that old sugar mill, and without the Fenner brothers or their bank loan. She didn't need to cast wishes on evening stars; she made her own dreams come true.

And she certainly didn't need to rely on that no-good Dr. Facilier.

Tiana hated to admit that, for the briefest second, she'd considered his offer to get her the restaurant when they'd made that deal last Mardi Gras. Thank goodness she'd quickly come to her senses. There was only one thing she relied on Facilier to provide. One thing she couldn't have possibly done herself.

She walked over to the pantry and moved aside the jar of preserved green beans from last year's crop. Behind it stood a tiny vial of the potion she'd agreed to add to her gumbo. She met with Facilier every couple of weeks, usually during her normal trip to the French Market, and exchanged the empty vial for a new one.

As long as he held up his end of their bargain, ensuring that her daddy stayed alive and the rest of her friends and family remained safe and well, this was all she would ever need from the Shadow Man.

She leaned forward, peering at the vial.

"Can't be," she said as she snatched it from the shelf.

But yes, it was empty.

"Oh, come on," she whispered.

Guess she had to add a trip to the French Quarter to the list of everything else she had to do before tonight's dinner service. She grabbed her bag and headed out.

5

Facilier

Dr. Facilier positioned himself against the wrought iron lamppost, hunching his back so that the dusty cloak he'd donned wouldn't slip from his shoulders. Of all the disguises in his repertoire, this one was by far his least favorite. But blending in with the riffraff who loitered about the French Quarter was paramount to keeping his identity concealed.

He forced a wretched cough from deep in his lungs, the kind that would send anyone who came near scurrying to the other side of the street. He was in no mood for company.

Not that he had that to worry about today. Most of the people hustling their way through the narrow streets and alleyways didn't seem to notice him. They were too busy complaining about the peculiar haze blanketing New Orleans. Facilier didn't mind it one bit. The gauzy cloud was the perfect distraction, providing extra cover for those deeds he'd rather keep hidden from the public eye.

Unlike the rest of the folks whining about this fog, Facilier chose to use it to his advantage.

And here came his opportunity to do just that.

He spotted his mark when he was still several yards away. The unsuspecting fool strolled along the sidewalk with a trumpet tucked underneath his arm and a derby hat pulled low over his forehead. He ambled right past Facilier, whistling to himself as if he didn't have a care in the world.

Because he didn't.

Prince Naveen of Maldonia never had to worry about anything. He'd been born into the kind of wealth most people couldn't fathom. Even after his parents had cut him off, he never faced any *real* hardships. His looks, charm, and connections were aces in his pocket, qualities he could count on to get him out of anything.

Facilier fought to keep the disgust from showing on his face as he set off to follow the young man.

He hung back, maintaining a respectable distance between himself and the prince while traveling along St. Ann Street. He waited until Naveen reached the crowded street corner before sidling up alongside him. Naveen paused while a horse-drawn carriage clomped by, and Facilier made his move.

"Oh, oh, excuse me," he said, fumbling into the prince.

"Whoa, whoa, whoa. You okay there?" Naveen asked.

Pretending to be a drunkard deep in his cups, Facilier slurred a mumbled "thank you" as he looped his arm around Naveen's shoulders. With sleight of hand, he pricked him at the base of his neck and collected several drops of his blood using a small bottle that he'd held hidden in his palm.

Naveen stiffened, but he wasn't in a position to let go lest he drop the poor drunk man he'd been kind enough to help.

"Steady there, my friend," Naveen said. He looked to a stately gentleman standing next to them and, with his free hand, motioned as if he were drinking. "It is a bit early in the day, eh?"

The other man turned his nose up at them both, then proceeded to cross the street.

"You okay?" Naveen asked as he righted Facilier.

"Yes. Yes, thank you," Facilier slurred.

"You take it easy." Naveen tipped his hat to Facilier and continued on his way.

Facilier smiled as he watched Naveen scratch at the place where he'd pricked his skin. He probably thought it was a mosquito.

He pocketed the small vessel he'd used to collect the prince's blood and quickly made it back to his residence deep in the French Quarter. The front room served as the storefront for Dr. Facilier's Emporium, but it was in the back where the real magic happened.

Unfortunately, when it came to *his* magic, real was relative. It was mostly sleight of hand, convincing illusions, simmering brews. And, of course, the borrowed powers.

Facilier removed the dusty cloak and tossed it aside on his way to the nondescript chest at the rear of the room. He lifted the lid from the chest and shielded his eyes from the streams of blinding light that burst forth and ricocheted off the walls.

Carefully, he retrieved the bowl from the bowels of the chest. Its smooth opal exterior made it cold to the touch, but the contents bubbled like the brew in a witch's cauldron. He carried it to a nearby table and added the drops of blood he'd just confiscated from Naveen to the bowl. Using the tip of his cane, he swirled around the concoction that had been fermenting for the better part of a year and intoned the initial verses of the spell he'd cast on Prince Naveen with the help from his friends on the other side.

Bitterness festered on Facilier's tongue, its intensity growing with every word that poured forth from him. His reliance on his *friends* was a source of constant fury, but he had no other choice.

Facilier closed his eyes tight around the image of his mother as his mind brought him back to those days when he would sit at her knee, observing her service to the people of their community. She had been a healer, practicing sacred rituals passed down from her mother and her mother's mother and beyond. But none of those rituals had been enough to heal *her*. No words, no dancing, no burning of alms had been enough to keep her here.

The day his mother's soul passed on was the day he vowed to get back at this cruel world. It was what it deserved for ridding itself of her.

He'd shunned his mother's religion, refusing to learn its practices, now knowing for once and for all it could do nothing for him. What was the point? None of it had saved her.

So to achieve the power and fortune he had coveted, he had turned to his friends from the other side. And now the price of doing business with them continued to increase.

Facilier unhooked a wooden spoon from the wall and

scooped up some of the concoction. Careful not to spill even a drop, he cupped his hand underneath the spoon and carried it to the brass plate that held the gold crest of Maldonia that had once hung around Naveen's neck. Pilfering the crest was about the only thing that useless Lawrence had done right after their misguided scheme backfired and Facilier had decided he was done using the amulet.

Facilier slowly drizzled the piping hot liquid over the crest as he murmured the final lines of the spell.

The spell didn't give him total control over Naveen's mind—the price for that particular trick had been much too high—but his friends had offered the next best thing. As long as Facilier performed the ritual of covering something Naveen still held near and dear to his heart with Naveen's own blood, he would be susceptible to Facilier's wishes. Similar to the potion he supplied Tiana, though this was tailored specifically to the prince and his memories.

There was just one caveat: the spell became less potent with each day that passed. Lately, all it seemed to be doing was making sure he forgot about the incidents of last Mardi Gras. Timing was important in these deals. And Facilier was up against the clock.

That dunderheaded prince and LaBouff's daughter were always together, yet no official wedding announcement had made it to the newspapers. Their dillydallying was costing Facilier precious time. The longer he had to wait to get his hands on LaBouff's fortune, the longer he had to remain beholden to his friends on the other side.

He'd considered discarding the spell he'd cast on Naveen after Tiana opened that little supper club in Tremé, especially once LaBouff became a frequent visitor. The man loved to indulge in Tiana's cooking. Facilier figured it would be only a matter of time before he could get the wealthy sugar baron under his control.

Except LaBouff seemed immune!

Facilier didn't doubt that Tiana was using the potion as promised. He'd swindled enough of her customers as they left the supper club to know that she dutifully added it to her gumbo exactly as he'd directed. But when it came to LaBouff and the rich cronies who often accompanied him to the restaurant, the magical concoction seemed to have no effect.

Facilier tightened his fist around the handle of the wooden spoon to the point of cracking it.

He had to get to the bottom of this. He had to get to LaBouff.

He had so many cards built into houses. One wrong move and—poof. It would all fall down.

Mardi Gras was less than a week away, which meant the

Shadows would be expecting their payment for that deal he'd made with them almost one year ago. If Facilier had any chance of getting to LaBouff through Tiana's gumbo, it had to be soon. Because once the sun dipped below the horizon on Mardi Gras night, Tiana would no longer be around to add his potion to her gumbo.

She just didn't know it yet.

6

Tiana

Tiana fidgeted with the pleats in her gingham dress as a familiar mix of anxiety and dread curdled in the pit of her stomach. She glanced over her shoulders, searching for signs of Dr. Facilier. She'd sent word that she was in need of more of the potion for her gumbo by way of their usual method: tying a white kerchief to the door handle of an abandoned factory just around the corner. She'd seen his nearby emporium from afar, but she had no desire to ever visit. These clandestine meetings were nauseating enough.

They followed the same protocol whenever she needed

to replenish her supply of the potion. She was to sit on this particular bench, underneath the canopy of a towering oak tree in Jackson Square, and wait. She'd repeated this ritual five times over the past three months, and she hated it more and more each time.

But Facilier had fulfilled his end of their bargain, and she vowed to do the same. She had kept a close eye, and as far as she could tell, the potion hadn't caused harm to any of the customers who'd consumed it. Adding it to her gumbo was a small price to pay in exchange for having her father back.

Tiana stood and looked around. Facilier had never been this late before. The dinner service would be starting in less than two hours, and she still had vegetables to chop, sauces to make, and beignet dough to prepare.

"Looking for me?"

Tiana spun around. She slapped her palm to her chest to calm her heart.

He'd done that on purpose.

"I didn't expect to see you again so soon," Facilier said in that vexing drawl Tiana had come to despise.

"We're busy down at the supper club," she said. "And my gumbo is our top seller. I'm making more batches of it than ever."

His expression darkened as he leaned in close. "Have you been stretching this potion? Trying to make it last longer?"

"No! I put the exact amount you instructed into each pot. That's why I ran out sooner than expected," she said, making no effort to mask her offense. "I would never take a chance like that, not when—" She glanced on either side of her, and in a lowered voice, said, "Not when my daddy's life depends on it." Tiana opened her palm, revealing the empty vial. "Are we making this trade or not? I have a restaurant to run, Dr. Facilier."

Facilier snarled as he reached into the breast pocket of his purple vest and retrieved the vial.

"Five drops," he said, distrust still teeming in his eyes. "Make sure you put it in every pot of gumbo you cook, Tiana."

Tiana slipped the vial in her bag, experiencing a rush of relief now that she had a full bottle of the potion once again. She'd warred with these contrasting emotions for the past three months—abhorring the fact that she'd had to make a deal with this vile man at all, while at the same time cherishing what it had made possible.

Facilier tipped his top hat to her. "Until next time."

Tiana turned on her heel without uttering a parting

word. There was nothing in their deal that said she had to treat him with any sort of kindness.

She tucked her bag to her side and left through the side gate of Jackson Square. She attempted to walk up St. Philip Street, but an upturned horse cart had dumped manure onto the sidewalk. Tiana quickly pivoted, heading back toward the river. She would cut through the French Market and follow Esplanade Avenue back to Tremé.

The afternoon rush had descended on the market, with women carrying wicker baskets on their arms, picking through the selection of produce, meats, and fresh pasta brought in from the French Quarter factories. This was just one of the reasons Tiana preferred to visit the market in the early morning hours. Not only were the offerings fresher, but she didn't have to wrestle with other shoppers.

She shouldered her way through the throng of pedestrians. When she arrived at the edge of the market, she felt an odd sensation tugging at her, an undeniable pull that drew her attention toward the water. Her stomach twinged uneasily. She looked over and found Ms. Rose staring at her, framed by the vivid purple wisteria that grew along the flower stall's walls and awning.

Tiana released a relieved laugh and waved.

Ms. Rose nodded in acknowledgment, but her expression remained austere. Tiana didn't know what to make of it. She started to walk toward the flower stall to ask Ms. Rose if something was wrong, but then a customer grabbed the woman's attention and she broke eye contact.

Tiana disregarded the unsettling episode and continued toward Tremé, her mind jumping to everything that still needed to be done before they opened up the supper club.

She stopped.

There was that feeling again, as if something was . . . was following her. She quickly turned, positive that she'd seen a fleeting shadow of some kind out of the corner of her eyes. She whipped her head around the other way.

Nothing.

"It must be this fog," Tiana muttered.

She continued on her swift walk up Esplanade Avenue, clucking her tongue at her own foolish antics.

Still, she couldn't shake the feeling that something was very, very wrong.

7

Naveen

The pungent aroma of coal fire and burning sugarcane permeated the air surrounding LaBouff Sugars' massive sugar mill. The red brick building stood out boldly among the smaller structures along the banks of the Mississippi River, its prominence a physical testimony to its significance to the local economy.

Naveen roamed about the production floor, checking in with the workers at the heart of the operation to make sure they had everything they needed. He came upon one of the contraptions—he still didn't know what they were officially called—where dark molasses percolated, gurgling and splattering over the edges of the large copper pots. Puffs of white smoke plumed from the vessels and lingered in the air above their heads.

The foreman had tried to explain the process that was used to turn the willowy stalks of sugarcane that were brought in by the truckload into crystallized sugar and molasses, but Naveen was still a bit shaky on the mechanics of it all.

He flagged down one of the workers he'd befriended since he'd begun working here the year before.

"Hey, Jacob. What is this called again?" Naveen asked.

"Why, that's the boiler," the man replied, a smile stretching across his soot-covered face.

"Oh, yes. Thank you." He would have to remember that if he wanted to convince the others that he was serious about the sugar business.

And he was. He was determined to learn everything about this industry. He preferred being on the factory floor with the workers over sitting behind a desk.

Naveen wasn't as naive as many thought him to be; he knew Mr. LaBouff had only offered him this job because of his friendship with Charlotte. He didn't even have an official title, or any real duties. He wanted to prove to everyone that he had more to offer than just his charm.

He had yet to figure out exactly what that more was, of course, but that's why he was here now.

Naveen pointed at the thermometer on the side of the massive kettle. "So when the temperature reaches—"

A piercing whistle rent the air.

Naveen jumped back. His hands shot up in the air. "It was not me!"

That was why he never touched any of the equipment. He knew his limitations.

"You might wanna get outta the way, boss," Jacob said.

"I am not the boss!" Naveen called out, but no one could hear him above the ruckus that ensued as the men set about extracting the heated liquid from the boiler.

He stood back and watched, fascinated by the choreography of it all. It was like a graceful dance, the way the factory workers moved about the equipment, each confident in his role. Observing the backbreaking work these men put in day after day gave Naveen a greater appreciation for the sugar he had always enjoyed, yet taken for granted.

He now recognized that he'd taken *a lot* of things for granted. It was easy to do that when you spent most of your life having everything handed to you.

Did he miss living in the lap of luxury? Sometimes. But if his parents sent passage for him to return to Maldonia that very day, with the promise of giving him everything he asked for, Naveen would turn them down. He liked this new life he'd built for himself in New Orleans. There was something very freeing about earning his own money and not being under his parents' thumb.

Except now, it felt as if he was under Mr. LaBouff's.

His boss didn't make demands the way his parents had, but how could Naveen ever feel that he was earning his own way with a job that had been given to him as a favor? He wanted to prove to Mr. LaBouff that he could be an asset to this company.

And, well, maybe he wanted to prove that to himself as well. He wasn't sure what had sparked this new ambition, but he couldn't shake it and didn't think he wanted to anyway.

Naveen shoved his hands in his pockets and tried to fight off the familiar uneasy feeling that settled in the pit of his stomach. Like he was forgetting something important. It wasn't the first time he'd had to brush off such feelings in recent weeks. Something seemed . . . off.

He entered the milling room and leaned against the wall, giving a wide berth to the sharp blades that swung like pendulums from huge pulleys, slicing the pulpy cane into shreds. He pulled his trusty notepad from his back pocket and scribbled a reminder to research how the boiler worked. As he made his way to the rear of the room, he caught the tail end of a conversation between two workers who were maneuvering a bushel of sugarcane stalks onto the massive scale.

"Uh, excuse me, gentlemen," Naveen said. "What were you just saying about the candy company?"

The worker took his hat off and fidgeted with it, his expression suddenly apprehensive.

Naveen did his best to mask his exasperation. He wanted these men to like him—to think of him as one of the guys. But because of his proximity to Mr. LaBouff, they treated him as if he were in charge.

"I am just curious," Naveen said.

"Well . . . uh, my brother works over at Dugas's. Said they had some kinda fallin' out with their sugar supplier. They may be lookin' for a new one."

"Really?" His gaze shifted from the worker to the milling machine and back. "Dugas's, they make those little chocolates with the marshmallow center, yes? I see them everywhere."

The man nodded. "Yessir."

Naveen began to pace back and forth between the scale and the nearby bushels of sugarcane waiting to be weighed. His pulse pounded like a thunderous drumbeat within his chest as an idea began to take shape.

LaBouff Sugars was the king of sugar in the South.

Dugas's was the king of candy. A partnership between those two companies could be the start of an empire.

And if *he* was the one to broker the deal . . .

He turned to the two workers. "Can you keep the news of this . . . uh, what is the saying? Under wraps?" Naveen asked.

"Sure thing, boss," the man said. "But this isn't just rumor. My brother works there. He knows."

"No! No! I believe you," Naveen said. "I just want to . . . investigate a little on my own. And it is just Naveen. No boss here."

"Right, boss." The man tipped his hat to him.

Naveen let out a sigh, but his frustration at his fellow mill workers refusing to treat him like a regular guy was quickly replaced with his excitement over this new development. This was his chance. If he could convince Dugas Candy Company to partner with LaBouff Sugars, he could prove to everyone that he belonged here and that he was capable of doing more than simply being a friend to the real boss's daughter.

"Naveen!"

His head popped up. Had he conjured Charlotte just by thinking about her?

"Naveen, where are you?"

He quickly made it out of the milling room just in time

to see Charlotte LaBouff rounding the corner of one of the huge boilers, her blond curls bouncing with each step.

"Charlotte, what are you doing here? You know it is not safe for you on the factory floor."

"Well, *you're* here," she said. She grabbed him by the hand and started for the winding staircase that led to the upper floor. "But I don't like all this grime and dust anyway."

Naveen followed her to the suite of offices that lined the left side of the building. Mr. LaBouff's office was the biggest, of course, but Naveen's wasn't much smaller. In a way, he could understand why the factory workers had yet to warm up to him. They all shared a lunchroom that equaled the size of the office he had for himself.

Charlotte pushed through the door and plopped into the chair behind Naveen's mostly empty desk. She pointed at him.

"I need you to be my date for tonight," Charlotte said.

"Charlotte." Naveen rubbed the bridge of his nose. "We have been over this, have we not? You and I are friends. We should not mess that up by—" He ducked just in time to miss the fountain pen she pitched at his head. "Hey, that is dangerous."

"I'm not talking about a *real* date, Naveen," she said with an exasperated huff. "Daddy is bringing two members of the city council to Tiana's supper club tonight, and Mr.

Dubois will probably bring his son Rubin with him." She made a gagging motion. "He's been trying to get with me since we were in grade school together, and I don't want him getting any ideas."

"So you want to lie to him."

"Yes," she answered without the slightest hint of remorse.

Naveen chuckled at her audacity, but it was what he'd come to expect of Charlotte.

Once she'd decided to no longer pursue him as a husband, she had become an unlikely friend. In fact, she was his *best* friend. He wasn't sure he would have made it through this past year in New Orleans without her.

And not just because she had gotten him this cushy job at her father's sugar mill.

It turned out he and Charlotte had more in common than Naveen first realized, with both of them coming from significant wealth. Although Charlotte didn't seem interested in proving that she could earn her keep in the same way he felt compelled to lately. She was more than happy to spend her father's fortune.

But their wealthy families were only one of the similarities he and Charlotte shared. They both loved to dance and had spent the past year cutting a rug at dance halls all around New Orleans. It took him a little longer to catch on to the latest moves, but Charlotte was a surprisingly patient teacher. She also shared his love of art. She joined him at the museum whenever there was a new exhibition on display.

And Tiana. They both shared a particular interest in Tiana.

Though his interest in her was decidedly different from Charlotte's.

"Well?" Charlotte asked with a tinge of frustration. "Are you gonna be my date tonight, or what?"

A night of good food, jazz music, and the chance to see Tiana again?

Naveen gave her his best smile. "What time do we leave?"

8

Tiana

"Baby girl, looks like we're running low on corn bread."

Tiana poked her head out of the pantry long enough to call out to her daddy, "I'm on it."

She grabbed a bag of cornmeal from the shelf, then added baking soda, flour, and her secret weapon: sweet molasses from LaBouff Sugars. Cradling her haul close to her chest, she kicked the door open with her foot and raced past the waitresses lined up at the counter, collecting meals to take to the hungry customers who had descended on the restaurant tonight. The crowd started rolling in as soon as Tiana opened the doors for the dinner service, and the stream of people lining up to enter T&J's Supper Club had been steady ever since.

Tiana deposited the ingredients for the corn bread onto the counter. She turned to the stove and, with a big cooking spoon, stirred the pot of simmering collard greens. She picked up a fork and used it to flip over the catfish fillet she'd left frying in her daddy's cast-iron skillet. It was flaky, golden, and perfect, exactly as she'd intended.

The swinging door that separated the kitchen from the dining room swung open, and her head waitress, Addie Mae Jones, came bursting through it, her arms piled high with dirty dishes.

"Tiana, how much longer on those beignets?" Addie Mae called.

"Just a few more minutes," Tiana answered. She quickly grabbed the last of the beignet dough from the icebox, rolled it out, and cut it into squares. She carefully dropped them into a waiting pan of hot grease, giving each the chance to take shape before adding the next.

Tiana used her forearm to wipe the sweat from her brow as she skirted around the prep table to grab a couple of plates for this latest order. She'd lost count of how many she'd made already tonight.

"You need help over there?" her mother called.

"I got it, Mama. And what are you doing in here? You're supposed to be out in the dining room, enjoying the band. I told Louis to have the Crawfish Crooners play 'St. Louis Blues' just for you."

Back at the stove, she used a spatula to dunk the puffed-up pastries into the hot oil, making sure the edges were a warm golden brown before she scooped them out of the fryer. That was the key to making sure her beignets were crispy on the outside and pillow-soft on the inside.

She plated them on one of T&J's Supper Club's signature emerald-green plates and sprinkled just the right amount of powdery confectioners' sugar on the top.

Perfect.

"All right, Addie Mae, here are those beignets you've been asking for."

"You'd better mix up another batch of dough," her head waitress said as she grabbed hold of the plate Tiana handed to her. "As usual, these beignets are our biggest seller. Behind the gumbo, of course."

Her mother was tying an apron around her waist as she walked up to the stove.

"Mama, what are you doing?"

"Helping," Eudora said. "Until you two hire another cook, I am making it my mission to be of use."

Tiana dropped her head back and sighed up at the

ceiling. For the past two months, she and her mother had had this same discussion at least once a week. Tiana didn't know what else she could do to make her understand that she didn't want to hire another cook. She didn't need one. She could handle it.

Besides, they used recipes her daddy had been crafting ever since he was a little boy; was she supposed to just allow anyone to come into this kitchen and learn those secrets? Not in this lifetime.

Tiana looked over at her daddy, who stood at the shelf chopping onions without shedding a single tear. "Would you tell her that we're fine?" Tiana asked him.

"My baby girl knows what she's doing, Eudora," James said.

Her mother held her hands up in surrender. "If you say so. But I still think you could use an extra set of hands or two. Maybe that way Tiana can get out and enjoy the band a bit herself." Her eyes brightened. "Why don't you see if Charlotte's out there? I'll bet she brought along that nice young man."

Tiana shook her head. She would not take the bait.

Her mother had made several not-so-subtle mentions of that "nice young man" who always came by with Charlotte over the past few months. She would rather have her mother as a third cook than a matchmaker.

But at that moment, Eudora untied the apron from around her waist and rolled it into a ball. "Anyway, I hear you. You've got things under control. I'll go listen to the band." She grinned as she leaned in and planted a kiss on Tiana's cheek. "You know to come and get me if you need me. Even if it's just to give yourself a breather."

"Thank you, Mama," Tiana said, softening.

As she turned back to the dough, Tiana took a deep breath, trying to remind herself what was important. Here she was preparing all her favorite foods with her daddy, their loved ones showering them with praise over the success of their new endeavor. Her mama was smiling and happy. It was everything she'd ever wanted.

So despite the awful feeling she got in her gut whenever she even thought about the deal she'd made with Facilier, Tiana remembered everything she'd gained.

Her family was whole again. How could she *ever* regret that?

Addie Mae burst through the door with another set of dirty dishes. "What did I just say about those beignets? I've got three more orders. Do you need some help?"

"I've got it," Tiana assured her.

If Tiana ever did consider bringing someone else into this kitchen, it would be Addie Mae Jones. The waitress had come highly recommended by an old coworker from Duke's

Cafe. Like Tiana, Addie Mae had dreams of opening her own restaurant. She would get there one day, too. She was a hard worker, and she had a way about her that made each customer feel as if they were the most important person in the restaurant.

It was probably why Tiana had hired her on the spot, and after her first hour on the job, had declared Addie Mae the best waitress in town. She could only imagine how chaotic this place would be without her here to keep the rest of the waitstaff in check.

Of course, the fact that the rest of the waitstaff was Addie Mae's younger cousins, Jodie and Carol Anne, made it easy for her to keep them in line. They both worshiped their older cousin.

Now that this latest order of beignets was done, Tiana turned her attention back to the pot of gumbo gurgling on the stovetop. She took in the dents and pings along the walls of her daddy's big gumbo pot. Every imperfection was perfect in her eyes.

"How's that gumbo coming along, baby girl?"

"It's almost there," Tiana called.

Her father came over and pulled her into a side hug. "Smells good."

"And it tastes even better." She scooped up a big spoonful of the gumbo and blew lightly across it. Then she held the spoon up to him and grinned as he sipped a bit of the dark brown liquid.

"Just like your daddy taught you to make it," he said. His big belly laugh was the sweetest sound in the world. She would have made a deal with the devil himself in exchange for hearing that sound every day.

The Shadow Man is close enough to the devil.

She ignored the pinch of unease that threatened to crop up again.

"Let me see about these catfish," her daddy said. "As much as the folks out there love the gumbo, they can't get enough of this fried catfish. Well, that and the music."

"Does the band have them dancing out there?" Tiana asked.

"Oh, yeah. They're sounding real good tonight. Your mama's right; you should go and see for yourself." He gestured with his head toward the swinging door that led out to the dining room. "I can handle things in here for a bit. Go have a listen, and make the rounds. People been asking 'bout ya."

When they'd first opened the restaurant, Tiana had made a point of dropping in at each table for a few minutes to make sure their patrons were having a good time. She wanted people to feel at home when dining at T&J's Supper Club, as if they were having a meal with family.

But her desire to move beyond the walls of this kitchen and visit with the crowd had diminished the moment Naveen started visiting regularly.

Just as Facilier had warned, Naveen had no recollection of the days the two of them had spent together, journeying through the dark, brackish waters of the Louisiana bayou. As far as Naveen was concerned, Tiana was simply the owner of the restaurant where he occasionally indulged his love of beignets and jazz music.

It's better this way, she reminded herself.

Saying the words was easy. Accepting them was another thing.

"I'll go out in a minute, Daddy," she said as she tried to think up an excuse to hang back.

She often wondered if it would have been better if she had never attended the LaBouffs' Mardi Gras ball last year. If she had never met Naveen at all.

But then, did that mean he would have actually *married* Charlotte?

She almost laughed out loud.

Tiana wasn't convinced winning his heart had ever been Lottie's true objective. Shortly after last year's eventful Mardi Gras, Charlotte had declared she still wanted to marry royalty, but the title of princess came with too many responsibilities. She'd set her sights on becoming a duchess and had spent the past year trying to convince Mr. LaBouff to allow her to travel to England.

But her father was adamant that she remain right here in New Orleans. It was the first time Tiana had ever witnessed Mr. LaBouff deny Lottie something she'd asked of him.

Tiana started, suddenly remembering she needed to make tonight's crawfish étouffée. It had become Mr. LaBouff's favorite, and Tiana always made sure she had a fresh batch just for him.

"Hey, Addie Mae," Tiana called as she put together the fragrant stew. "Can you go out there and let me know if Mr. LaBouff is here?"

"He sure is," Addie Mae answered. "And he has Mr. LeBlanc and Mr. Dubois from the city council, along with Dubois's son, with him. He asked if there's any—"

"Étouffée," Tiana supplied. "Coming right up. In fact, I'll bring it to him myself."

Tiana dished up several bowls and set them on a serving tray. She cut thick slices of corn bread and added a slice to each serving. But when she picked up the tray, she immediately set it back on the counter.

Tiana closed her eyes and sucked in a deep breath. She had to prepare herself for the prospect of seeing Naveen.

She could tell Charlotte was starting to get suspicious. The last few times they had come, Tiana had made sure to maintain her distance. On their most recent visit, Lottie had tried to get her friend's attention by yoo-hooing across the whole supper club before Tiana had waved and scurried away.

"All you have to do is avoid going near their table," Tiana whispered to herself.

Mr. LaBouff would make that easy enough. He'd be sitting in the far right corner of the dining room, far from where the band played. As he'd explained it to her, he liked the music, but needed to be somewhere a bit quieter in order to conduct business with the gentlemen he brought to the restaurant.

Charlotte, on the other hand, always sat at a table as close to the stage as possible. That would work in Tiana's favor. She would take Mr. LaBouffs' meal, stop in on a few other tables to make sure folks were enjoying themselves, and get back to the kitchen.

"See, it'll be easy."

At least that was what she told herself.

9

Tiana

Sucking in another fortifying breath, Tiana lifted the serving tray and carried it out to the dining room. She avoided even glancing toward the stage, where the band was playing a rousing rendition of Jelly Roll Morton's "Smoke House Blues." She didn't want to take the chance of catching either Charlotte's or Naveen's eye.

As she looked out over the packed restaurant, pride made her chest swell up like the giant silver airship she'd seen in the paper. Everyone seemed to be having the grandest time, their smiles and jubilant chatter mingling with the music from the band.

She moved forward, spotting the three gentlemen sitting with Mr. LaBouff. He looked as if he were holding court, his ample belly and overwhelming presence taking up more space than any of the night's other patrons. There wasn't an official monarch in this city, but if there had been, Tiana had no doubt who would reign as the King of New Orleans. There was no one more powerful living here than her best friend Charlotte's daddy. Not even the mayor.

As Tiana had come to learn over the years, politics only got you so far. The *real* power in this city—and probably the world—was money.

And Eli LaBouff had a lot of it. As did the other men at the table, it seemed, judging by their posh clothes. What had Addie Mae said—they were councilmen?

Tiana sighed, thinking about her own daddy and how, despite the fact that he was now a business owner, he would never fit in with Mr. LaBouff's crowd. Not because he wasn't smart enough or didn't work hard enough. Simply because of a matter of his birth and station in life. Because of the color of his skin. Same reason the Fenner brothers had refused to sell her the old sugar mill. The unfairness of it rankled.

Tiana pushed the infuriating thoughts away as she came upon the table, focusing on the task at hand.

"Tiana!" Mr. LaBouff's jovial voice resonated throughout the dining room. "How's it going tonight?" Before she could speak, he continued, "Well, heck. I don't have to ask you that. Just look at all the people in this place! No better restaurant in town."

"Why, thank you, Mr. LaBouff. And thank you, gentlemen, for spending this Thursday before Mardi Gras at T&J's Supper Club. We're honored to have you here." She placed a bowl of étouffée before each of them, then said, "Are you sure you don't want to try the jambalaya pasta? It's brand new, and everyone seems to like it."

"It can't be better than this here étouffée," Mr. LaBouff said. "It's all I eat whenever I'm here."

"Well, all right." Tiana lifted her shoulders in a hapless shrug. "You all enjoy your étouffée. If there's anything else I can get you, just let me know, you hear?"

"How about getting rid of that fog out there?" one of the councilmen said with a laugh.

"Is it still foggy?" Tiana asked.

"And it's getting thicker by the minute. You reckon it's something going on with the water? It seems to be worse down by the river."

"I thought maybe it was the stacks of the sugar mill, or some of the other factories in the Quarter, but your guess is as good as mine," she said. "I just hope it clears up before the Mardi Gras parades start rolling. No one wants a foggy Mardi Gras."

The effects on the Fat Tuesday celebrations weren't her only concern when it came to the bad weather. Tiana feared people would be afraid to venture away from home if things got so bad that it made traveling along the roads too danger-ous. There were more and more of the new Ford Model Ts on the roadways these days, and there was no doubt one of them would crash into another if drivers couldn't see.

The folks there in the Tremé neighborhood loved to dine at the restaurant, but T&J's was beginning to see a fair num-ber of patrons from other parts of the city. She wanted them all to be able to travel safely to and from the supper club.

"I should tend to some of the other tables," Tiana said. "Remember, if y'all need anything, just let me know."

When she turned, a stiff breeze ruffled the hem of her dress as a gentleman from a nearby table whizzed past her, his face hidden behind a newspaper. An eerie sensation skidded along Tiana's spine, raising the tiny hairs on her arms and at the back of her neck.

She shook off the strange feeling and turned her atten-tion to the table where a bunch of her friends from the neighborhood sat. She'd known Georgia, Donald, Maddy, and Eugene since grade school, back when they all sat like quiet little mice in Mrs. Brown's classroom. Well, except for

Georgia. That one never could keep her lips from flapping for very long.

"Hey there, y'all," Tiana greeted. "Y'all having a good time?"

"Sure are."

"We're having the best time."

"I just wish we were closer to the stage," Georgia remarked. "Your place is so popular; people have to get here really early if they want a good seat."

"It does get crowded," Tiana agreed with a smile.

"I gotta hand it to you, Tiana. You said you were gonna open your restaurant one day and you sure did it. This place is the best spot in Tremé."

"In all of N'awlins," Donald chimed in.

Once again, Tiana's chest expanded with pride. It wasn't all that long ago that this same group of friends would hound her to go out with them. And here they all were, spending their night out at *her* restaurant.

"And I love the Crawfish Crooners," Maddy said. "I'm surprised that I hadn't heard of them before they started playing here."

"The band leader, Louis, just moved down from Shreveport," Tiana said quickly. "But he's making a name for himself here in N'awlins. Y'all should come back tomorrow, because we have a special guest band."

"Oh, yeah? Which one?" Donald asked.

"Rudy Davis and the Allstars!"

The entire table gasped as Tiana's smile widened.

"How'd you get Rudy Davis to agree to play at your restaurant?" Georgia asked. "Ain't he up in Chicago now?"

"New York, last I heard," Eugene said.

"Well, he's back in town for a few days, and he owed Louis a favor." Tiana nodded up at the stage. "He filled in for Mr. Davis down at a jazz club in the Quarter a while back and convinced him to stop by. And after Rudy had some of Daddy's gumbo, he agreed to perform next time he was here. It's like y'all said, T&J's Supper Club is the best spot in all of N'awlins."

"Wow!" Georgia said.

Suddenly, a new high-pitched voice cut through the crowd. "Tia!"

Tiana turned to see Charlotte at a table just steps away from the stage. She frantically waved her hands in the air, motioning for Tiana to join her. Tiana glanced just past Charlotte and locked eyes with Naveen, who was staring directly at her.

Her heart caught in her throat.

Tiana quickly looked away.

"Well, thank y'all for coming tonight," she told her

friends. "But I need to get back to the kitchen. Gotta keep the hot food coming if I want to keep people happy."

"Tia!" Lottie called again.

But Tiana ignored her. She tucked the serving tray underneath her arm and rushed past the other tables and through the swinging door, desperate for the sanctuary the kitchen provided.

10

Tiana

"Back so soon?" her daddy asked as soon as Tiana stepped into the kitchen.

She walked over to where he stood before the stove, tending to a large cast-iron skillet with several fillets of golden-brown catfish. Tiana picked up a spatula and nudged the catfish, causing the hot oil to sizzle even more.

"I can't spend all night out there," she said in a shaky voice. Goodness, how could simply seeing Naveen rattle her this much? "It's unfair to leave you with all the work," Tiana tacked on, hoping her daddy bought her excuse.

"I told you I have everything under control, baby girl," he replied. "Go and enjoy yourself a little while longer."

"I don't think—"

"Tia!" Charlotte burst through the swinging door, whizzing around the kitchen like a tornado. She came upon Tiana and plopped a hand on her hip. "Didn't you hear me calling you out there?"

"Oh! Lottie, hey!" Tiana forced as much false cheer into her voice as she could muster. "No, I didn't hear you," she lied. "It's so noisy out there with the band and all."

"Hello there, Charlotte," James greeted. "Glad to see you could make it here tonight."

"Hey there, Mr. James." Lottie waved to him before grabbing hold of Tiana's arm. "You don't mind if I steal Tia for a spell, do you? I promise to have her back here before the second dinner rush."

"No problem at all," her daddy said. "I was just telling her to go out there and enjoy the band."

"Yes, the music is fabulous tonight. And I have the best seat in the house, so come and join me."

Tiana wanted to dig in her heels—literally—as Lottie tugged on her arm, but she stood no chance when pitted against both her best friend and her daddy. Instead, she braced herself for the impact of having to be near Naveen and pretend he had no effect whatsoever on her. She was no Evelyn Preer, but a few more months of this and her acting skills might get her all the way to Hollywood.

But when they arrived at Charlotte's table, it was empty, save for two dishes that held the remnants of the pasta jambalaya both had eaten tonight. Tiana was confused by the unnerving mix of relief and disappointment that assaulted her at finding Naveen's chair unoccupied.

"Where's Naveen?" Tiana asked. "Did he leave?"

"He had better not have," Charlotte said, looking around. She gasped and pointed to the center of the room. "Oh, my word! Look to the dance floor, Tia!"

Tiana swung around and did a double take. Was that Naveen dancing with her mother?

Goodness.

"Just look at Ms. Eudora out there cutting a rug." Charlotte clapped excitedly. "Who knew your mama was such a hoot!"

"I sure didn't." Tiana had to admit it was nice to see her mother having a good time. She just wished it were with anybody else. Tiana had no doubt her mother was talking her up.

"You look great, by the way," Charlotte said as she reclaimed her seat. "Did your mama make that dress?"

Tiana looked down at the simple yellow-and-white

gingham sheath. It was one of her nicer dresses, but it was nothing compared to the creations Charlotte wore every day. Creations that Tiana's mother had made with her own two hands.

"Actually, I made this one myself." Tiana preened as she sat. "I guess I inherited skills from both Mama and Daddy."

"Oh, Tia, you are just unbelievable! I wish I had half your talent." Charlotte lifted her hands in the air. In a wistful voice, she said, "I'm still trying to figure out what I'm good at doing. I'm not sure I'll *ever* figure it out."

"Don't talk that way about yourself, Lottie. You can do amazing things if you put your mind to it." Tiana reached across the table and gave Charlotte's hand a reassuring squeeze. "I know you can."

"Maybe," her friend said with a shrug. "I do have a knack for shopping. Maybe I can do *that* professionally one day."

"That's a . . . thought," Tiana finished. She had never heard of such a job, but if there ever were a job out there for Lottie, that would be the one.

Suddenly Charlotte looked at her seriously, squeezing Tiana's hand. "Hey, Tia, I miss you. I know you're busy, but I feel like maybe you've been avoiding me?"

"Oh, no, no, I haven't . . ." *Been avoiding* you, Tiana added silently.

"Good." Charlotte suddenly brightened. "Then you can come to Maison Blanche with me tomorrow. Please? Ms. Eudora is making my dress for *my* Mardi Gras ball, but I have about a half dozen others to attend over the next five days and I need a different gown for all of them. I need your help picking them out. Maybe you can get something, too! I'd love for you to join me for some of these parties."

Tiana hesitated. She'd never had time to go shopping with Charlotte before.

"Please, please, please?"

Charlotte looked so genuinely hopeful, Tiana felt a twinge of guilt for not spending much time with her friend this past year.

"Well, I don't think I'll have time for parties," Tiana started. She watched her friend deflate a little. "But I'll go with you tomorrow—as long as we're done in time for me to get back here so that I can start prepping for our big Mardi Gras kickoff," Tiana added.

"Eep!" Charlotte got up and threw her arms around Tiana. "Yes, all right, deal! Gosh, I still can't believe you have Rudy Davis and the Allstars playing at your supper club! It's gonna be so fabulous." She moved to sit back down. "And speaking of, oh, Tia! Tia! Tia! How could I forget to tell you! I had an epiphany today."

"Another one?" Tiana couldn't help laughing. She had missed Charlotte's unflappable energy.

"Yes, a *real* one this time. Are you ready for this?"

"Ready as I'll ever be," Tiana said.

"You know how much I love art, right? Naveen and I are always at the museum together."

"Yes, I know," Tiana said, praying her envy didn't show on her face.

"Well, I've discovered that I love British art. And do you know the best place to see *British* art?"

"In England?" Tiana asked.

"That's right!" Charlotte waved her hands in the air. "You see, if I tell Big Daddy that I want to study with the artists who live in London, then he *has* to send me there, because it's educational. And while I'm educating myself on British art, I can search for my duke!" She squealed. "Isn't my plan the best?"

"Uh . . . sounds like the bee's knees to me," Tiana said.

"It's just brilliant, and I know it will work. Besides, I need to do something. Big Daddy has brought that dull Rubin Dubois around again."

The band brought their song to a close, and Louis announced that they would be taking a ten-minute break. Panic surged through Tiana as the band members set down their instruments. She quickly glanced to the dance floor and spotted Naveen striding toward them, his charming smile as bright as always. Her heart immediately began to thump wildly within her chest. For a moment, she couldn't breathe.

"Uh, Lottie, I need to get back to the kitchen."

"But Mr. James said that you should sit and enjoy the band. They'll be back to playing in just a bit."

"No, really. I have to go," Tiana said. She stood and moved swiftly through the maze of tables to the kitchen. Before pushing past the swinging door, she chanced a glance over her shoulder. Naveen had stopped in his tracks. The light had drained from his eyes, and a look of hurt and confusion had taken its place.

Tiana bypassed the cooking and serving areas and headed for the small storeroom. She closed herself inside of it and plopped down on an empty milk crate, sucking in several breaths as she tried to calm her erratically beating heart.

"Who knew you were such a coward?" Tiana whispered.

After agreeing to Facilier's deal, Tiana had selfishly hoped that Naveen would return to Maldonia. It would have made things easier for her. But then, she knew that wasn't true. It didn't matter where he lived; this private agony of knowing what she had given up would remain.

It's been a year!

She had to find a way to move on. She could not go on like this, feeling such heartache every time she saw him.

"Has anyone seen Tia?" Charlotte's voice carried throughout the kitchen. Tiana closed her eyes and counted the seconds until her friend would find her. It didn't take long.

Charlotte knocked twice on the door to the storeroom before opening. "Tia?" she called. "What are you doing in here? Why did you run away again like that?"

"I'm sorry, Lottie. I've got too much to do."

"Really?" Charlotte drawled. She cocked her hip to the side and perched a fist on it. "I can tell. You're so very busy right now, sitting in a closet." She peered at Tiana. "Do you know what I think? I think maybe you've been avoiding someone after all. And maybe that someone is *Naveen*. The question is why?"

"Lottie, please."

"I want to know, Tia. Is it because you're—"

But before Charlotte could finish, Louis burst through the partially opened door. "We've got a problem."

11

Facilier

Facilier exploded out of the door to the supper club. His blood pounded in his ears as his mounting rage reached unprecedented levels. He shouldered past the line of patrons still hoping to make their way into Tiana's restaurant, glaring at them, baring his teeth. But he didn't take any satisfaction in the way they recoiled.

LaBouff wasn't eating the gumbo!

That was why the potion he'd given to Tiana hadn't worked on the sugar baron and his cronies. Because LaBouff had been eating that blasted étouffée this entire time. Facilier whacked at a pile of garbage with his cane, sending the refuse flying across the uneven cobblestone streets in this seedier part of the Vieux Carré.

Fury consumed him, rising in his throat until it unleashed with a raw scream into the dark, foggy night sky.

Once home, he ripped the fedora from his head and flung it onto the hat rack next to the door. He hadn't needed much of a disguise tonight. With the number of people crammed inside Tiana's little supper club, he'd gone unnoticed as he slipped inside and parked himself at the table near LaBouff's.

Tiana thought she was so clever, but he was the brains of this operation. He had been visiting her little supper club for months now. Always cloaked in a different disguise, he'd been right there in the same room with them, observing from afar how she interacted with all her customers, especially those fat cats Eli LaBouff brought in. But he had never gotten close enough to notice that LaBouff wasn't eating the gumbo.

Facilier peeled off his black gloves and tossed them aside as he made his way through the emporium to the back rooms of his home.

Disgust pooled in his stomach, recollections of the conversation he'd overheard tonight between LaBouff and those two from the city council swirling around in his head. The wealthy sugar baron had pledged to invest fifty thousand dollars in a new set of railroad tracks being added to those that already lined the riverfront as if it were play money.

What a ridiculous man with ridiculous ambitions. He didn't deserve his fortune, nor his influence. The things Facilier would do with that type of wealth, with men bending over backward to heed his every word. . . . He snarled as he recalled an incident years ago when he'd encountered Eli LaBouff in Jackson Square. The sugar baron had not been nearly as wealthy and powerful as he was now, yet still carried himself as if the world were his to control. Facilier had held his hand out for a gentlemanly handshake, but LaBouff had walked past him without so much as a glance.

Well, LaBouff and his cronies would take notice of him. And soon. Facilier would make sure of it.

He squeezed the handle on his cane so hard it was a wonder the wood didn't break under the strain. He tossed the cane aside and went to work, gathering everything he needed to create more of the potion he'd given to Tiana for her gumbo.

Before long *he* would be on his way to owning this city.

His arms brimming with the ingredients he'd collected from the shelves, Facilier turned and sneered at the dark, dank room. He was better than this musty hovel that was just steps above living in squalor. He should have been living in a mansion like the ones Eli LaBouff and those other fat cats lived in along St. Charles Avenue.

He had thought he would be satisfied with their wealth and power, but now Facilier decided he wanted more.

He wanted their *envy*.

He wanted them to seethe with jealousy when he walked by, to crave his attention. He wanted LaBouff to choke on his own bitterness and resentment. It was only right that he experience what Facilier had endured all these years.

And the only way to accomplish that was to take hold of the power they all had over this city. Once he was able to manipulate their minds, the rest would fall into place. He was sure of it.

A knock at the door jarred Facilier out of his fervent musings. He tilted his head toward it, waiting for the second double knock. When it came, he smiled.

He went over to the door and opened it with a flourish.

"Mr. Bruce, my dear friend. Back so soon?" He stepped aside. "Why don't you step into my humble abode."

The stout man barged into the room. He held up a bottle.

"Regina smiled at me yesterday!" Bruce exclaimed. His eyes were eager, but his pudgy jowls still sagged like the fish-filled nets the fishermen pulled out of the Mississippi River.

Facilier had been expecting him. The concoction he'd

sold the cobbler just a few days ago should have lasted him well into next week, but Mr. Bruce's infatuation with the war widow who frequented his shop grew stronger with each bottle he consumed. That was always a good sign for business.

"If you give me just a moment, I will provide everything you need," Facilier said. He turned to the shelf stocked with neatly arranged jars and bottles of various sizes, each filled with assorted liquids and salves. He might not have the knowledge his dear mother had, having been taught by the Vodou spiritual leaders of her homeland, but he'd learned a trick or two in his day.

He emptied dried rose petals into a black marble mortar and crushed them into a fine powder with the pestle. He added a bit of honey, a little sage, and the juice of one red cherry. Then he mixed it up using a wand made of rose quartz.

Facilier motioned for the man to hand him the empty bottle he'd brought with him. "Let me have that there bottle," he said. He slowly poured the concoction into it and swirled the bottle around. As he did so, Facilier mumbled gibberish. The words didn't matter as long as Mr. Bruce believed they held the power to make sweet Mrs. Dupre fall in love with him.

"There," Facilier said. "A few sips and your lady friend will be at your door."

The bits of gravel Facilier had sprinkled at the widow's doorstep would ensure her trip to the cobbler. The jagged stones were hell on shoe soles.

Mr. Bruce reached for the bottle, but Facilier pulled it out of his reach and stretched out his other hand, passing his thumb over his fingers.

"Ah, ah, ah," he crooned. "I think you're forgetting something."

Bruce handed over several folded bills. Facilier fanned them out, counting the money before finally releasing the bottle into his customer's stubby hand.

"Now, remember, you need only a small teaspoon of it in the morning. Of course, you can take more at night before bed, if you think Mrs. Dupre needs a bit more urging."

The man nodded excitedly as he tucked the bottle into his pocket and exited the door, disappearing into the dark, foggy night.

Facilier smiled as he closed the door behind him, but his grin quickly turned into a glower.

He shouldn't have had to peddle silly love potions to numbskulls like Bruce. Done were his days of performing two-bit schemes for pennies; he wanted bigger things for himself. His plans for LaBouff might have been stalled, but they weren't completely thwarted.

"Wait. Wait a minute," Facilier said.

He rushed back to the door and wrenched it open. The fog was even thicker than it had been on his walk home from the supper club.

Something strange permeated the air. Literally. Facilier had no idea what was behind this curious phenomenon, but he now realized that he could use it to his advantage.

His low, deep chuckle grew louder as he shut the door and returned to his laboratory.

His first plan might have failed, but this one wouldn't. He searched the shelves until he caught sight of a large jar with a particularly potent ingredient—one that could stop a grown man in his tracks and make him wait for his fate.

He knew exactly what he had to do.

12

Tiana

Trepidation thundered throughout Tiana's bloodstream as she stared into Louis's worried eyes. She was almost afraid to ask, but running away from a problem was never the way to solve it.

Of course, it would help to know exactly what the problem was.

"What's the matter?" Tiana asked Louis.

He backed out of the way and motioned to the man standing behind him.

The *bleeding* man standing behind him.

Tiana scrambled up from the floor. She scurried out

of the storeroom and into the kitchen, where the other four members of the Crawfish Crooners stood.

Charlie, their other trumpet player, held a dish towel up to his lips. Tiana took notice of the large splotches of bright red blood seeping into the towel and immediately knew they had more than just a problem on their hands. This was an emergency. And a disaster.

"What happened?" she asked, rushing to Charlie's side.

"Charlie split his lip on the horn," Louis said. "We were playing a rendition of 'Tin Roof Blues,' and his bottom lip just split open like a banana peel."

"Ooh," Charlotte said, covering her mouth. She looked on the verge of losing the pasta jambalaya she'd eaten for dinner. "I'll be in the dining room if you need me, Tia," she mumbled from behind her hand.

Louis hooked a thumb toward Charlotte's retreating form. "What's wrong with her?"

"Lottie's just a little scared of blood. She'll be okay," Tiana said. "Let's focus on Charlie." She set a comforting hand on the trumpet player's shoulder. "Do you think you need a doctor?"

He nodded.

"Gerald here is gonna take him," Louis said. "It's a bad split. He'll need a doc to sew that lip up."

She did her best to hide it, but Tiana was on the verge of losing her own dinner. She looked on in horror as the crimson stain imbuing the towel began to spread. The color seemed to drain from Charlie's face, turning his skin ashen.

"Now," Tiana said, ushering Charlie and Gerald, the band's trombone player, out of the kitchen through the back door that led to the alley. "Get him there safely."

"We're gonna get set up for the final set," Harold, their drummer, said.

"Don't know how good we'll sound being down a trombone and a trumpet," Walter, the bass player, added as he followed Harold out of the kitchen.

Tiana slapped her palm to her forehead. "How did that even happen, Louis?"

Louis hunched his broad shoulders. "I dunno. Charlie was just blowing his horn as usual, and next thing you know . . ." He flapped his hands open, providing a visual Tiana really could have done without. "Strangest thing I've seen." He leaned in close and whispered, "And I've seen some pretty strange things in my day. Though I don't have to tell you that."

"Shhh," Tiana said, looking over her shoulder to make sure no one had overheard. She inched close and lowered her voice. "Tell me, Louis, have you sensed that *more* strange things are happening lately?"

His scabrous forehead creased even more with his frown. "How do you mean?"

She opened her mouth, about to tell him that she thought she was being followed by murky shadows. But it seemed so ridiculous she decided against it. Tiana still wasn't convinced those shadows were real. More than likely, her mind was playing tricks on her due to the stress of pulling off a successful Mardi Gras season.

Instead, she waved off his question. "Forget I said anything. I'm just . . . just a bit out of sorts these days; still nervous about this weekend."

"Well, your first real test will be tomorrow night, when Rudy Davis and the Allstars pack this place," Louis said. "Charlie couldn't have picked a better time to split his lip."

"Louis!" Tiana smacked him on the arm.

"What?"

"That's an awful thing to say." She plopped her hands on her hips. "You do bring up a good point, though. This is going to sound horrible, but do you think the rest of the band will still be able to play tonight?" Tiana asked. "We still have the second dinner service to get through."

"I don't know." Louis shook his head. "I handle the

melody, but I count on Charlie's trumpet to harmonize. Maybe if—"

"Umm . . . I can play trumpet."

Tiana whipped around. Naveen stood several feet behind them, holding up a shiny brass horn.

"Sorry. I just wanted to make sure everything was okay back here. There seemed to be a lot of frantic running," he explained. He gestured to the trumpet in his hand. "The ukulele is still my first love, but I've taught myself how to play the trumpet this past year. I never leave home without it."

"All right, man," Louis said.

Panic seized Tiana's chest. "No!"

Louis and Naveen both stared at her.

"Why not? It's the perfect solution," Louis stated. "We'll only need Naveen here for this final set. I can play Gerald's trombone, and then you've got Rudy Davis and the Allstars tomorrow."

"I know . . . I just . . ." she said, unable to come up with a rationale that wouldn't make her sound like a terrible person, or worse, a lovestruck fool.

She couldn't admit that having to watch Naveen up on that bandstand would rend her soul in two. But that's exactly how she felt. It was hard enough when he was only a guest here at her restaurant, but to have him actually working here?

But what choice did she have?

"Very well," Tiana said. She looked over at Naveen and suppressed the whimper that nearly escaped. Bracing herself, she stuck her hand out.

"Welcome to the band."

13

Naveen

Excitement surged through Naveen's veins, his euphoria building with every song the Crawfish Crooners played. His obsession with jazz music was one of the things that had first drawn him to New Orleans, but never had he imagined he would get the chance to play with a live band. He felt like a real musician, not just someone with a hobby.

He could get used to this.

Naveen peered out at the crowd from his perch on the raised dais, hoping to spot Tiana. He had noticed her sticking her head out of the kitchen door a few minutes ago, but it appeared she had not followed Charlotte out to the dining room.

Disappointment and exasperation warred within him as he recalled the abject horror that raced across her face when he'd offered to step in for the injured trumpet player. It wasn't as if he'd suggested he take over cooking duties in her kitchen—*that* would be a disaster. But he knew his way around a trumpet, and he'd practiced enough of the American jazz standards to blend right in with the Crawfish Crooners.

Naveen had hoped Tiana would be grateful that he'd offered to help. Or, at the very least, that she would be relieved the band would be able to play through the second dinner rush even though they were down two members.

Alas, it would appear that no smiles of appreciation were anywhere in his future. Not from Tiana.

If only he could understand why she hated him so.

Well, that was not fair. He did not know if Tiana hated him—he did not know how she felt about him at all! Every time he came near her, she scurried away like a frightened little church mouse.

Her behavior was peculiar. And frustrating.

And . . . confusing.

At first, he'd thought Tiana was just shy. He would visit that diner where she had worked as a waitress just to see her.

Of course, he could not let her know that was why he frequented it, so he'd order beignets. He ate so many of those luscious fried doughnuts during his first few months in New Orleans that his pants started to get tight at the waist.

Once he and Charlotte became friends, his encounters with Tiana also became more frequent. Naveen waited impatiently for her to warm up to him, but when she remained skittish, he figured that was just her nature.

Then, after she opened her restaurant, he observed how vibrant she was with all her other guests. That was when Naveen realized that Tiana's timidity seemed to be reserved only for him. She constantly turned away from him, almost in a rebuff. He couldn't understand it.

Had he done something to her?

He tried to tell himself that it didn't matter, but that would be a lie. He spent much of his spare time playing jazz music or learning more about the sugar industry, but when he was not doing either of those, he was trying to solve the mystery of the beautiful Tiana.

Louis held his hand up, indicating that this would be their final song of the night, which meant his experience as a real musician was coming to a close. Naveen managed to clear his mind. He wanted to soak in the last drops of this remarkable feeling.

The song ended, and the crowd erupted in applause.

It was exhilarating. Seeing the joy on everyone's faces, knowing he'd entertained them with his music—it sent a rush of pride and gratitude galloping through his bloodstream.

If only Tiana had been out in the dining room to see it.

"Hey, man, you should be on top of the world after that performance," Louis said. "Why you looking so down and out?"

Naveen glanced over to find Louis smiling at him, his toothy grin a mile wide. He had been so caught up in his thoughts of Tiana that Naveen hadn't realized he was frowning.

"I'm not," Naveen assured him. "This was great. I was just . . . just thinking."

"Well, maybe you should stop thinking about whatever it is that put that frown on your face," Louis said as he slapped a broad palm on Naveen's shoulder. "Not if it makes you this sad."

That was the problem. He *couldn't* stop thinking about Tiana.

"I'm not sad," Naveen said. He covered Louis's hand. "Thanks for letting me play with the guys, eh? This was like . . . what do they say? Like a dream come true?"

"Aw, man. Any time," Louis said. "In fact, you should

think about joining the band. We can always use a new guy on the trumpet."

"It would be like old times," Naveen said automatically.

Louis's eyes widened. "What did you say?"

"Uh, like old times?" Naveen said. He frowned. "Wait, have we done this before? Played music together, I mean?"

"I . . . I don't think so," Louis said.

"I could have sworn . . ." Naveen shook his head, wondering what had gotten into him. "Anyway, thank you for the invitation, but things are getting pretty busy down at the sugar mill." He clapped Louis on the shoulder. "This was fun, my friend."

Naveen had started to think of Louis as a friend in the year since he'd arrived on the shores of America. Despite his extremely big teeth and the skin condition that required him to constantly rub lanolin onto his skin, Louis was approachable and always had a ready smile. Naveen was grateful for him. He was grateful for all of the friends he'd made since moving to New Orleans.

More and more, Naveen was coming to realize that traveling to this country was the best decision he'd ever made. He was meeting new people and working hard . . . if one could call persuading restaurants and stores to partner with LaBouff Sugars hard work. For a guy like him, it came naturally.

But what else could he do with his life?

Naveen considered Louis's invitation to join in with the Crawfish Crooners. If he could spend the rest of his days playing jazz music with his friends, he would die a happy man.

Well, maybe not *completely* happy.

Convincing Tiana that she did not have to run away whenever he was near would be nice. She and Louis were good friends. Maybe he could ask Louis to put in a good word for him.

Naveen's back went ramrod straight.

Achidanza!

Why hadn't he thought of this before?

He swiftly climbed down from the stage and went in search of Tiana's other friend—her *best* friend. Charlotte. He spotted her sitting at the table Mr. LaBouff always occupied when he dined at the supper club, toward the rear of the dining room.

Given the look on Charlotte's face, the fella sitting next to her was the one she'd hoped to avoid. Maybe if he rescued her from this conversation she obviously did not want to be a part of, she would return the favor.

"Hello, gentlemen," Naveen greeted the table at large. "Mr. LaBouff, I wonder if I could speak to Charlotte for—"

"Oh, yes!" Charlotte yelled. She pushed back from the

table so quickly that her chair landed on the floor behind her. "I don't mean to be rude, but now that Naveen is done filling in for that trumpet player with the busted lip, we can go back to our date."

She gripped his arm like a vise and pinched him.

"Yes," Naveen yelped. "Yes, let us continue our . . . our date."

"Oh, thank goodness!" Charlotte released a relieved sigh as they quickly made their way back toward their table near the stage. "I swear, if I had to listen to Rubin Dubois talk about his bunions a second longer, I may have murdered him. Heavens to Betsy, that man is irritating."

Naveen's forehead wrinkled. "Umm . . . who is Betsy?"

"I don't know. It's just something people say around here." She waved him off. "Now, what is it that you wanted? Or did you come over because you could see on my face that I was ready to commit a felony?"

"Uh, both, actually," Naveen said. He pulled out the chair at their table and waited until she sat before taking a seat himself. He scooted his chair closer to her and, in a lowered voice, said, "I need you to put in a good word for me with Tiana."

Charlotte's head jerked back. The suspicion in her eyes caused Naveen to squirm like a bug under a microscope. But then a cagey smile drew across her lips.

"I *knew* you had designs on Tia," Charlotte mused as she pointed a finger at him. "I could sense something happening between you two."

"I just—"

She held up her hands. "But before you get your hopes up, I can already tell you exactly what Tiana will say. She'll say that she's too busy and doesn't have time for romantic foolishness."

"But—"

"Now, usually, I would disagree with that sentiment, because I believe there is nothing more important than love. However, I've known Tia a long time, and I know how hard she's worked for this restaurant. I don't want anything to distract her, either."

"I don't want to be a distraction. I only—"

"Of course, that girl really does need to loosen up a bit."

"I just want to get to know her better," Naveen rushed out before she could interrupt him again. "That is all, Charlotte." He hunched his shoulders. "I am not sure why, but Tiana does not seem to like me very much. Maybe if you tell her that I am not such a bad guy, she won't run away when she sees me, eh?"

Charlotte tipped her head to the side. After several moments ticked by, she pointed at Naveen and said, "Okay, here's what I'll do. I'll tell Tia that you are madly in love with her—"

"No, no, no, no!" Naveen said.

Charlotte slapped him on the arm. "I'm only teasing, Naveen. Lighten up! I know what I'm doing here," she said. "I will casually mention how interesting you are." She snapped her fingers. "Quick, give me something interesting about you."

"Uhh . . . I have been learning to juggle?"

"I'll make something up. Besides, I'm hoping to drag her to some Mardi Gras balls, and she'll need a date." She narrowed her eyes at Naveen once more. "But you better not make me regret it. Tiana is my best friend, and I will not see her hurt."

Naveen shook his head. "No way. I would never hurt her." His pulse quickened at the thought of accompanying Tiana to a ball, seeing her all dolled up in a beautiful gown. He could see her now!

Actually, he *could* see it.

Naveen squinted in confusion.

Had he seen her in a ball gown already?

"Of course, we'll have to work our way up to the Mardi Gras ball. I think you need to start slow, like asking her out for coffee tomorrow." Charlotte's eyes brightened as she looked over Naveen's shoulder. "Here's your chance."

Naveen whipped around.

Tiana had just stepped out of the kitchen. She carried a tray laden with dishes on her shoulder, probably beignets or bread pudding. Both were hot ticket items when it came to dessert at T&J's Supper Club.

"You ready, sugar?" Charlotte asked.

He stopped and took a breath. Before he could nod, Charlotte grabbed him by the hand and jerked him from his seat.

"Come on! Operation: Make a Match with My Two Best Friends is on."

14

Tiana

Given the current tranquility of the empty dining room, one would never believe that less than an hour earlier this place had been packed to the gills with a boisterous crowd and rousing jazz music. Tiana shoved away the guilt that tried to creep in at the notion of her sitting here doing nothing. She'd worked hard tonight—they all had. She deserved to relax for a spell, to steal just a few minutes and quietly celebrate yet another successful night at T&J's Supper Club.

If she was being honest, she also needed a minute to ruminate over that *other* thing that had happened about an hour ago.

She was still reeling from Charlotte's outlandish suggestion that Tiana and Naveen meet up for café au lait the next day. Tiana had reminded her that they already had plans to go shopping, and then she'd raced back to the kitchen.

What was Lottie thinking?

Although, to be fair, Charlotte had no way of knowing the turmoil Tiana endured whenever she was near Naveen. None of her friends knew what she'd sacrificed in order to keep them all safe. Still, her *best* friend, who had known her all her life, should have known better than to propose such a preposterous idea. And in front of Naveen, no less!

With a sigh, Tiana pushed up from her seat. This was enough relaxing for the week.

She went around to all the tables and wiped them down with an old dishrag. Using as much muscle as she could muster, she scrubbed at a particularly stubborn stain on the table next to Mr. LaBouff's, then picked up a tray stacked with dirty dishes and hauled it into the kitchen.

She walked past one of the paintings that Ms. Rose had given her and stopped short. The portrait, depicting a rainy evening in the French Quarter, was one of her favorites of those that hung in the restaurant. But something seemed . . . off.

Tiana tilted her head to the side, trying to figure out exactly what bothered her. She peered more closely and blinked several times. She was sure that the flowers hanging along the wrought iron balcony had been more vibrant. The same with the deep red brick of the building. Now they seemed obscured by the rain. Was the mist in the painting thicker?

"Don't be ridiculous," Tiana murmured.

That thickening fog outside must have been fogging her brain. Or maybe it was just that she was bone-tired after the night she'd had and wasn't thinking clearly.

She continued to the kitchen, carting the last of the dirty dishes with her. She backed her way through the swinging door. When she turned, she yelped in surprise.

"Addie Mae!" Tiana nearly dropped the tray. "My goodness, you scared me. What are you still doing here?"

"Mr. James made me promise not to leave you here by yourself," Addie Mae answered.

"I should have known." Tiana rolled her eyes. And to think she'd felt such a sense of triumph after convincing Daddy to go home early. "Well, let's get these cleaned up so that we can both get out of here."

She and Addie Mae made quick work of the dishes and had the kitchen looking spotless in no time. Of course, it would be a mess again the next night, but that was how things worked in the restaurant business; she wouldn't have had it any other way.

"Thanks for the help," Tiana said as she followed Addie Mae out the back door that led to the alley behind the restaurant. She snapped her fingers. "I forgot Mama's dessert," she said, remembering the bread pudding she'd promised to bring home. Her mother had left early with a headache, probably from all that dancing.

"I'll wait for you," Addie Mae said.

"No, you go on home," Tiana said. "I'll see you tomorrow."

She went back inside and found the thick wedge of bread pudding wrapped in tinfoil sitting where she'd left it near the coffee percolator. She slid it into her bag, then looked over the kitchen one last time to make sure all was in order.

Letting out a deep breath, she tried to make the stress of the night dissipate. *This is all yours and Daddy's.*

And no one could take it from her.

Tiana walked back into the alley and gasped, struck by how thick the fog had become in just a few minutes. She could barely see a foot in front of her.

"My goodness," she whispered.

She kept the alley behind her restaurant clear of clutter, but she still tiptoed about, making sure she didn't trip over anything she couldn't see.

Despite its still being February, a sultry heat lingered in the air, making the night warm and damp. Tiana hefted her bag more securely onto her shoulder and took off for the Rampart streetcar line. If she didn't make it in time for the last ride to the Ninth Ward, she would find herself walking home.

At least the walk from Tremé would be shorter than if she'd bought that old sugar mill from the Fenner brothers. In fact, maybe it was a blessing that the realtors had sold it to someone else.

"Yeah, you keep telling yourself that," Tiana said with a huff.

"You always go around talking to yourself?"

A streak of cold rushed through Tiana's veins. She took a step back. "Who's there?" she called.

A low, distinct laugh came from just over her shoulder. Tiana quickly turned. She blinked twice as the thick fog parted and the Shadow Man appeared.

"Well, hello there, Tiana," he greeted in that deceptively cordial voice of his. "Fine night out, isn't it?"

She straightened her shoulders, refusing to show an ounce of fear. "What can I do for you, Mr. Facilier?"

"Why so formal? We're old friends at this point, aren't we? And it's *Doctor* Facilier."

"We are *not* friends, *Doctor*. The bottle of the potion I got from you this morning should last for at least two weeks, so we have no further dealings with each other until after

Mardi Gras." Tiana hefted her bag higher on her shoulder and began to walk past him. "Now, if you'll excuse me, it's late and I need to get to the streetcar stop. I have another long and busy day ahead of me tomorrow."

"I can imagine," he said, stepping in front of her and blocking her path. "This little restaurant of yours is all any-one can talk about." He looked toward the building. "It's . . . nice." He didn't sound impressed. "Of course, the one I offered you would make this look like a shabby shack in comparison."

Tiana stuck her chin in the air, ready to defend her res-taurant, but he spoke again before she could.

"Your guests don't seem to mind, so why should I?" he said with a casual shrug of his bony shoulders. "It appears your food makes up for the lack of . . . ambience, shall we say."

"The food *is* the most important thing at a restaurant, and yes, my guests love the dishes Daddy and I prepare here. That's all that matters."

"Yes, it is," he said. "I'm particularly interested in that étouffée you cooked tonight for Mr. Eli LaBouff."

Tiana's eyes shot to his. "How do you know that I served Mr. LaBouff étouffée?"

A wicked smile curved up the corners of his mouth.

Tiana suddenly recalled the stranger who had stalked past her, nearly knocking her over.

"You were here tonight," Tiana said in an accusatory tone.

Facilier peered down at his fingernails, then buffed them on his shoulder. "I may have stepped inside for a moment. I wanted to see what all the buzz was about."

Tiana narrowed her eyes at him. She didn't trust this one as far as she could throw him.

"I need to get going," she repeated. She tried to move past, but this time he stopped her with his cane, shoving the long stick out in front of her.

"Not so fast," Facilier said. "I have a proposition for you. Call it an amendment to our original arrangement."

Tiana shook her head. "No. I'm fine with how things are now. I'm not making any more deals with you."

He moved in close, his voice growing more sinister. "Look, girlie. You got off easy with that first deal. And if you want things to continue as they are, you'd better listen to what I have to say. It would be a shame if there was a horrible accident at this restaurant you've opened, but we all know how quickly fires start. Don't we?"

Tiana gasped. "You wouldn't."

He tilted his head to the side. "Now that I think about

it, it would be far worse for you if something were to happen to that dear father of yours. Or your mother."

Dread sliced through Tiana like a knife through an onion.

"You keep my family out of this," she hissed. "That was part of the deal."

"Things change." Facilier shrugged. "You of all people should understand *transformations*." He reached inside his jacket and drew out a vial similar to the one she'd gotten from him earlier today, but bigger. "You can still avoid harm coming to your family. All you have to do is add this potion to *all* of your food from now on. It's simple, Tiana."

"But why?" she asked. "Everything has been going just fine with me adding the potion to the gumbo. What difference will it make putting it in everything?"

"Enough," he snarled.

Tiana flinched at his harshness, then cursed herself for showing even a hint of fear. She'd learned over the course of this year that the best way to handle Dr. Facilier was to show that he couldn't intimidate her.

"My question is legitimate," she countered. "What's the point of putting this potion in all of my dishes? You said I had to put it in Daddy's gumbo because that's the dish he's known for."

"I've cautioned you before about questioning my friends

on the other side. Ask yourself, Tiana. Is it worth risking your daddy's life when you just got him back? Is it worth your *prince's* life when all you have to do is what you've been doing all this time? Why must you make things so difficult?"

"Because I don't trust you," she said. "I'm never going to just do something simply because you asked, *Doctor* Facilier."

He grabbed her wrist and turned her hand palm up. He slapped the vial into the center of her palm. "Every single dish, Tiana."

She threw the vial directly at his face. He snatched it as if he had been expecting her to do just that.

"I don't have to do anything," Tiana said. "I've held up my end of our bargain. You hold up yours."

She knocked his cane out of the way and brushed past him. She moved like her feet were on fire, refusing to look over her shoulder to see if he was following her. Her entire body trembled as she ran on shaking legs for the streetcar stop. Tiana could hear the bells jingling, indicating its arrival.

She was still yards away from the stop.

"Hold on there!" she shouted, frantically waving her hands even though the conductor wouldn't be able to see her through the thick fog. "Please! Don't leave!"

She reached the corner of Ursulines and South Rampart

and looked both ways through the haze before stepping into the street. The moment her foot hit the roadway, the headlights of a Model T blasted through the fog.

Tiana yelped, jumping back onto the curb.

She slapped her hand over her erratically beating heart.

"Goodness," she whispered. She looked again for vehicles, then crossed the street, grateful that the streetcar was still at the stop. Tiana climbed aboard and paid her fare, then made her way to the back of the streetcar. She collapsed onto a seat and covered her face with her hands.

What was she going to do? Could Facilier really hurt her parents? Or Naveen?

Of course he could. The man had turned both her and Naveen into frogs. He could do whatever he wanted to do with that strange power he wielded.

She never should have made that deal with him. She knew better than to get involved with the likes of the Shadow Man.

But if you hadn't, Naveen wouldn't be human. And Daddy wouldn't be here.

Once she reached her stop, Tiana alighted from the streetcar. She could barely see her hand in front of her face. The relentlessness of this fog took her breath away.

She traveled this route so often she could probably have made it home with her eyes closed, but it was still unnerving not being able to see where she was going. Not knowing if anyone was out here with her.

"Don't be ridiculous," Tiana whispered.

This was Facilier's fault. Her run-in with him had her on edge, causing her heartbeat to escalate and tendrils of anxiety to cascade down her spine. But she was in her own neighborhood now. She didn't have anything to worry about. Right?

Taking a deep breath, Tiana couldn't help running the rest of the way.

15
Tiana

The Ninth Ward, New Orleans
Friday, February 1927
Four days before Mardi Gras

Tiana lifted her favorite camel-brown hat from the rack in the corner of her room and fixed it over her hair. She turned to face the mirror and frowned.

"You look like you're off to shovel manure in this getup," she said to the image staring back at her.

She expelled a frustrated sigh as she tossed the hat on the bed and went back to her chifforobe for what had to have been the dozenth time this morning. There must have been *something* in there that would be appropriate for shopping at the most prestigious department store in all of New Orleans.

"Ah, yes! This one should work."

She pulled out her green-and-white polka-dot dress with the satin ribbon that tied at the waist, and the matching satin trim that ran along the hem of its ruffled skirt. She would normally only wear a dress like this to a wedding, or on Easter Sunday, but if she was going on this outing with Lottie to Maison Blanche, she had to look the part of someone who belonged there.

Because she *did* belong there.

She was just as good as anybody else who set foot in that establishment, and she was going to make sure everyone who was there knew it.

Tiana pulled the dress over her head and pinned the barrette Ms. Rose had given her as a gift behind her ear. It had tiny gardenias attached to it, adding an elegant touch to her ensemble. She swished around from left to right in the mirror, admiring the way her dress twirled about her legs.

She stopped.

"Wait . . ." Tiana murmured.

She stepped closer to the mirror and peered at the barrette. She could have sworn the two flowers on either end of the trinket had been buds. Now all four of them were full gardenia blooms.

She must have been mistaken about the buds. Had to have been.

But she had specifically remembered those buds. She'd remarked on how pretty they would be if they could bloom.

She shook her head. There had to be a logical explanation. Maybe she'd bought a second barrette and had forgotten about it? Or perhaps someone had switched them on her.

With shaking hands, she slowly slipped the barrette out of her hair and returned it to her jewelry box. She tried her best to ignore the uneasiness that continued to build within her gut.

Tiana closed her eyes tight and sucked in several deep breaths. When she opened them, all would be okay. She popped her eyes open and forced herself to smile at her reflection.

"See, everything is fine. You're just tired."

She looked back at the clock on her bedside table and realized if she didn't get going, she would be late. When she walked into the kitchen, she was greeted with a surprised murmur from her mother, who sat behind her sewing machine.

"Well, look at you," Eudora said after removing the

needle she'd had sandwiched between her lips. "You're dressed pretty fancy for making fried chicken and jambalaya, aren't you?"

"I'm not going to the restaurant just yet," Tiana said. She drew a cup of water from the tap and leaned against the counter as she took a sip. She stood up straight. "Wait, where's Daddy?"

"He went out to Jefferson Parish to look at some gardening equipment. He said to tell you he'll be back by this afternoon to start preparing for the Mardi Gras weekend kickoff." Eudora threaded a second needle with purple thread. "I should have the last of these done just in time."

Her mother had spent the past week making tablecloths in the traditional Mardi Gras colors as part of the decorations for the supper club's weekend-long celebration. Tiana couldn't wait to see how they would look.

Eudora glanced at Tiana. "You still didn't tell me why you're all dolled up."

Tiana finished her water, rinsed the cup in the empty sink, and returned it to the cupboard.

"I'm going over to the LaBouffs', and then Charlotte and I are going to Maison Blanche."

Her mother's eyebrows shot up. "Oh, you've got Maison Blanche money now?"

"I'm not planning on buying anything," Tiana assured her. "I'm only going with Lottie because she invited me."

"Well, you have been working hard. You deserve to treat yourself to something from the department store." Eudora pushed away from her sewing machine and came around the table. She reached into the pocket of her dress and pulled out a five-dollar bill.

"Five dollars?" Tiana cried. She backed away when her mother tried to hand her the money.

"Didn't I just say that you deserve to treat yourself? Go on and buy yourself something fun."

Tiana shook her head. "No way, Mama. I'm not wasting five whole dollars on foolishness."

"It's not foolishness. What's the point of working so hard if you don't enjoy the fruits of your labor?"

Eudora cupped Tiana's cheeks with her hands. They were slightly callused from years of working with needle and thread. "I haven't said this enough lately, but I am *so* proud of all the work you've put into the supper club. Your daddy is, too."

A lump of emotion immediately formed in Tiana's throat. There were few things in this world that meant more to her than making her parents proud. She closed her eyes and smiled, relishing the safety and comfort of her mother's tender touch.

"Thank you, Mama." She opened her eyes. "But I'm still not taking your five dollars." She slipped out of her mother's hold and quickly made her way to the front door. "Tell Daddy I'll meet him at the restaurant later."

"Tiana!" her mother called, her hands on her hips.

"Love you, Mama." Tiana blew her a kiss before grabbing her purse and leaving the house.

Tiana headed south toward the river this time, opposite her usual route. That way she could hop on the St. Charles Avenue streetcar line, which would take her directly to the LaBouff mansion.

She greeted neighbors while simultaneously calculating the various tasks she had to complete before that night's special dinner service.

The streetcar pulled up to the stop just as Tiana arrived.

"Hey there, Tiana," the streetcar operator greeted. "I hear you've got a big name playing at your restaurant tonight."

"I sure do," she answered as she slid a nickel in the box. She spoke loud enough for everyone on the streetcar to hear. "Rudy Davis is kicking off Mardi Gras weekend at T&J's Supper Club. Make sure you stop on by once your workday is done."

Tiana smiled as she heard murmurs of excitement while she made her way to the back. She took an empty seat on the side that faced the river, and was immediately taken aback by the thick grayish cloud that hovered over the water—even thicker than yesterday. There might have been something to Councilman Dubois's theory that this peculiar fog was coming from the river.

Tiana put her chin in her upturned palm and marveled at the activity buzzing along the riverfront. Despite the lingering mist, she could make out the fishermen casting wide nets off the pier that stretched along the banks of the Mississippi River. She and her daddy made a trip to that same pier at least once a week, making deals for fresh catfish, dreaming up new recipes.

A medley of worry, alarm, and sheer rage bubbled up inside as she recalled Facilier's threat.

To ignore it outright would be unwise, but she did not want to bow down to his whims, either.

She now recognized her folly. She'd become too comfortable, foolishly trusting that a known con man would remain true to his word. She should have been expecting him to pull something like this all along.

Well, it wasn't going to work. Unless he could give her a good reason to add that potion to everything she served at the restaurant, she wasn't going to do it. Who knew what was in this new version, if it was even the same magical concoction keeping her daddy alive . . . or something more nefarious? And who knew what else he would ask if she complied?

Attempting to put Facilier out of her mind, she took in the sights and sounds of the city. The streetcar sailed past LaBouff's enormous brick sugar mill. Plumes of white smoke bellowed from metal stacks, mixing in with the fog.

As she stared at the deep red bricks of the mill, another unwelcome thought made its way to her mind. Was Naveen somewhere inside? What was he doing? Was he considering asking her out for coffee again?

Stop that, Tiana!

She could *not* have coffee with him. She needed to focus on her future. And as much as she wished things could be different, Naveen was not and never could be part of it.

She pulled her bottom lip between her teeth to stop it from quivering, cursing even that tiny display of weakness.

The streetcar rolled along St. Charles Avenue, past the imposing homes that lined the wide boulevard. Tiana couldn't imagine what it would be like to live in one of these, despite the fact that she'd been a frequent guest at the largest one in the city since childhood.

Even at a young age, she'd noticed that the people who looked like her never *lived* in those houses—they only cleaned them or provided some other kind of service. Her youthful mind thought it was happenstance, but as she got older, Tiana gradually became aware of disparities between how the Black people who lived in Tremé and the Ninth Ward—and even the poor white people living in the tenement buildings—were treated, compared with those who lived uptown. She would ask Mama about it, but after hearing her say "It's just the way things are" so many times, Tiana stopped asking. Tiana always wished she could do something to help end those disparities.

When the streetcar pulled up in front of the LaBouffs' large white mansion, Tiana bade farewell to the conductor and climbed down the steps. She waited for several Model Ts to drive past—they were common in this more affluent part of the city—before she crossed the busy street and entered through the heavy wrought iron gate.

New Orleans was home to many grand residences, but there was none more magnificent than the two-story Greek Revival home Mr. Eli LaBouff had commissioned right in the heart of the city's Garden District. Stately columns surrounded the wraparound porch, each archway adorned with ornate ironwork. The house, with its intricately carved trim and elaborate front door, was a work of art.

"Tia!"

Tiana looked up to find Charlotte waving at her from the second-floor balcony. Feathers from the fluffy pink plumes that lined the edges of the silk dressing gown she wore flittered to the ground.

"I'll be right down," Charlotte said. "I just need a minute to finish getting dressed."

Shaking her head with a small laugh, Tiana didn't bother to point out to Lottie that she was the one who had said to be here at 10 a.m. sharp. She'd known her friend long enough to understand that 10 a.m. in Charlotte's time meant no sooner than 10:30 a.m. to everyone else.

She entered the house and was instantly pummeled by Stella, Charlotte's gentle giant of a hound. She hunched to the ground and rubbed the dog behind both ears. "How's it going, girl? You mind telling your mama to hurry it up?"

Stella's tail wagged back and forth as she looked excitedly at Tiana.

"Stella doesn't have to tell me anything, because I'm ready," Charlotte said.

Tiana looked toward the top of the gargantuan staircase. Lottie descended the steps, wearing a pristine white suit with a form-fitting skirt and a wide-brimmed hat. Tiana knew she'd made the right choice in choosing the green-and-white polka-dot dress.

"Well, come on. Let's get going," Charlotte said, putting her arm through Tiana's as if she hadn't been the one who'd left Tiana waiting. Tiana had to hand it to her—only Lottie had the charm to get away with such things.

They exited through the front door and walked to a car idling at the curb. Ten minutes later, the car pulled up to the multi-storied department store in the heart of downtown. If the prime Canal Street location wasn't enough to convince people of its prominence, Maison Blanche's towering white edifice, with its lofty columns and fancy carvings, should.

Tiana tamped down the bit of nerves that suddenly tried to surface. This wasn't her first time shopping here. She and her mother frequented Krauss Department Store a few blocks away because of their fabrics selection, but she'd come to Maison Blanche with Daddy just a few months ago to buy a present for Mama's birthday.

She just knew that shopping here was a completely different experience for her than for her friend.

"I know exactly what I want," Charlotte said as they walked through the door. "Well, I know the exact colors I want—I'm thinking something violet and maybe a blush pink. Ooh, and midnight blue!"

She led Tiana to the gown section and proceeded to run the store attendants ragged as they catered to her every whim.

Tiana was mindful of the store clerk who lurked near

the display of rayon stockings. The woman had been watching her like a hawk from the moment they arrived.

Charlotte emerged from the changing room wearing a sparkly navy blue flapper dress with crystal embellishments along the neckline.

"What about this one, Tia?" she asked, turning left, then right in front of the mirror.

"That dress was made for dancing," Tiana replied.

"Yeah, but it's missing something."

Charlotte marched to the row of mannequins and lifted a navy cloche from one of them. She tugged the tight-fitting hat over her bouncy blond curls.

"You know, I actually think this would look better on you," she said. Charlotte tried to fit the hat on Tiana's head, but she moved out of the way.

"Lottie, no," Tiana said. Yet the lurking store clerk had already noticed.

She rounded the display case and rushed to where Charlotte and Tiana stood.

"Excuse me—she cannot try on the merchandise," the woman stated.

Lottie looked over at her. "Why not? We're shopping."

"She cannot try on the merchandise," the woman repeated, her voice even harder. Colder. "It's store policy."

Lottie plopped a hand on her hip, but Tiana intervened before she could say more. "It's okay, Lottie."

"No, it is not!"

"Ma'am, if you do not calm down, we will have to ask you to leave," the clerk said.

"Excuse me!" Charlotte gasped. "Do you know who my daddy is?"

Tiana took Charlotte by the hand. "We're leaving," she said.

Charlotte wrenched her hand away. "We are not! We have every right to be here. And you have every right to try on whatever you want."

"Charlotte, please," Tiana hissed. "Let's just go. Please."

It must have been the plea in Tiana's voice that finally caught Lottie's attention. Or maybe it was the use of her full name, something Tiana rarely did.

"Okay," she said with a nod. "We'll leave."

She stuck her nose up in the air in the most Charlotte way possible and marched into the changing room. She came out a few minutes later dressed in her white suit.

"I will never, ever step foot in this store again," Charlotte said.

Tiana did her level best to keep her own head held high as she followed Lottie out of the department store, but when she slid into the back seat of the car, the adrenaline released from her body in a rush. Her hands shook.

"The nerve of that woman!" Charlotte huffed. "We shouldn't have left, Tia. In fact, Jefferson, turn the car around."

"No," Tiana said. "No, Lottie. I'm not going back there."

"You can't let people tell you what you can and cannot do. I never back down from—"

"I can't do what you do!" Tiana said. She fisted her hands in her lap, fighting for control over her emotions. She hated this feeling, and she resented Charlotte for putting her in this position, even if her friend's heart was in the right place. And at the moment, that felt worse than Dr. Facilier's magical bind.

"You don't understand," Tiana said. "They can forbid me from trying on their merchandise, and if I don't comply, they can call the authorities. That's my reality."

"But it doesn't have to be that way."

"But it *is*," Tiana said. "Who knows, maybe one day I will be able to try on that hat at Maison Blanche, but today is not that day."

"And not that store," Lottie said.

"Never that store," Tiana reiterated. She paused. "I do appreciate you standing up for me that way."

"I will always stand up for you, Tia," Charlotte said, grabbing her friend's hand.

But as the car moved through the city, they both fell into silence, wrapped up in their own thoughts.

16

Tiana

Tiana sifted flour into the steel bowl she'd dubbed her beignet-making bowl, then added in two heaping cups of sugar direct from the LaBouff Sugars mill. She relished in the comforting chaos of the busy kitchen, trusting that it would get her mind off what had occurred this morning at Maison Blanche department store.

It wasn't working out as planned.

Now that she thought about it, making beignets wasn't the best distraction method. She made them so often that her mind tended to wander, and right now, it remained fixated on the horridness of that morning's encounter. What had happened with that snobby sales clerk was a stark reminder of what she knew all too well: that unfairness lurked around every corner, especially for people who looked like her.

Once again, Mr. Fenner's words from the year before echoed—the ones he'd uttered after selling that abandoned sugar mill right from under her. A woman of her *background* wasn't fit to run a big business like this.

"Did that dough do something to you?"

Tiana startled at Addie Mae's question. "What?"

Addie Mae nodded at the bowl Tiana held. "You're whipping that dough up like it stole your favorite pair of shoes or something. Too much of that and the beignets will come out tough and chewy instead of fluffy."

Tiana cursed under her breath as she dumped the contents of the bowl into the garbage and started over.

That clerk at the department store might have ruined her morning, but Tiana darn sure wouldn't allow her to ruin the rest of Tiana's day. Not with the crowd she was expecting at her restaurant tonight—especially after spreading word about Rudy Davis and the Allstars.

Tiana started to hum her favorite of his tunes, "Jump, Skip, and a Hop," under her breath as she cracked an egg and added it to the bowl. She measured and poured in the sugar and threw in a pinch of salt, getting back into the familiar rhythm and focus. On her way to the icebox for milk, she noticed the wire basket that she used to store the pasta was empty. For a moment she just stared at the basket, baffled.

She'd quickly gone through the pasta Mr. Salvaggio had delivered yesterday and had put in an emergency order to be delivered first thing this morning. Tiana went into the pantry to see if Addie Mae had mistakenly put it there, but there were only canned vegetables, tomato sauce, and rice on the shelves.

"Addie Mae." Tiana walked over to where her head waitress was stacking salad bowls. "Where's the pasta I ordered?"

"You made jambalaya with it, didn't you?"

"That was yesterday's order. I put in another for today. Mr. Salvaggio assured me that it would be delivered this morning. Did he not bring it?"

Addie Mae shook her head. "No, I don't think so. And I haven't seen any packages out back."

Tiana frowned. Mr. Salvaggio was one of her most reliable vendors. It wasn't like him not to follow through.

"I hope he isn't unwell," she murmured. She untied the apron from around her waist. "You know what, I think I'll just take a walk down to the French Market. I need a few extra ingredients anyway. I found a recipe for greens with salt meat in Mama's cupboard that will go mighty fine with tonight's menu."

Tiana hung the apron on the nail next to the door, then grabbed the wicker basket she used whenever she went to the outdoor market, which lined the huge bend along the mighty Mississippi. It was only a fifteen-minute walk through the French Quarter. That is, if she didn't run into anyone she knew on the way there. A fifteen-minute journey could take an hour with chatty neighbors stopping her to inquire about how her mama and the rest of the family were doing.

Tiana was walking near one of the brick tenement houses when she caught sight of a silhouette out of the corner of her eye. She moved to the side, assuming it was some hardworking factory worker on his way to one of the many warehouses in the Quarter. When the blurred figure didn't emerge after she'd walked several yards, Tiana slowed her steps so that whoever it was behind her could move along.

They didn't.

She stopped walking and turned around.

No one.

Unease crept up Tiana's spine in the same way that ever-thickening fog crept along the city streets. She couldn't dismiss this as fatigue or her mind playing tricks on her. Something—or some*one*—was definitely following her.

"Hello?"

No answer.

Was it the Shadow Man? But no—for all his tricks, Facilier couldn't resist hearing himself talk. He would have shown himself by now.

Heart starting to pound in her chest, Tiana hurried along the sidewalk, barely stopping at the street corners to check for traffic.

Relief washed over her when she arrived at the covered outdoor market and found it bustling with people. She waved to the egg vendor, Mr. Taylor, and his son, Lil Johnny, lifted his cap in greeting. The strong smell of fish hit her square in the face, but Tiana didn't mind. She waded through the throng of people at the seafood stalls that were set up at the very end of the market, making her way to the plethora of vegetable stands lined up on both sides of the pedestrian walkway.

Tiana did a double take when she glanced over at the river.

It was green. *Grassy.* A thick moss skimmed the top of the water.

"What's happening here?" she asked.

"Strange, ain't it?" a fisherman said. He held up a foot-long catfish. "Can I interest ya in one of these?"

"No, thank you," Tiana said. She hooked her thumb at the river. "When did this start?"

The craggy-faced man hunched a shoulder. "All was just fine yesterday. Got outta my boat this morning and this stuff was covering the water. Strange, indeed."

"There has to be something to account for it. Could it be the fog?" she remarked.

"Don't know. Not making it easy for us fishermen, I can tell ya that."

From the conversations she caught on the way to her favorite vegetable stand, the baffling algae bloom on the river was the talk of the market.

Tiana sidled up to the stand run by the Galvez family from St. Bernard Parish. They always had the freshest, most flavorful vegetables, and if you offered a fair price, they would throw in a little something extra.

Tiana picked up several bunches of dark leafy greens, a few radishes, some onions, and a basket of strawberries. She'd been wanting to try her hand at making a strawberry sauce to drizzle on top of her beignets. After paying for her purchases, she went over to the Rinella family's pasta stand for her last order. It didn't measure up to Mr. Salvaggio's spaghetti, but then again, little could.

She was moving away from the stand when a sense of foreboding tingled along Tiana's spine. Just then, an encroaching shadow fell over her. She spun around to find Dr. Facilier standing just over her shoulder. She quickly squelched the cry that rose in her throat.

"What do you want?" she whispered harshly.

"You know why I'm here."

She narrowed her eyes. "Were you following me earlier?" Confusion flashed in his eyes, telling Tiana all she needed to know. He wasn't the one who had trailed her to the market after all. Tiana waved off her question. "Forget it. I told you that I am not making any more deals, so leave me alone."

She turned and started to walk away, but before she could get past the next vegetable stall, Facilier was suddenly in front of her, blocking her path. Tiana yelped, but the buzz and chatter around the busy market drowned out her cry.

Facilier lowered his head until he was eye level with her. "I've been polite. You don't want me to get nasty."

She waved her arms in front of his face, inches from her own. "What do you call this?"

"You see this little bit of fog that's been hanging around this city?" Facilier scoffed. "It's nothing. My friends can show you what *real* smoke looks like."

"Are you saying that they're the reason behind this strange weather?"

"I'm saying *you're* the reason this fog is here. I warned you things would get ugly if you didn't do what I said." He pulled the large vial he'd tried to give her the last time they'd met from the inside pocket of his vest. "Take it. Use it tonight."

Facilier shoved it into her hands, looking like he wanted to say more. But then he looked past Tiana, his eyes widening in dismay. He quickly pivoted and stalked away, disappearing into the heavy fog.

Tiana turned to see what had motivated his abrupt departure. "Oh, Ms. Rose!"

"Hello, Tiana. Who was your friend?" the woman asked as she approached.

"He's . . . he's nobody," Tiana muttered darkly, watching Facilier retreat further into the fog. She threw the new concoction into her bag.

"You know, Tiana, my mother used to say all the time, *bel dan pa di zanmi.* Just because someone is smiling at you, it doesn't mean they're your friend. One must be careful of the company one keeps."

"He's no friend of mine," Tiana said.

The woman only nodded. Then, after a beat, she said,

"Were you going to leave the market without visiting my flower stand?"

"Well, I'm in a bit of a rush." Tiana hedged. Ms. Rose had the ability to make her feel as if she'd just been scolded in the most gentle way possible. "But I must say that those beautiful flowers you gave me yesterday are gorgeous," Tiana added. "They really do brighten up the restaurant."

"I'm happy to hear that," the woman said in her soothing voice. She nodded in the opposite direction. "Follow me. I have another gift for you."

"I really can't," Tiana called, but Ms. Rose was already heading to her flower stand, and the woman had been much too nice to her over these past few months for Tiana to rudely walk away.

"Ms. Rose, I appreciate the gifts, but I can't continue to accept them, especially without payment," Tiana said as she trailed after her.

"But I insist," Ms. Rose replied. "My painting is a hobby. They would remain unseen in my home if you weren't kind enough to display them. And this one is very special. I think you will like it."

She lifted a purple cloth from the framed picture, unveiling an absolutely stunning portrait of the Mardi Gras Indians. The bright colors of their elaborate headdresses were so brilliant; they gave the picture an almost lifelike appearance.

The scene displayed the tradition, which had originated in Tremé, of the formerly enslaved Africans paying homage at Mardi Gras to the Native people who had aided them during troubled times. How could she say no to a painting that held such meaning to the neighborhood that had embraced her restaurant?

"It's beautiful," Tiana said. "I know exactly where I'm going to put it."

"You must hang it in the very center of the back wall, facing the stage."

Tiana blinked. "That's . . . uh . . . very specific."

Ms. Rose shrugged her delicate shoulders. "There's a symmetry to the placement, yes? The rhythm of the band paired with the rhythm of the Indians' tambourine?" She tapped the side of her leg as if she were playing one of the percussion instruments.

"Yes." Tiana slowly nodded. "Yes, I agree."

"You should probably get back," Ms. Rose said. "Word on the street is that you have quite the celebration taking place at your restaurant tonight."

Tiana shook her head, trying to clear it. "Yes—yes, I do," she said. "Thank you again for the painting."

"Thank you for giving it a home," she returned.

Tiana secured the gift underneath her arm before leaving the French Market. She decided against going back the way she'd come, choosing to head west, past the Cabildo and St. Louis Cathedral. As she came upon the huge limestone Louisiana Supreme Court building that had just recently been built, she watched as a brand-new Model T pulled up to the curb and one of the Fenner brothers—the taller of the two—got out of the car.

As if the day could get any stranger.

"Well, if it isn't Tiana. How are you doing?"

"I'm doing well, Mr. Fenner. How are you?"

"Oh, well, you know. All is good, except for this fog that doesn't want to go away. Strange thing, isn't it?"

"That it is. And it seems to be getting thicker by the day."

"Yes, it does." He looked her up and down through the monocle that hung from a chain on his neck. "You know, Tiana, I hope there are no hard feelings about what happened with that old sugar mill. Your restaurant never would have survived in that area. Where it is now, over there in Tremé, is much more suited for your type of establishment."

She straightened her shoulders. "Forgive me for being so bold, Mr. Fenner, but I happen to disagree. I think my restaurant would thrive no matter where it's located. And I haven't given up on the riverfront. Me and my daddy are gonna eventually open an even bigger restaurant one day. In fact, we plan to open *several*."

She gave him a sweet smile as she hefted her basket of vegetables up higher on her forearm. "Now, if you would excuse me, I have a very big night ahead. If you would like some good food and good jazz music, might I suggest you come over to Tremé and give T&J's Supper Club a try? The doors are always open to *any*one."

Tiana's heart pounded like a bass drum within her chest as she continued along Royal Street. She could feel Mr. Fenner's eyes boring into her retreating form, but she wouldn't take back a word she'd said, and she refused to apologize for her tone. She was tired of everyone telling her what to do, where to be. This weekend's Mardi Gras celebration would give her the boost she needed to do things her own way. She would make it so.

Even if that constant unease in the pit of her stomach made her wonder what other forces were at work.

17
Naveen

Naveen paced the length of the porch, counting his steps as he traveled from one end to the other. It spanned the entire front of the café where he was set to meet a representative of Dugas Candy Company, and if the man didn't show up soon, Naveen feared he would wear a trench into the wooden planks.

Setting up the meeting on such short notice had taken a bit of finessing, but if there was one thing Naveen was good at, finessing was it. Now, he had to parlay that skill into convincing the area's largest candy company to partner with LaBouff Sugars.

He stopped his pacing long enough to look out at the street for signs of John Dugas, the son of the owner of the company. The fog made it difficult to make out the faces of the people who walked by. Not that it would make much of a difference to him. He had never seen John Dugas before. But he'd been in America long enough to recognize that the people here displayed their status by the clothes they wore. Naveen was certain that, being the son of a rich candy maker, John Dugas would arrive in a suit and tie, and possibly a top hat.

If the average person were to look at Naveen on any given day, they would probably think he had grown up a pauper. He'd worn his best pair of pants, but he favored comfort over formality. Stuffy attire made him itchy, and he only wore it when absolutely necessary.

He stopped pacing as panic seized him.

Maybe more formal dress *was* necessary for a day like today. Maybe Dugas would take one look at him and think he wasn't serious enough to go into business with. What did Mr. LaBouff always tell him? He had to look the part of a businessman if he wanted to succeed in business.

Did he have time to run home and change into something more conventional?

Naveen took off for the porch steps, but stopped at the

sight of a young man wearing brown slacks and a sweater vest not much different from the one Naveen wore.

"Mr. Dugas?" he asked.

"Yes! Are you Naveen?" He tipped the bill of his derby hat. "Pleasure to meet you."

John Dugas was about his age, with a cheery smile that Naveen could make out even through the fog.

Naveen suddenly felt foolish for being so worried. He and this man would get along just fine.

They talked for two hours over cups of coffee and tea biscuits. Naveen had strategically chosen a café that used LaBouff Sugars in all their desserts. But it soon became apparent that Dugas could not be so easily sweet-talked into a deal.

"I have to warn you," the man said as he stirred another teaspoon of sugar into his café au lait, "LaBouff Sugars has some stiff competition. This area is full of sugar mills that have been vying for our business for years. What makes you think LaBouff's is the one for us?"

"Because none of those other mills are bigger or more successful than LaBouff's," Naveen stated with certainty.

Dugas nodded. "True. But there are logistical issues, as well. Dugas Candy Company is headquartered across Lake

Pontchartrain. Will LaBouff make that extra inconvenience worth our while?"

"We will," Naveen assured him, although he had no idea what it would entail to deliver the product across the vast lake. It didn't matter. If he landed this contract for LaBouff's, he would do whatever it took to make sure it was a success.

Not only did he want this for himself, but after his recent interaction with Tiana, Naveen had a burning need to show her that he, too, could prosper. Seeing how hard she worked to make her restaurant a success made him want to do the same in his job.

"I can personally guarantee that no other sugar mill will provide the same service as LaBouff's," Naveen continued. "Nor will anyone else provide a superior product. With LaBouff's, you get the best."

Naveen wasn't sure how John Dugas could turn down such a fabulous sales pitch.

"You drive a hard bargain. But I have one more question," Dugas said. "How did you know we were in the market for a new supplier? We just got rid of our previous one a couple of days ago."

Naveen leaned in closer and smiled. "It's my job to stay on top of such things. And if you go with LaBouff Sugars, we will bring that same diligence."

By the time Naveen walked out of the café, he felt so

light he practically floated down the steps. It wasn't a sure thing—John Dugas was much too savvy a businessman to show his hand. But it was close, Naveen could feel it.

And *he* would be the one to make it happen.

Possibly. Maybe. *Right?*

He cursed that little nugget of doubt, but after being a screwup for so long, how could he be certain that this time things would be different? Dugas could very well be meeting with other sugar suppliers that very minute, having the same friendly conversation.

Naveen returned to the sugar mill and went on his daily tour of the factory floor. He spotted Randy Boudreaux coming out of the boiler room.

"Hey, Randy!" Naveen called. He looped an arm over the man's shoulder. "Thanks for that inside information about Dugas's." Even though he could barely hear his own thoughts above the noisy industrial equipment, Naveen still leaned in close so that no one would overhear. "This is only between me and you, my friend, but LaBouff Sugars may be their next supplier. Pretty good, eh?"

"Oh yeah?" Randy asked. "Was it the new cane seeds we're using that did it for him? That ribbon cane produces a much sweeter juice."

"I—" Naveen frowned. "I didn't think to tell him about that." Naveen cursed under his breath.

"Aw, don't beat yourself up, boss. I don't think it'll make a difference."

But it *could*. Competition was fierce—Dugas had said so himself. Any leg up Naveen could give LaBouff Sugars would be a good thing.

Naveen looked at Randy's soot-covered face with the same curiosity he'd felt every time he'd chatted with the man.

"I should have brought you along to my meeting," Naveen said. "Your mind is sharp, Randy. How did you end up working on the shop floor?" He immediately held up his hands. "Not that there is anything wrong with that. You guys do incredible work down here; I just wondered why you don't try your hands at sales. I think you would do a good job."

Randy shrugged. "I come from poor folks on the bayou. Folks like me don't get to wear them fancy sweaters to work." Another shrug. "That's just how it is."

Naveen watched him as he walked back toward the boiler room.

He wasn't so clueless as to not recognize what it meant to be born into privilege, but he had never thought about those who were held back simply by the chance of their birth. What would he have done with his life had he not been the son of the king and queen of Maldonia? Would he even have the fortitude to work at LaBouff's?

What was he without the royal blood that ran through his veins?

Naveen's head was buzzing as he climbed the stairs up to his office. He was so distracted that he almost missed the fine linen envelope on his desk. His pulse quickened as he picked it up and turned it over.

Naveen sucked in a swift breath.

The royal crest of Maldonia was branded into a seal of gold wax. He quickly loosened the seal and pulled out the letter.

Our dearest Naveen,

It has been a year since you embarked on your journey to North America. Your mother and I now see that we were harsh in our initial decision to cut you off from your rightful inheritance.

Please accept this correspondence as an apology and an invitation to return to your home in Maldonia. We have already prepared the southwest wing of the palace to serve as your residence. This comes with a slate of servants to tend to your needs and a healthy stipend to cover your expenses.

*I expect your response to our invitation within
the next two weeks.*

  In congruence with your mother, the Queen,
     Your father, the King of Maldonia.

Naveen stared at his father's bold handwriting so long that the letters began to swim on the page.

Home.

They wanted him to come home. He would have servants. A luxurious place to lay his head.

Money! He would have all the money he could possibly spend, and more.

So why did it suddenly feel as if he'd eaten too many biscuits at the café?

Perhaps because, as easily as he could think of all he would gain by returning home, it was just as easy to consider all he would lose. Like the friends he'd made here in America. Like the satisfaction he experienced after an honest day's work, the fulfillment that came only with knowing he was earning his own way.

Like the chance to get to know Tiana better.

He was meeting Charlotte at Tiana's place tonight for her big celebration to ring in the Mardi Gras season. He felt a lurch of excitement just knowing he would get the chance to see her soon. Who knew, maybe this time she wouldn't run away from him.

But that would all be irrelevant if he returned home.

Naveen pressed a fist to his stomach and slumped into his chair. He brought his elbows up onto the desk and cradled his head in his hands. The decision his father had put before him felt like an anchor in his gut.

Would it make him foolish to turn down their invitation to return to the life he'd known back in Maldonia?

Or would it make him a failure to accept it?

18

Tiana

Anticipation thumped like a drum throughout Tiana's bloodstream as she raced from one end of the dining room to another, putting the finishing touches on the decorations for tonight's celebration.

She tugged on the green cloth covering Mr. LaBouff's table, then turned to the one at the very rear of the dining room. She frowned. The flowers at the table's center that had looked so vibrant that morning were suddenly all wrong. The marigolds were clumped together on one side of the vase, while the stalks of lavender congregated on the other.

She plunked her hands on her hips. "Okay, now who is messing with my centerpieces?"

"Tiana?" She turned to find Addie Mae peeking out of the door to the kitchen. "I don't know the last time you looked outside, but folks are lining up around the building. If we don't start this dinner service soon, those people are going to barge in."

"Oh, goodness, all right," Tiana said. "But first, Addie Mae, did you tinker with these?" she asked, gesturing toward the table.

"I serve food, I do not decorate," was her head waitress's answer.

"Hmm," she murmured. "Maybe it was one of the other girls."

Tiana quickly rearranged the flowers, but when she turned for the door, something else caught her attention out of the corner of her eye. She whipped around to look at Ms. Rose's painting of the Mardi Gras Indians that she'd hung up earlier.

She tapped her fingers against her lips, counting in her head as she studied the portrait.

"Weren't there six men?" she whispered. Tiana was sure there had been at least a half dozen colorfully dressed men in the painting, but now she only counted five.

"Tiana!" Addie Mae called again, motioning to the door.

"I'm on it," Tiana said. She glanced once more at the painting, thinking that she really needed to get some sleep once she was sure this kickoff celebration was a success.

She rushed over to the kitchen and opened the door a crack, poking her head inside. "Are we ready?"

"Ready," Jodie and Carol Anne replied in unison.

"Ready as we'll ever be, baby girl." Tiana smiled at her daddy, who wore one of the new aprons her mother had surprised them both with earlier that day. She'd painstakingly embroidered their initials on the front panel.

"Okay," Tiana said. "It's time for T&J's Supper Club to kick off the Mardi Gras season in style!"

She headed to the front door. Though Addie Mae had warned her, she could scarcely believe the line of people waiting. Tiana smiled wide as she welcomed the patrons filing inside. Although people tended to dress a bit fancier on Friday nights, many had gone all out this evening. The women wore flapper dresses and long gloves, and most of the men were in well-tailored suits and homburg hats.

Just as she'd predicted, her dining room would be bursting at the seams with people eager to hear Rudy Davis and the Allstars.

Tiana's smile grew even wider as she spotted Buford,

the cook at Duke's Cafe, where she'd once worked, walking toward her.

"Well, hello there, Buford."

"Tiana," he replied with a nod. He gestured at the door, a sheepish look on his face. "I . . . uh . . . I thought I'd come check out your new restaurant. I've been hearing good things about it."

"Have you now?" she asked. "Well, come on in." She held her hand out with a flourish.

It would be rude to revel in his obvious discomfort. But, then again, Buford *had* taken every opportunity to make fun of her dream back when she worked at Duke's.

"Oh, Buford," Tiana called. "Why don't you bring that trophy you got for winning the Kentucky Derby next time?"

His forehead creased in confusion, making Tiana wonder if he remembered the time he'd told her that he had a better chance of winning the horse race than she had of opening a restaurant.

But then understanding dawned in his eyes. "I guess I deserve that," Buford said.

Tiana decided to take pity on him. "I'm just messing with you," she said teasingly. "There are no hard feelings. In fact, I'll be sure to make my way down to Duke's soon. It's been a while since I had your flapjacks."

"Flapjacks? Why, I haven't made those in quite some time," Buford said.

"Why not? They were your bestsellers, after my beignets, of course."

"Well, Duke's has been closed for a while, so—"

"Closed?" Tiana's head snapped back in surprise. "Since when?"

"Going on a year now," Buford said. He looked at her as if she'd lost a few of her marbles.

Tiana's heart skipped a beat.

"But, Buford, I . . . ?" She'd only left her job at Duke's Cafe about five months earlier, just as she and Daddy were gearing up to buy the restaurant. He had to have been mistaken.

"I'm gonna go in and get myself a seat," Buford said.

"Yeah," Tiana whispered. "Go on in."

She put a hand to her stomach. She thought about her conversation with Ms. Margery at the streetcar stop yesterday. And with her butcher, Mr. Phillips, and Mr. Smith at the fabric shop. All of them had behaved as if parts of the past didn't exist. She recalled the strange buds on the barrettes, the changing painting, the wilting flowers. Once again, she felt like she was losing it.

Could this be . . .

No. The Shadow Man didn't have that kind of power. He didn't have access to her possessions, let alone the memories of random people.

But they weren't just random people, a little voice in Tiana's head countered. They were all people she had a connection to—albeit loosely—in one way or another. Hadn't he warned that he would bring harm to folks she knew? What if this was the start of it? What if her loved ones—the friends and family she was closest to—were next?

"It's all one big coincidence," Tiana murmured. Although that was becoming harder and harder to believe.

Tiana forced herself to return her attention to the guests still filing into the restaurant. Once every table was filled to capacity, she went into the kitchen and took her place by her daddy's side, focusing on the food. They cooked up a pot of red beans and rice, and another filled to the brim with her pasta jambalaya. She expected a lot of sales of the jambalaya, but the star for tonight was smothered pork chops with a little of the greens she'd whipped up on the side.

"These sure do take me back," her daddy said. "Your grandmother used to cook them every Sunday."

"I can't wait for Mama to try them," Tiana said.

"She should be here in a few minutes. She said she didn't want to miss any of Rudy Davis."

Tiana looked at the clock that hung above the door and frowned. She'd asked Addie Mae to come and get her when the band arrived. They should have been here by now.

"Speaking of Rudy Davis," she said as she untied her apron. "Let me see if he and his band need help setting up."

Just as she started for the door that led to the dining room, Lil Johnny Taylor, the egg vendor's son, came bursting through.

"Miss Tiana!" he shouted. "Miss Tiana, you'll never believe it!"

The young boy was out of breath, his chest heaving with each word.

"Calm down, Lil Johnny," Tiana said as she hurried to the faucet to draw him a glass of water. "Here, drink this."

Lil Johnny took the glass and gulped down half before wiping his mouth with his sleeve.

"Now, what's going on?" Tiana asked.

"There was a fire!" he finally said. "I never seen anything like it."

"A fire?" Tiana gasped. "Was anyone hurt?"

He shook his head. "I don't think so, but it sure was scary."

Her daddy came up behind her, wiping his hands on a dish towel. "Any idea what caused it?" he asked.

Lil Johnny hunched his bony shoulders. "No, sir. Strangest thing. It just happened out of nowhere."

"And you're sure no one got hurt?" Tiana asked.

He nodded his head so fast the pageboy cap he always wore nearly fell off.

"I'm pretty sure, ma'am. But I got a message. From Rudy Davis."

"Rudy Davis?" What was Rudy Davis doing sending her messages through Lil Johnny Taylor?

"Yes, ma'am. You see, it was the Allstars' instruments that caught fire. They're all burnt up. Mr. Davis said to give you his regrets, but he and the Allstars won't be able to perform tonight."

19

Facilier

"Good evening, sir." Facilier smiled at the well-dressed gentleman approaching his table in Jackson Square. "Can I interest you in a game of cards?"

"Out of my way," the man said, swatting at him with the folded newspaper he carried.

Facilier glowered at the man's back as he continued down the sidewalk. If only he hadn't been in so much debt to his friends on the other side, Facilier would have had them burn the man to a crisp, right on the spot.

Alas, he owed too much already, and he was incapable of producing a fire by sheer will alone. He had to rely on more conventional methods, like the kerosene he'd poured over Rudy Davis and the Allstars' instruments.

He chuckled at the havoc he'd caused with that stroke of genius. Or, should he say, the havoc *Tiana* had caused. Because that was what he planned to tell her.

He already had her thinking she was the reason this peculiar fog had overtaken the city, but the fog didn't go far enough. It wasn't dangerous enough to those close to Tiana.

But this fire? The fire was personal. He would make her believe that it was punishment from his friends on the other side. And that was only the start!

The potion was still his easiest route to LaBouff—to making sure all of this hadn't been for nothing—so Facilier wouldn't count solely on the mysterious fog and the fire to make Tiana fall in line. She was too smart for him to take that chance. This fog could disappear as quickly as it had shown up, and she could write the fire off as some sort of fluke. No, he had yet another ace in his pocket.

Actually, his aces were tied up in a room back at his emporium.

He'd ambushed the pasta maker on his way to Tiana's restaurant that morning. Not only did she rely on old man Salvaggio for his wares, but Facilier had witnessed their new friendship. She was chummy with just about every person who set foot in that restaurant.

And he was going to *remove* each and every one of them until he convinced her that his friends on the other side were behind the disappearances. He already had a nice collection going.

If he could make her see that her stubborn resistance to using his special new potion was causing others to suffer, she would come to heel.

Well, she had *better* come to heel. He had less than a week to trick her into feeding LaBouff that concoction before his friends on the other side came calling.

Realizing he needed to check in on his captives, Facilier started packing up his cards and table. He might be a bit deceitful, but he wasn't a complete monster. Besides, they could possibly prove useful in other ways.

He navigated through the green fog toward his home in Pirate's Alley. When he entered, a blast of cold air hit him.

Facilier shut his eyes for a brief moment. It was as if he'd summoned them with his thoughts.

The Shadows.

The low moans and groans emerged from somewhere deep within the walls of the drafty space, the air becoming colder as their groans grew louder, until both reached a crescendo when they appeared. They slithered along the walls and on the floor at his feet.

"Friends, it's so nice to see you again," Facilier lied. A

gust of wind billowed. "Yes, yes, I agree. The time for small talk is over."

He canted his head to the side, listening to the rhythmic intonations that only those indebted to them could understand.

"Yes, I know. Payment is coming due."

The Shadows didn't know it yet, but this would be their final collection. Because this was the last deal he planned to make with them. He nodded and murmured in agreement as their lamentations continued.

Until they said something that made him stiffen in shock.

"What was that?" Facilier asked. "Has Tiana signed the contract?"

A high-pitched keening accompanied a frigid blast of cold air. The Shadows didn't like repeating themselves.

"But . . . but why would that matter? I made the request on her behalf, and it was done," Facilier said. "It was a verbal agreement. We've done those before."

Their answering chant sent a chill down Facilier's spine that had nothing to do with the brutally cold temperature of the room.

Had he heard them correctly?

The exchanging of a soul required more than just a verbal agreement?

No. No, that couldn't be right.

"I . . . I think you're mistaken," Facilier said.

Gale-force winds blasted across his face. Facilier held up his forearm to shield himself from the fierce gust.

Read the governing covenant?

He raced to the cabinet where contracts for the numerous bargains he'd made with the Shadows over the years were stored. A collection of scrolls sprang forth from the drawer. He pitched them left and right, clearing out the drawer until he reached the bottom, where the very first agreement he'd made with them lay.

He unfurled the crumpled parchment and scanned the document, his hands shaking so badly he could barely make out the words.

"See, here it is," he said once he got to the end. He held up the document so the faceless creatures could see his wobbly ten-year-old signature scrawled across the bottom. "It says right here that I can make requests on behalf of others."

They spoke in sighs and grunts, the juxtaposition of the soft and sharp sounds a brutal cacophony that sent Facilier's head reeling.

What was that? He had missed the clause on the exchanging of souls?

Fear caught in his throat as his eyes continued down the

document. The verbiage on the exchange of souls was at the very end, in print that was tiny and faded.

He squinted at the minuscule words, but there they were. Right there in black and white.

> *The soul of the one who requested the deed shall vacate the body one year from the signing of an agreement in exchange for the soul of another being returned to the earth. All knowledge of the returned soul's previous death shall be wiped clean from the consciousness of all who knew him, with the exception of those who are party to the agreement. Payment shall be rendered by signatories of the agreement.*

Tiana wasn't a signatory.

"What . . . what does this mean?" Facilier said.

More moans. More deep, intense, ghastly moans.

This final warning from the Shadows was the most terrifying thing Facilier had ever heard.

If Tiana did not physically sign over her soul, he, as the lone signatory, must forfeit his own.

20

Tiana

This could not be happening. It could *not* be happening.

"This is a disaster," Tiana said.

She'd promised Rudy Davis and the Allstars. If she went out there and told the crowd there would be no show, they would rebel. Even worse, they might never come to her restaurant again. This was the kind of thing that could ruin T&J's Supper Club's reputation and make the success they'd achieved short lived.

In the few months since they'd opened, Tiana had learned just how difficult it was to run a restaurant in a city known for its cuisine. Serving great food was only a small part; if you alienated your customers, they could easily spend their dollars somewhere else.

And this was supposed to be their weekend!

"Now, just stay calm, baby girl," James said. He put an arm around her shoulders and gave her a gentle squeeze.

She leaned into her daddy's comforting embrace, wanting nothing more in this moment than to soak in the support he provided. But she had an emergency on her hands. She couldn't just stand there doing nothing.

"I have to figure out a way to fix this," Tiana said. "People are expecting dinner and a show."

"The way Lil Johnny described it makes no sense," Addie Mae said. "Why would only the instruments burn up?"

"That's what I don't understand, either," Tiana said. "It almost makes me wonder if it was intentional—"

My friends can show you what real *smoke looks like. . . .*

Was this Facilier's doing? Had he sicced his friends on Rudy Davis's band just to get back at her for not wanting to add his latest potion to all her dishes?

"How can T&J's have a Mardi Gras celebration without a band?" Addie Mae asked. "People are going to be so disappointed."

"Or they're gonna go down the street to listen to The Shiny Walter Band," Carol Anne said.

Tiana whipped around. "Where's Shiny Walter playing?"

"Smokey Joe's over on Rampart. I heard folks talking about it earlier."

Tiana quickly tried to come up with a backup option. But she couldn't call on Louis and the rest of the Crawfish Crooners. She'd given them the night off, and they were surely all scattered about the city.

She walked over to the swinging door, nudging it just wide enough to observe the crowd. She fidgeted with the top button of her dress as her eyes scanned the packed dining room. Tiana was relieved to see so many cheerful smiles. People were enjoying their food, and everyone seemed to be having a grand time.

But how long would that last if she went out there and informed them that the band everyone had come to see tonight would not be performing? That *no* band would be performing?

Trepidation tiptoed up and down her spine, the feeling of dread escalating as each second passed.

As she looked over the crowd, she caught sight of Charlotte's blond curls at her favorite table near the stage. Naveen was there with her.

Naveen!

You can't ask him.

But Naveen was the only musician here. And when he'd played for the crowd the night before, everyone seemed to love him.

She'd promised her patrons dinner and a show. What choice did she have?

"This is what you get for making promises," Tiana whispered to herself.

She sucked in a deep breath and slowly blew it out, then pushed open the kitchen door and headed straight for Lottie and Naveen's table. Tiana did her best to quell the butterflies that instantly began to flitter around her stomach as she drew closer.

"Hi, Lottie. Naveen," Tiana said as she came upon their table. She cursed her voice for shaking.

"Tia, everything looks so beautiful tonight," Charlotte said. "But where's the band? I'm ready to dance."

"Well, that's why I'm here." She turned her attention to Naveen, her breath catching in her throat. It was hard to believe that, at one time, she'd found him annoying. She would gladly put up with his exasperating habits if it meant they could be together.

But you can't. So get on with what you came here to do.

Tiana swallowed deeply, then allowed the words to rush out of her. "Rudy Davis and the Allstars' instruments burned up in a fire tonight, and they won't be able to make it, so can you please play your trumpet for the crowd, Naveen?"

"Oh, goodness." Lottie's hand flew to her chest. "Is everyone okay?"

"I think they are," Tiana said. "But, of course, they can no longer perform tonight. And I have no way of contacting Louis. I would if I—"

"Yes," Naveen said.

"Yes?" Hope surged through her. "You'll do it?"

"Of course I will, Tiana."

There was something about the way he said her name—the way it rolled off his tongue in that lyrical way he spoke. If she didn't know any better, Tiana would have thought the Shadow Man had taken away her ability to speak. She was transfixed by the subtle hint of longing in Naveen's hazel-colored eyes.

The butterflies returned. But Tiana didn't try to suppress them; she didn't want to. Because *this* flutter was filled with excitement and yearning and all those feelings she'd tried so hard to ignore this past year when it came to Naveen.

For one brief moment, Tiana allowed herself to just feel.

"Thank you," she finally answered, her voice once again catching in her throat.

"Anything for you," he said.

Before Tiana could respond, he grabbed his trumpet and climbed onto the stage.

"Good evening, good people," Naveen greeted the crowd. "I trust everyone is having a great time tonight? Have you tried that jambalaya?" He rubbed his belly and licked his lips. "Fantastic!"

Rousing applause and calls of "here, here" reverberated around the restaurant.

"Now, I bet you're wondering, 'What is this guy doing here,' eh? Where's Rudy Davis?" He hunched his shoulders. "Well, unfortunately, there was a bit of an incident with Mr. Davis's band. They won't be able to make it."

Disturbed murmurs began to hum throughout the dining room.

"But never fear," Naveen continued. "You will get a great show tonight. That is a promise!"

He tipped his trumpet to the crowd, brought it to his lips, and opened with a rousing rendition of an old Fats Waller tune. Before Tiana knew it, she was swaying back and forth with the rest of the crowd, her distress from a minute ago a thing of the past. He really was charismatic.

She glanced toward the kitchen and caught sight of her mother and father dancing just outside the door, her heart nearly bursting at the sight.

"Naveen sure is good with that horn, isn't he?" Lottie asked.

"That he is," Tiana said, bringing her attention back to the stage. "Thank goodness for that. He's saved me from what could have been a catastrophe."

"You know, Tia," Lottie said, her voice taking on a teasing tone, "Naveen really likes you. Now, don't tell him I told you that, because he's trying to take things slow. But y'all are moving *too* slow for me."

"There is no 'y'all' when it comes to me and Naveen," Tiana said.

"But there could be. What do you have against him?"

Tiana closed her eyes. "Lottie, please. You know I don't—"

"Don't have time for romance," Lottie singsonged. "Yeah, yeah, I know. I'm not saying you have to marry the man, Tia. You can spare an hour for coffee, can't you? I think it would do you some good."

Tiana watched as he belted out a slow ballad on the trumpet. What she wouldn't give to sit across a table from Naveen in a quaint café in the Quarter. Laughing. Joking. Just enjoying his company.

Was that too much to ask? Would that violate the terms of the bargain she'd made with Facilier? Did relinquishing her love for Naveen mean she couldn't have any dealings with him whatsoever?

What if it wasn't just her and Naveen on a date? What if there were others around, and she and Naveen just so happened to meet up?

Her eyes still fixated on the stage, Tiana said, "The annual neighborhood picnic crowning the King of Zulu is tomorrow in Congo Square. Me and Mama . . . and Daddy take part every year. We start early in the morning, and it lasts all day long." She glanced over at Lottie. "Why don't you join us?" She returned her eyes to the stage, hesitating only a moment before she added, "And bring Naveen with you."

21

Tiana

Congo Square, New Orleans
Saturday, February 1927
Three days before Mardi Gras

Tiana stood on the periphery of the crowd that had formed in the center of Congo Square. She clapped along to the rhythmic beat of the drum, cheering on the brave folks who took their turn in the center of the circle.

It was a longstanding tradition to honor the ancestors who had been brought here against their will and forced to work the land by commemorating their sacrifice through song and dance. The Mardi Gras Indians, just like those in the painting Ms. Rose had given her, led the ceremonial celebration.

Their elaborate headdresses and colorful costumes sparkled in the rays of sun. Remarkably, the thick fog that continued to plague the city had thinned into a gauzy haze, as if it knew how important today was to the people gathered here and didn't want to ruin it. The light mist that did remain cast an ethereal quality over everything, making it seem almost dreamlike.

"You wanna dance, baby girl?" Her daddy gestured to the circle.

Before she could talk herself out of it, Tiana nodded, grabbed him by the arm, and entered the fray.

She mimicked the steps of the other dancers, joining in the traditional African folk dance she'd been taught as a little girl. Her daddy danced alongside her, stomping his big feet and twisting his torso from left to right.

Tiana tilted her head back and held her arms to the sky, unable to restrain her smile. She felt a sense of weightlessness, as if she could take flight at any moment. It was a feeling she never wanted to let go of, a freeness she hadn't allowed herself to feel in far too long.

Once the dance ended, the crowd erupted in cheers.

Her daddy wrapped her up in a big bear hug and

swung her around like he used to do when she was a little girl. Tiana clung to his big frame, soaking in the safety and security and love he embodied. Her throat tightened with emotions that threatened to overwhelm her.

"That felt like old times, baby girl."

"It felt like the *best* times," Tiana answered.

He set her back down and rubbed a hand over his stomach. "All that dancing has made me hungry. I think it's time for some of that fried chicken and corn bread."

Her daddy headed for the spot they'd commandeered on the left side of the square, where her mother was busy setting up the lunch.

Charlotte and Naveen both ran up to Tiana.

"That was fabulous!" Naveen said.

"Oh, it was, Tia! Just fabulous," Charlotte said. "Who knew Mr. James could move like that?" She flapped her arms like a crazed flamingo in what Tiana could only guess was her attempt to mimic the folk dance. "I've never seen such dancing before."

"Really?" Tiana asked. She considered the fact that the celebration at Congo Square was a sacred ritual, but only to certain communities in New Orleans. Tiana had never thought to invite Charlotte to join them before. "No. No, I guess you haven't," Tiana said.

"Show me how you did that spin," Charlotte said. She twirled and fell flat on her backside.

"Ouch." Tiana grimaced.

"Well, that didn't go the way I thought it would." Charlotte held her arms out so that Tiana and Naveen could help her up. She took a step and yelped. "I think I broke my ankle!"

"But you didn't land on your ankle," Tiana said.

"Hmm . . . well, *some*thing's broken. Naveen, sugar," Charlotte called. "Why don't you help me over to where Ms. Eudora is setting up the picnic. I think some peach cobbler will make me feel better."

Tiana shook her head but chuckled as Naveen looped Charlotte's arm around his neck. Together, they hobbled toward Tiana's parents.

"Hey, Tiana!"

She spotted Maddy jogging toward her.

"I'll meet y'all over there in just a minute," Tiana told Charlotte and Naveen, then waved over her friend. "Hey, Maddy," Tiana said as she approached. "How's it going?"

"I saw you dancing out there, girl! Good to know you can still kick up your heels and have a good time."

"Maybe you should tell Georgia that so she can get off my case about going out," Tiana answered with a smile.

"That's if I can find her. I haven't seen her or Eugene since leaving your supper club Thursday evening. I thought they would show up last night, because Georgia loves her some Rudy Davis, but I guess it's just as well they didn't." Maddy leaned in close. "Although, I must say, that trumpet player from last night sure is something." She wiggled her eyebrows. "He's been looking at you the entire time we've been talking."

Tiana felt a telltale blush creeping up on her cheeks. "I need to go help Mama set up lunch," she told Maddy. "I'll talk to you later. And if I run into Georgia and Eugene, I'll let them know you've been looking for them."

Tiana continued to the lunch that her mother had spread out on the massive patchwork quilt she'd created from fabric scraps. The quilt made an appearance only once a year, for this very celebration. It was soft and colorful, and filled with memories that Tiana had learned to cherish even more during those years when her daddy was gone.

She wouldn't think about those times. Their family was whole again. That was what mattered.

Tiana was grateful that talk of postponing the picnic until after the fog retreated had turned out to be nothing but talk. More and more people were looking toward the river as the culprit. Based on snippets of conversation she'd caught as she'd moved about the square, that green algae growing on the river had also gotten thicker overnight.

Whatever had caused this phenomenon, it was beginning to wreak havoc for too many people, especially for people who relied on the river for their livelihood, like the fishermen she did business with. Tiana didn't want to give any credence to what the Shadow Man had told her, but the thought continued to linger in the back of her mind.

Was this all her fault?

"Don't be ridiculous," she whispered to herself.

Refusing to allow thoughts about the Shadow Man to steal another minute of her day, she joined the others over on the picnic blanket and feasted on fried chicken, corn bread, deviled eggs, fruit salad, and peach cobbler.

Full and satisfied, Tiana braced her hands on either side of her and stretched her face upward toward the sky, basking in the warmth of the sun trying to peek through the haze.

"Uh, Tiana?" Naveen's voice came from somewhere just to the left of her.

She tilted her head to the side and opened one eye. "Yes?" She could see Charlotte a few feet away, holding her thumb up and smiling.

"I—I wondered if you would like to dance?" Naveen asked.

She wasn't sure if it was the raw hope she saw in his eyes, but something compelled her to say, "Okay."

Tiana almost laughed at Naveen's shocked expression. His mouth opened and closed several times before he spoke. "Really?" he asked.

This was her chance to backtrack, to tell him that she hadn't heard him correctly, or that she'd simply changed her mind.

But she didn't.

She no longer hoped for a day when there could be anything more between them; she knew it was impossible in order to keep him safe.

But she selfishly wanted this one dance. One little dance. That wasn't too much to ask, was it? And here at the picnic, they seemed so far from the Shadow Man and his tricks.

Tiana held out her hand.

Naveen helped her up from the quilt, beaming. Together, they joined the others who were dancing to the lively brass band that had started up a few minutes ago.

In that moment, at least, every single thing was right in her world.

22

Naveen

The energy pulsating throughout Congo Square captured everything that Naveen loved about New Orleans. The music, the people, the vibrancy of this place and all who lived here was like nothing he'd ever encountered. Could he honestly consider leaving now?

Maybe it was not the best time to entertain such a question, not when standing across from a carefree—dare he say silly?—Tiana as she tried to teach him the current dance moves. As much as he loved his home, it was no match for Tiana's radiance. If given the choice between being here with her or returning to his home in Maldonia, he would choose Tiana every single time.

"Are you paying attention?" she asked him.

"Hold on," Naveen said. "You are going too fast. Now, what am I supposed to do with my legs?"

"It goes like this," she said. She bent her knees and pivoted her toes in and out. Then she executed alternating kicks in time with the music, all while counting the steps and trying to direct him to follow along.

Naveen overexaggerated the move in hopes of eliciting a certain response from her. She rewarded him by throwing her head back and letting out a peal of that magical laugh of hers.

Yes, *that* was the response he was looking for. Goodness, but he loved her laugh.

"I'm not sure the Charleston is your thing," Tiana said, wiping tears of mirth from her eyes.

"No, no. I think I've got it," Naveen said.

This time, he actually *did* try to get it right, thinking he would impress her with how quickly he was able to catch on to the dance. But he tipped too far to the side with one of his kicks and nearly fell to the ground.

"Whoa," Tiana said as she reached for him.

"I am fine." Naveen raised his hands. "Just embarrassingly clumsy all of a sudden."

So much for impressing her.

But maybe this was better. Her lyrical mirth wrapped around him, cocooning him like a warm, comforting blanket.

"Oh, my," Tiana said, slapping a hand to her forehead. "I can't recall the last time I laughed so much."

"It is a beautiful sound."

"I . . . uh . . . thank you," she said.

Their eyes met, and his heart felt as if it would beat out of his chest.

Achidanza!

Naveen had a hard time breathing. The sight of Tiana's eyes staring at him with such feeling had stolen all the air from his lungs.

Suddenly, it felt as if no one else was in the park, as if this one moment in time was made for the two of them alone.

"Tiana, I . . ." Naveen began, but the words caught in his throat. He knew what he felt, but he couldn't figure out how to express it. Because he didn't understand it. He couldn't explain this pull he had toward her, as if they were destined for each other.

You can't talk that way. She will think you are loose in the head.

But that was the way she made him feel. He didn't recognize who he was when he was around her. Or maybe he did—a version of himself that felt both new and familiar somehow.

"Tiana, I was hoping—"

"What is that?" she said suddenly, her eyes going wide.

"Uh, I am trying to find the words—"

"No!" She pointed over his shoulder. "That!"

That was when Naveen heard it: a low hum reverberating in the air, a mixture of the murmurs from the picnic goers and something else. Something that sounded like . . . buzzing?

He turned to where Tiana pointed.

A dark cloud seemed to be shifting through the greenish fog, swaying like a pendulum through the air. The closer it got to them, the louder the hum became.

"What is that?" Naveen repeated her question.

The buzz grew even louder, along with yells and screams from the crowd on the far end of the square.

Something bit his neck. He slapped the spot. When he removed his hand, there was a black-and-red smear on his palm. "This looks like some kind of—"

"Mosquitoes!" someone shouted.

Chaos ensued as the thick black cloud descended on them. But it wasn't a cloud; it was a swarm of insects. Monstrous mosquitoes, at least ten times the normal size, twirled around like a twister, attacking the crowd with stinging bites.

"Run!" Naveen shouted. He provided cover for Tiana, shielding her from the torrent of bugs and dodging the people who scattered around the square, seeking shelter from the invasion. Grown men fell to the ground as the enormous insects ambushed them, jabbing at them with their extra-long beaks.

He and Tiana raced over to where Mr. James, Ms. Eudora, and Charlotte all huddled underneath the blanket where they'd just picnicked. Mr. James lifted the edge, motioning for Tiana and Naveen to join.

Naveen remained huddled close to Tiana, doing all he could to protect her as the stinging insects attacked his back even through the fabric of his shirt. It felt as if someone were firing pellets into his skin, each bite a hot, searing assault upon his flesh.

Finally, he and Tiana crawled under the large blanket. The five of them all huddled together as screams from the crowd rent the air.

"Are you okay?" Tiana asked.

Naveen grimaced. "It is just . . . a few bites," he said through clenched teeth.

"I've never seen such big mosquitoes in all my life!" Charlotte said.

"Neither have I," Naveen said. He lifted his arm to reveal ghastly welts forming on his skin. "I did not think bugs were capable of this."

"Is this what you call a few bites?" Tiana cried. She reached for his arm, but he instinctively pulled away. Naveen immediately cursed himself. Tiana was offering to tend to his wounds; why not let her?

He held his forearm up to her and tried not to yelp as she inspected the carnage. She gently wiped away the blood with her thumb, showing no concern for her dress, which was now stained.

"Where did those mosquitoes come from?" Charlotte cried. "It's not even summertime!"

"You're right, Charlotte," Ms. Eudora said. "These are early."

"Much too early," Tiana said. Naveen was not sure he'd ever seen such venom in her eyes.

"And I think I know what brought them here."

23

Tiana

They all went home following the harrowing mosquito attack in Congo Square, but despite her exhaustion, Tiana didn't take a moment to rest. She went straight to her room and dressed for war, pulling on a blue cotton top with long sleeves and the denim coveralls she reserved for when she really had to get her hands dirty. She tugged her hair back and tied it with a blue ribbon, then slipped on her leather boots.

She took a moment to mentally prepare, then stalked out of her bedroom.

When she entered the kitchen, her mother and father were both at the table, holding onto mugs.

"Where you going?" Eudora asked.

"I'm going to check on Naveen," Tiana lied. "I want to make sure he's okay."

She would eventually call on Naveen, but there was someone else she needed to see first.

"Can't you wait until tomorrow?" her father asked. "We've all been through quite an ordeal today, Tiana."

"Your father's right. You need to rest for a bit."

"I'm fine," Tiana reassured them. She appealed to her father's sense of duty, knowing that would do the trick. "Besides, after the way Naveen shielded me from that swarm, I owe him."

He nodded, and cautioned, "Be careful."

"I always am," Tiana replied.

She grabbed her bag from where it hung on a peg next to the front door and stepped outside. She was hit by the wall of thick, suffocating fog. It had returned with a vengeance.

It really was all the Shadow Man's doing—him making good on his threat. Now she had no doubt about it.

Tiana quickly made her way to his emporium in the French Quarter. If ever there had been an occasion to break her rule to only meet in public, this was it.

She stopped when she came upon his bright purple

door, the same color as the vest Facilier wore. There was a menacing skull and crossbones etched in the lintel above it.

Tiana clenched her fists at her sides, shoring up her nerve.

You can do this. You have to.

Facilier had warned her of what would happen if she didn't follow his commands, but she hadn't listened. He'd all but promised that his friends on the other side would begin to wreak havoc on the lives of those around her if she did not start adding that potion to all her dishes.

And because of her, people had suffered.

It was *her* fault for not taking his initial threats seriously. *Her* fault for trusting that he would stick to his word, for getting involved with him in the first place.

But despairing over what she should or shouldn't have done would do her no good now. It was time she ended this madness with the Shadow Man once and for all.

Tiana pounded on the door. "Open up, Shadow Man."

She jiggled the handle. It turned.

Unlocked?

Suspicion traveled down Tiana's spine like thick molasses. This had all the makings of a trap. Facilier wasn't the type to leave himself exposed.

But she'd come too far to back down now. She pushed the door open and took a step inside. Then another.

It was dark. Not a single window in the place, as far as she could tell. The only light in the room came from the door she still held open. Tiana pushed it open a bit more so that she could see her way inside.

As she came upon a table of some sort, she could make out the silhouette of an oil lamp sitting on top of it. She felt around the base of the lamp, searching for the knob. Once she found it, she said a small prayer that the lamp had fuel and gave the knob a turn.

A small flame flickered to life, giving off just enough light to illuminate the area around her. She picked the lamp up by its wire handle and made her way around the room. A shelf held what must have been hundreds of bottles. Some short and squat, others tall and slim. Some filled with liquids, others with seeds and pebbles of various kinds.

"I knew you would come to your senses."

With a gasp, Tiana spun around. Her heart slammed against her chest at the sound of the familiar voice. Yet, despite the glow from the lamp, the room appeared as empty as it had been when she first arrived.

"Where . . . where are you?" she stammered.

Facilier's deep, awful laugh rumbled around the room. A moment later, he emerged from the darkness, striding toward her with that ever-present walking stick.

"Smart girl like you knows what's best," he drawled.

"I'm not here to make any deals," Tiana said. "I'm here to tell you that you'd better stop whatever it is you're doing."

"And what is it you think I'm doing, Tiana?"

"Don't play coy with me. You all but said you and your friends are behind this fog. I'm guessing you're also the reason Buford thinks that Duke's Cafe has been closed for a year, why Ms. Margery doesn't remember making me a caramel cake for my birthday. And I'm pretty sure you set fire to Rudy Davis's band's instruments last night, and sent those mosquitoes to attack us this morning."

Facilier paused, holding his grin. "I told you things would start happening if you didn't do what I say," he said finally.

"We had a deal. I've been adding that potion to my gumbo ever since we opened the supper club."

He waved his hand. "This isn't about the potion. We can take care of that later. This is about your contract. It's time for you to sign the amendment."

"Amendment?" Tiana put her hands up. "I don't know what you're talking about. What I *do* know is that I have been fulfilling my end of our bargain. You have no right to demand I do anything more than what I agreed to."

"It seems you've forgotten part of the contract you signed."

"What are you talking about?" Tiana balked. "I didn't sign anything."

"Except that you *did*!"

He snatched the lamp from her hand and strode to a rickety wooden desk on the other side of the room. He picked up a tattered scroll and stalked back to where she stood.

"The proof is right here." Facilier held out the rolled parchment.

Tiana took a step back. "What is this?"

"It's the deal you signed," he said.

She shook her head and started to back away. "I . . . I didn't sign anything," she said again.

"Yes. You. Did."

Facilier opened his hand and blew a cloud of iridescent purple dust into her face.

Tiana's head shot back as if sustaining a blow. She lifted off the ground, suspended in a slow yet dizzying twirl high above the floor of the cavernous room. She started to spin faster and faster, her head swimming.

With a thud, she landed on her hands and knees. The ground underneath her was cold, the dirt and crumbling stone pressing into the fleshy part of her palms. Tiana lifted her head and found herself surrounded by towering catacombs and rusted wrought iron gates.

The cemetery.

Dread sluiced down her spine.

"Why am I here?" she whispered.

"That's why," came Facilier's low growl.

Tiana's head seemed to turn of its own accord, drawn to a scene playing out like the moving picture shows on the big screen at the Prytania Theatre.

It was her—wearing a sparkling white dress and glittery shoes.

Tiana suddenly realized what she was looking at. This was the previous year, when she'd made that deal with Facilier. She was unable to hear the words being spoken, but she remembered it all so clearly that she could almost recite them in her head.

She froze when Facilier pulled a scroll from his jacket and unfurled it.

But that part hadn't happened!

A scream collected in her throat as she watched herself sign the scroll, then shake Facilier's hand.

"No!" Tiana said aloud. "That's . . . that can't be right."

"But it is," Facilier said.

In a flash she was back in Facilier's dark emporium, her mind muddled by what she'd just witnessed. How could she not remember that?

"You signed this contract, Tiana." One corner of his

mouth lifted in an ugly grin. "You just saw it with your own eyes."

Facilier set down the lamp and picked up a long wand made of smooth purple stone. Threads of gold twirled throughout it. Tiana looked on in dismay as he closed his eyes and spoke in a language she didn't understand.

The wand began to glow in his hand. As he glided it down the scroll, tiny writing appeared in gold lettering. He hovered the wand over the bottom portion of the document.

"Here," Facilier said. "This is the section you seem to have forgotten. It says that you must agree to an amendment every year, or this city and the people you love will suffer. We're coming up on the one-year mark, Tiana. If you don't sign again by sundown on Mardi Gras, hell will rain down on this city."

"No!" Tiana gasped, shaking her head. She put a hand to her mouth as her eyes read over the letters scrawled in glittery gold ink. "No, this can't be. I didn't sign any contract! I didn't agree to any amendment! I'm not doing any of this!"

Her head snapped back with another blast of the purple dust. She was instantly dropped into the middle of her parents' living room. Both her mother and father writhed on the floor, pain etched across their faces as they soundlessly screamed into the void.

Tiana tried to run to them, but her legs wouldn't move.

It felt as if she were stuck in quicksand. She reached for them, but they were too far away.

Watching them suffer was so excruciating, Tiana's knees gave out, sending her to the floor. She squirmed around like a bug stuck on its back.

When she opened her eyes, she was once again in Facilier's dreadful dungeon. He stood above her, his mouth screwed up in a twisted grimace.

"Is this what you want for Eudora and James?" Facilier asked.

"Where's Mama and Daddy?" she screamed.

"They're just fine. For now," Facilier added. "I wanted to show you what could happen if you don't sign this paper before Mardi Gras."

It was one of his mind tricks again. But that didn't mean it couldn't be reality one day.

Tiana scrambled up from the floor and snatched the scroll from his hands. She tried to rip it, but it was tough as leather and barely crinkled.

That deep laugh rumbled from Facilier's chest.

"It's binding," he said. "Sign it before Mardi Gras, or watch your mama and daddy suffer."

There had to be a way out. She hadn't agreed to this. She could not be indebted to the likes of the Shadow Man forever—under his thumb for the rest of her life.

"You won't get away with this," Tiana said.

"I already have." He snatched a quill from a pot of ink and shoved it at her.

"No!" Tiana started to turn, but he caught her by the back of her coveralls. Jerking out of his grasp, she ran out of the dark room, then raced out of the alley and back into the fog.

24

Tiana

Tiana ran like the wind. She ran until she was out of breath, until she was far away from the Shadow Man's dreadful French Quarter dungeon. She didn't stop running until she reached Canal Street. The wide boulevard teemed with people going about their day, as if nothing were amiss. As if they all weren't in danger because of *her* actions.

Tiana flattened her back against the rough brick of a nearby building. She shut her eyes tight, wishing for a moment that she could shut out the world.

What had she gotten herself into?

If she could travel back in time, she would have never

made that deal with the Shadow Man. She would have smashed his talisman to the ground and let the chips fall where they might.

Now she was tied to Facilier for life. Stuck playing his games.

As much as she loved having her daddy back, Tiana knew he would never want this for her. If he knew what she'd done—the power she'd given the Shadow Man—he would be so disappointed.

As for Naveen . . .

Well, she would have figured out another way to save him. Anything was better than the bind she now found herself in.

"Tiana?"

Her eyes popped opened to see the flower vendor in front of her. "Oh, Ms. Rose." Tiana held her palm against her chest. "You scared me." She took a moment to collect herself. "How . . . how are you doing?"

"It would seem I should ask you that question," the woman said. "You look troubled."

She blew out a sigh. "I've had a rough morning."

"Oh?" Ms. Rose transferred the basket of irises she carried from one arm to the other. "How so?"

Tiana wasn't up for rehashing what had happened, but she couldn't bring herself to ignore Ms. Rose.

"I'm not sure if you heard about the mosquito attack at Congo Square," Tiana started. When the woman shook her head, Tiana filled her in with a condensed version of the assault. "But that isn't the half of it. Something . . . strange is happening to people around me—my friends and associates. It's hard to explain."

"Hmm," Ms. Rose murmured. She reached over and patted Tiana's hand. "Actually, it's quite simple. There's an old saying—"

"From your mother?"

"From my grandmother," she said. "She would say, *tanbou bat nan raje, men se lakay li vin danse.* The drum is beaten in the grass, but it is at home that it comes to dance."

Tiana was much too distressed from her confrontation with Facilier to decipher Ms. Rose's idioms. "What does that mean?"

"It means that acts that are done outside the home can have repercussions for *all* those inside the home. Your actions affect more than just you, Tiana. It's something to remember." She patted her hand again. "You take care."

Tiana mulled over the woman's words as she watched her walk away. Her shoulders slumped as she experienced something she never allowed herself to feel: hopelessness.

Her head still reeling, Tiana started walking again,

heading to the only place she could think of where she felt in control. Where she felt safe.

When she reached the supper club, she went directly to the pantry and retrieved the ingredients for her beignet dough.

"Tia?"

She stiffened at the sound of Charlotte's voice coming from the dining room. Her friend entered the kitchen a moment later. "Hey, Tia, do you know if I left my shawl here or—?" Charlotte stopped midsentence. "Tiana, what's wrong? Is it the bugs from this morning? They were scary."

"N-no, but—" Before she could utter another word, Tiana burst into tears.

"Oh, my goodness, Tia! Is it Ms. Eudora? Is she okay?"

"Mama's fine. It's nothing"—she hiccupped—"nothing like that. But, Lottie. Oh, Lottie, I've messed up something *awful*."

Charlotte rushed over and wrapped an arm around her shoulders. She guided her into the dining room and urged her to take a seat. Using a dish towel she'd grabbed from the kitchen, she wiped the sticky dough from Tiana's fingers.

"Now, now," Charlotte crooned. "It can't be worse than what we all just went through at Congo Square."

"But it is," Tiana lamented. She picked at a piece of fuzz on the tablecloth as she tried to come up with a way to describe the pickle she was in without betraying the terms of her and Facilier's deal. "Do you . . . do you know who the Shadow Man is?"

Charlotte's head jerked back. "You mean that man with the emporium in the Quarter? I've heard he's bad news, Tia."

"I know he is," she said. Oh, how she knew.

How could she explain the situation to Lottie without her friend thinking she'd gone off the deep end? She couldn't very well tell Lottie that Naveen had once been a frog and would have remained that way if not for Tiana's deal with Facilier. And her daddy? Could she honestly tell Lottie that her strong, vibrant daddy had passed away, but was now back because of the Shadow Man's friends on the other side?

She looked up from the table and into Charlotte's confused eyes.

"I can't go into any details, but I got involved with him. And now he's threatening to ruin my life."

"But, Tia . . . why?" Charlotte asked.

"I had no other choice," Tiana said. She fidgeted, scraping at bits of dough that remained on her fingers. "You wouldn't understand."

"I can try," her friend said. She pulled at one of Tiana's hands until Tiana looked at her. "Tell me."

Tiana chose her words carefully, knowing that one slip

of the tongue could prove to be dangerous. She didn't want to involve Charlotte in this mess with Facilier in any way.

"I came into possession of something the Shadow Man really wanted, and in exchange for it, he offered . . . well, something that I couldn't pass up. But then he changed the terms of our deal," Tiana continued. "And lately he's been hounding me to do more. He says that I have to keep doing whatever he asks or he'll hurt the people I love."

"Why, that . . . that's awful, Tia."

"I need a way out, Lottie. I can't allow him to have this kind of hold on me for the rest of my life. And I can't allow other people to be hurt because I was foolish enough to get involved with the likes of him."

"What are you going to do? There has to be something—someone that you can go to for help. Maybe I can ask Big Daddy. . . ."

Someone she could go to . . .

That was it!

Tiana plopped her palm to her forehead. "Why didn't I think of this before?" she whispered.

Her heart pounded against her ribcage as the first bead of hope she'd felt all day began to blossom in her chest. "There *is* someone!"

"Who is it? I can have our driver bring us to him right now."

"It's not a him, it's a her," Tiana said. "And you can't get there by car. She lives on the bayou." Tiana stood and began to pace between the stage and the table. "I need to go to Mama Odie."

"Who's Mama Odie?" Lottie asked with a frown.

"You don't know her," Tiana said. "But she's the only person I know who can help me get out of this mess. I'll have to find a boat. Maybe I can rent one from one of the fishermen at the dock."

"A boat? The bayou? Tia, this doesn't sound safe." Charlotte moved closer. "Listen, Big Daddy knows lots of people—"

"No." Tiana clamped her hands over Charlotte's shoulders. "Trust me, Lottie. I know what I'm doing." She pressed a kiss to Lottie's cheek. "Thanks for lending an ear. I appreciate it."

"Of course, Tia. You know I'm always here for you. . . . But I can't let you go traipsing off to this Mama Odie person, either."

"I'll be fine, Lottie," Tiana said as she moved to grab her bag. When she turned, Charlotte looked ready to put up another argument. "Don't," Tiana said. "Mama Odie is the only person who can help.

"The quicker I get to her, the better off we'll all be."

25

Naveen

Naveen stood in front of his desk, mumbling the words he'd practiced over and over again. Too much hinged on this meeting with Mr. LaBouff for him to screw it up. He absently rubbed at the welts on his arm, remnants of the mosquito attack earlier that day. Somehow it felt like a million years ago now.

He'd come to the mill after leaving Congo Square—assuring Tiana and Charlotte that he would clean his wounds as soon as he got there, since the mill was closer than home. And to his surprise, he'd found John Dugas waiting for him.

The man had countered with several uncustomary demands, stipulations that the mill's other customers would never dream of requesting. But Dugas Candy Company would not be an ordinary customer. It was Naveen's job to convince Mr. LaBouff of that.

If he could not, he just might have to give more thought to that invitation from his parents.

Naveen glanced over at the missive on his desk. It taunted him, silently insisting that he pack up and return to the life of luxury he had once lived. Asserting that he was a fool to think he could handle anything on his own.

But he could do this. He would show Mr. LaBouff that partnering with the candy company was in the sugar mill's best interest. And maybe even help Mr. LaBouff notice the contributions of the guys on the floor like Randy, see that they had more to give.

Naveen resumed his pacing. He stuck out his hand and engaged in an imaginary handshake.

"Thank you for seeing me, Mr. LaBouff. Have I got a proposal for you." Naveen shook his head. "No, no. That is all wrong. Not enough enthusiasm. Maybe if I—"

"Naveen! Naveen, sugar, where are you?"

Naveen ran out of his office at the sound of that very distinct voice calling his name. A moment later, he saw Charlotte climbing the stairs to the balcony.

Was she wearing . . . trousers?

Naveen was so shocked that he could have knocked himself over with a feather.

Wait. Was he supposed to knock *himself* with the feather? That didn't seem right. These American sayings still baffled him.

"There you are," Charlotte exclaimed as she made it to the landing.

"Charlotte, what are you wearing?" Naveen asked.

"Forget about my clothes," she said. "I need you to come with me. Now!"

"No. No. I can't," he said. "I have an important meeting with your father."

"There is nothing more important than this!" Charlotte said. "Then again, I don't know if I should even tell you. She told me not to tell anyone." She wrung her hands together, dismay evident in her worried eyes. "Oh, but I have to, because *some*body needs to talk some sense into that girl."

"To who? What girl?"

"It's Tiana," Charlotte said. "She's in trouble."

Panic instantly knotted in his chest. He thought about the picnic, about the look in her eyes when she'd spoken about the strangely aggressive insects. "Trouble? Where? What has happened?"

"That's just it. I'm not even sure. She gave me bits and

pieces, but I've known her far too long not to understand when she's not giving me the full story."

She began to relay what Tiana had shared with her, but Naveen had a hard time following. Something about her getting involved with a man known for cheating folks around the French Quarter out of their money.

"Charlotte, are you sure about this?" Naveen asked with an incredulous frown. "Tiana doesn't seem like one who is so easily swindled."

"She told me with her own mouth. She made some kind of deal with the Shadow Man, and now she wants out of it. I offered Big Daddy's help, but she doesn't want me to tell him. She says the only person who can help is a lady who lives on the bayou."

"Mama Odie?" he asked automatically.

Charlotte's eyes widened. "You know her?"

Naveen frowned. "I . . . I am not sure."

"How did you know her name?"

How did *I know that name?* It had popped into his head the minute Charlotte said "the bayou."

"Maybe Tiana mentioned her before?" Naveen tried.

Charlotte started that thing with her hands again, nervously twisting them. "I just don't know what to do about any of this, Naveen. It's too dangerous. Tiana's talking about renting a boat and going out there on her own, but I can't let her do that. That's why I'm wearing these blasted pants."

"So you're going, too?"

"I have to," Charlotte said. "I can't very well let my best friend go sailing in the middle of nowhere by herself. But I would feel so much better if you joined us."

Naveen reared his head back. "Me and Tiana? On a boat?"

Together?

Why did that seem somehow *familiar?*

"Oh, please say you'll come with us," Charlotte said.

Naveen glanced at the letter from his parents again, then at Charlotte. He thought about Tiana in trouble and knew there was only one answer.

"Lead the way."

26

Tiana

"Eighty-five cents a day?" Tiana cried. "To rent this rickety boat? I'll be lucky if it doesn't sink the moment I take it out on the water."

She couldn't waste time haggling. She needed to leave as soon as possible if she wanted to reach Mama Odie's before sundown. Otherwise, she'd find herself trying to navigate those narrow bayou passageways at night.

But she was her daddy's daughter. She had to at least *try* to get the price down.

"I'll give you fifty cents, and not a penny more," Tiana said.

The grizzly fisherman moved his cigar from one side of his mouth to the other. "Sixty-five," he countered.

"Fine," she said. She looked at the washed-up pirogue, with its warped, weatherworn planks. The chances were pretty high that this thing really *would* end up at the bottom of the bayou, especially if the thick blanket of algae covering the river had made it out to the swamps. The insidious green scum had even started to grow along the sides of the posts holding up the pier.

"There she is!"

Tiana whipped around at the sound of Charlotte's voice. She caught sight of her friend traipsing around the thick fishing nets and ropes scattered along the busy pier. And she was wearing trousers! Though she still looked completely out of place in a pink silk top with an embroidered collar and T-strap heels.

Tiana peered at the figure coming up behind Charlotte and nearly tumbled off the pier. Goodness, Almighty! She'd brought Naveen with her!

"Charlotte LaBouff, what is going on?" Tiana hissed.

"I couldn't let you go out there all alone, Tia." Charlotte panted as if she'd run all the way there from the LaBouff mansion. "It's much too dangerous. Naveen and I are going with you."

"Hey! Hey, what y'all doing here?"

Tiana looked past Charlotte and Naveen to discover Louis heading toward them, carrying his ever-present trumpet.

Was everyone she knew at the docks?

"I thought that was y'all," Louis exclaimed in his boisterous voice. "What y'all doing here?"

"What are *you* doing here, my friend?" Naveen gestured to the trumpet in Louis's hand. "Entertaining the fishermen?"

"I come out here to play every now and again. I like being close to the water." He looked at Tiana. "Y'all going somewhere?"

"I am," Tiana said quickly.

"*We're* going to get help from a lady who lives in the swamp," Charlotte insisted.

"Y'all going to Mama Odie?" Louis asked excitedly.

"How does everyone know about this Mama Odie except me?" Charlotte asked.

"Can I come with y'all?" Louis asked. "I was telling Tiana just the other day that I haven't been home si—"

"Excuse us for just a moment," Tiana said, cutting Louis off before he revealed more than he should. She grabbed Charlotte by the arm and dragged her several feet away.

"Charlotte LaBouff, what in the world is going on?"

"I told you, Tia! It's too dangerous for you to go out

there alone. There are gators and snakes and who knows what else lurking out there in the bayou. Besides, I told you I missed you. This may not be a Mardi Gras ball, but we'll be spending time together."

Tiana was baffled. "And just what do you plan to do if I get attacked by a snake? Beat it with that parasol?" she asked, pointing to the dainty satin-and-lace umbrella hanging from Charlotte's wrist. "And you brought *Naveen*!"

"I figured he could help protect us." Charlotte plopped a hand on her hip. "You may not think you need a strong man around, but you'll think differently if we get attacked by gators."

"Gators? What you say over there about gators?"

"Nothing, Louis," Tiana called over her shoulder. She turned back to Charlotte. "Look, I don't have enough room in the boat for all of you to come with me."

"Well, we'll just get a bigger boat," her friend said, as if her words were final. She looked at the little pirogue Tiana had just paid her hard-earned money to rent. "I'm not sure this would have gotten you very far anyway." Charlotte waved her hand in the air as if she were hailing a taxicab. "Oh, fisherman! Fisherman, we'll need to rent a bigger boat. Something with a cover, if you have it."

Tiana dropped her head back and looked up at the sky, but there were no answers raining down on her from above.

She followed Charlotte back to where a collection of boats for rent were lined up against the dock.

"None of these look very accommodating," Charlotte told the fisherman. "Don't you have anything bigger?"

"It's the bayou, Lottie. It's not as if you can take the Steamboat *Natchez* through those narrow canals or underneath those low-hanging branches."

Charlotte tipped her head to the side, an inquisitive dip to her brow. "Since when did you learn so much about the bayou? You hardly ever leave the city."

"I . . . I've . . . uh . . . heard things." Tiana stumbled over her words. She couldn't very well tell Lottie about her previous trip to Mama Odie's. "The fishermen are always talking about it when I come down to the pier to buy fish for the restaurant. Can we just pick a boat and get on with it?" Tiana asked, changing the subject. "We're losing daylight. I want to get where I'm going before nightfall."

"Where exactly on the bayou are we going?" Naveen asked.

Goose bumps popped up along Tiana's arms at the sound of his deep voice.

She closed her eyes for a brief moment in an effort to collect herself. A dance at a picnic was one thing. Being confined to a small boat with Naveen for hours? That was a decidedly *different* thing.

"It's kinda hard to explain," Tiana said before quickly moving away from him.

She walked over to where the fisherman and Charlotte were looking at a set of gleaming mahogany wood runabouts. Tiana didn't want to even think about how much it would cost to rent one of those.

She spotted a boat a few feet down the pier. It looked a bit worse for the wear, but it was big enough for all of them and its flat bottom was just narrow enough not to give her pause at the thought of flowing through whatever shallow waters they might find.

"We'll take this one," Tiana told the fisherman.

"That one?" Charlotte screeched. "Tia, I don't—"

"You want to come along, you come in this boat," Tiana told her. She turned her attention back to the fisherman. "Can you have this ready to go in the next ten minutes?"

The man tipped his tattered cap to her. "That I can do."

Tiana replied with a firm nod. She hefted the linen sack she'd brought with her and realized that the few provisions she'd thrown in there during her quick trip back to the house wouldn't be nearly enough food for four.

She turned to her motley crew and pointed just past the dock to the French Market. "I'm going over to those stalls to get more supplies. Be ready to get going when I return."

As she made her way to the market, Tiana tried to come

up with answers to the inevitable questions Charlotte and Naveen would have. How was she supposed to explain her relationship with a two-hundred-year-old Vodou woman living in a tree house in the bayou?

"You'll figure it out," she said underneath her breath.

At the market, she bought bananas, apples, pears, and dried figs, along with several fresh loaves of French bread. She would find a way to make the canned sardines and beans she'd taken from home stretch between the four of them.

Tiana was scooping shelled pecans into a small sack when she noticed Ms. Rose walking up to her.

"Hi, Tiana," Ms. Rose greeted her.

"Hey there, Ms. Rose." Tiana tied off the sack of pecans with twine and handed it to the vendor to weigh. "I would love to chat, but—"

"You're in a rush," the woman finished for her. "You're taking a boat ride."

Tiana's brows arched. "Yes," she said. "How did you know?"

Ms. Rose jutted her chin toward the water. "I saw you on my daily walk along the dock."

Tiana wasn't sure why anyone would choose the pungent docks to take a stroll, but it wasn't her concern right now.

"Well, I better get going," she said, hefting the bag with her purchases higher on her shoulder.

"Where are you headed?" Ms. Rose asked.

"Umm . . . to see a friend." It was what she'd told her parents when she had gone back to the house to gather supplies. "She lives on the bayou."

"That's a long way to go to see a friend," Ms. Rose said.

"She's, ah . . . special," Tiana said. "And I really need to see her as soon as possible."

Ms. Rose nodded slowly. "Well, before you go, I have something for you." She reached into the bag she always carried with her. Then she took Tiana's hand and placed a pewter brooch shaped like a rose in its center.

"Oh," Tiana said, unsure exactly why the woman was giving her such a lovely piece of jewelry, especially when she knew Tiana was on her way to the swamps. "This is quite beautiful," she said. "But maybe you should hold on to it until I get back from my trip?"

"No." Ms. Rose closed Tiana's fingers over the brooch. "Take it with you. Maybe pin it to your shirt."

Tiana looked down at her coveralls. This brooch was as inappropriate as Lottie's dainty parasol and heels. But Tiana didn't have time to argue. "Thank you."

"Be careful," Ms. Rose told her. She glanced up at the

sky. "There's quite a storm coming." She brought her gaze back to Tiana's. "It's been brewing for a while."

Something in the woman's tone, in that piercing, intense look in her eyes, made the hair on the back of Tiana's neck stand on end.

Just then, a streak of lightning came from out of nowhere, striking close to the St. Louis Cathedral and putting a finer point on her statement.

"*Malè je wè pa kite l' rive*, Tiana," Ms. Rose said. "The eyes that see misfortune don't let it arrive. Keep your eyes open. Take heed of warnings. And be careful."

"I will," Tiana said, shivering despite the heat. She held up the brooch. "Thank you again."

She gave a shaky smile, then moved past Ms. Rose, toward the dock. When she glanced back over her shoulder, the woman was still standing there, watching her.

Tiana quickened her steps and tried to shake off the strange feeling suddenly prickling her skin. She looked up at the sky and, even through the fog, could see the voluminous storm clouds building.

She needed to get to Mama Odie's . . .

Before the sky ripped opened on all of them.

27

Tiana

By the time Tiana returned to the dock, Louis and Charlotte had already climbed aboard the boat, but Naveen was nowhere to be found. Tiana briefly wondered if he'd decided against joining them, but a moment later he came running along the pier.

"Here we are," he said, holding three fat beeswax candles to his chest. "I've heard the bayou can get murky, even during daylight hours. Thankfully, there was someone selling these in the market."

Tiana was touched by his thoughtfulness, despite the

impracticality of his suggestion. She reached into her bag and pulled out her kerosene lamp.

"I'm way ahead of you. Though we can use those as a backup if necessary."

"You think of everything, don't you?" he said.

Tiana couldn't tell if he was joking, so she just nodded. "Are we ready?"

"Ready!" Louis called. "Hey, Tiana, you need me to help guide you to Mama Odie's?"

Tiana hesitated. Louis was not the greatest at directions. Still, he'd grown up in these bayous, and she supposed having him here to help was better than relying on her memory alone.

"Start out that way," the fisherman chimed in, pointing east. "A few knots down, you'll see the entrance to the canal that'll take you to Bayou Bienvenue. That's the quickest route to Mercier, Maxent, and all the others."

Tiana had no idea exactly on which bayou Mama Odie's house was located. She would have to rely on her recollection of landmarks, and on Louis.

And prayer. Lots and lots of prayer.

"Thank you," she told the fisherman as he untied the last of the rope from the stout, algae-covered pole and gave their boat a firm push with his booted foot. He tipped his hat to them again as they started to drift out on the scummy water.

Tiana grabbed hold of the long handle that stuck out from the motor, holding it steady as they traveled along the busy river. She kept the boat close to the bank to avoid the wake from any of the larger vessels. The waves they created made the grassy film covering the water resemble short, rolling hills.

After about ten minutes, she spotted the turn the fisherman had told them about. The fog, which was thicker on the water, made it difficult to see. Fortunately, as they traveled farther away from the city, it began to let up, and she could see more than two feet ahead of the boat.

Tiana could sense they were getting closer by the odors lingering in the air—the briny aroma of the river mixed with the dank, vegetative smell of the murky bayou. It instantly brought back memories of the last time she had been there.

She firmly shut those thoughts out of her head. It was bad enough that she had to share this tiny boat with Naveen. She would not torture herself by reminiscing about the time they'd spent together, falling for each other.

"Aww, this takes me back to when I was little," Louis said.

"Really? I didn't know there were bayous in Shreveport," Charlotte said.

Tiana cut a glance at Louis and shook her head. "Uh,

Louis's family is originally from the bayous west of here," she said to Lottie.

"Yeah, I grew up in parts like this," Louis added. "Once you live here, it never leaves your blood."

"What made you come to N'awlins?" Charlotte asked.

Tiana looked back at Louis. When she'd made the deal with the Shadow Man to allow Louis to become human, the two of them had sketched out a story about how Louis had moved from North Louisiana in search of fun and excitement in the big city. It wasn't far off from the truth. She just hoped Louis didn't say anything that would rouse suspicion.

Louis gave Lottie a line about wanting to play jazz in the spot where the musical style was born, which seemed to satisfy her. Tiana breathed a sigh of relief and prayed that the subject wouldn't come up again. She would have a hard enough time explaining Mama Odie once they arrived at her boat house; she didn't have the energy to come up with another story about Louis's dubious origins.

The body of water they were in tapered into a much narrower canal. Large spindly tree branches hung overhead, with gossamer-thin moss draping from them like a lady's fine hair.

Tiana looked upward, squinting to see through the hovering fog. She couldn't be sure, but she thought this might be the place where she and Naveen had first fallen out of the sky on that fated balloon ride they'd taken a year before. She looked from side to side, keeping an eye out for the hollowed tree stump where they'd hidden away from that pack of gators.

A small smile tipped up one corner of her mouth as she remembered that first night, and how ridiculously out of his element Naveen had been. She glanced over at him now, taking in his strong and handsome profile. He'd changed so much in the year since she'd first met him. He was no longer the spoiled little rich boy who thought he could get by on his looks and charm.

Though he'd surely won *her* over with that charm in the end.

"Do you want to share what you find so amusing, Ms. Tiana?"

Tiana startled. "Huh?"

"You were smiling," Naveen said.

He lounged against the wooden bench as if it were a velvet-covered chair in a palace somewhere. Even in the middle of a humid bayou, he still had that regal way about him. Tiana figured it was ingrained in him. It was yet another example of how so very different they were.

She wondered—even if she hadn't made that deal with Facilier, were there too many things about his world that made it so that she would never fit in it?

"It's nothing," she finally answered him. "Just thinking back on happier times."

"Would those happier times include this morning? Before the insects, of course." He scooted a few inches closer to her and shimmied his shoulders. "Did I impress you with my smooth dancing moves?"

"Smooth?" Her brow arched.

"Was I not?"

Tiana bit her lip to suppress her grin. "You were . . . interesting."

"Hmm." He rubbed his chin. "I'm not sure how I feel about that. I've seen some pretty interesting things that were not very impressive. Quite the opposite, in fact."

She couldn't hold back her laugh any longer. "Entertaining? Is that better?"

"Eh." He wiggled his hand. "Not really, but I'll take it."

"If it makes you feel any better, I think with a little practice, you will be dancing the Charleston better than anyone else in N'awlins."

He peered over at her, a faint light twinkling in the depths of his hazel eyes. "Are you offering to be my teacher?"

The rich cadence of his voice sent Tiana's heart thumping triple time. She rebuffed his suggestion with a shaky laugh. "Now, Naveen, you should know better than to ask that. I hardly have time to think these days with as busy as we are down at the supper club."

"Hmm," he murmured again. "You know, I am pretty new to this having-a-job thing, but from what I have seen, most people will take a day off every now and then just for fun. Now, *that* is interesting, yes?"

"Prince Naveen, is that your way of chastising me for working too hard?"

"Yes," he said. "Is it working?"

"No."

"Ah, Tiana." He pitched his head back and sighed up at the sky. With a hunch of his shoulder, he said, "I tried."

"I know lately I've been working longer hours than some deem healthy—especially my parents—but it's an important time. And I have to work hard if I want my restaurant to be a success."

"I understand," he murmured, leaning forward. "Actually, I admire that about you. Maybe you can teach me what it takes to be a success, eh?" He winked. "Along with how to dance the Charleston, of course."

Tiana swallowed.

Oh, yes, his charm was as strong as ever.

This trip was going to be even more challenging than she'd thought.

28

Facilier

Facilier hustled through the crowd of dingy factory workers heading back to their humdrum jobs, their faces filthy with soot and grime. He hated that they worked so close to where he lived. He remembered a time when people such as these weren't allowed anywhere near the Quarter. Prior to when the railroad was built, when the wealthiest of the city lived here before migrating to those big mansions uptown.

Oh, to have those days back.

But it looked as if the riffraff was here to stay. The dreadful factories that had taken over the Quarter made it so.

Facilier arrived at his residence in Pirate's Alley. He

hung his top hat on the hat rack as he stepped inside, his mind filled with the myriad quandaries before him. His pursuit of Eli LaBouff's fortune had dominated his existence for years, but that was no longer his top priority. He now had a more pertinent goal: saving his own soul.

And in order to do that, he had to get Tiana's signature on that contract.

He regarded his bandaged hand with a scowl. He'd tried signing Tiana's name to the document himself, but a bolt of lightning had struck the contract, burning off a bit of his skin with it. He should have known his friends on the other side would have a provision in place to impede something like that.

Well, he was done playing games. He *would* get Tiana's signature on that contract, and he knew exactly how he would do it.

It was time for him to turn up the heat on Naveen.

Tiana was more than just smitten with the prince. He'd seen them out in Congo Square that morning, giggling like a couple of besotted lovebirds while they danced as if they didn't have a care in the world. He gathered Tiana would do just about anything for her little prince.

After all, it was the threat of Naveen remaining a frog forever that had finally propelled her to accept his deal a year before.

What should it be? Should he snatch him off the street and store him in that room with the others?

No. It wasn't enough for Naveen to go missing. Tiana needed to *see* his pain.

An unfortunate accident at LaBouff's sugar mill? A broken leg, maybe? Or how about a nasty burn from those big kettles filled with piping hot liquid sugar? Wouldn't it be a shame if that pretty face of his was scorched, leaving him scarred for life.

Facilier mulled over his options. He should have gone after her prince from the very beginning, but it was too late for recriminations. The only thing that mattered was getting her to comply before his friends on the other side came to collect.

As if he'd conjured them just by thinking about them, the floor underneath his feet started to shake, and the temperature around him grew cold as ice. Facilier braced himself as shadows slithered along the floor and walls.

"Well . . . hello," he said, injecting false cheer into his voice.

They spoke in their typical moans and groans.

If he closed his eyes Facilier could still see that dirty, disheveled little boy, curled up on the filthy floor of an abandoned building. Nowhere to go, no mother to take care of him.

The Shadows had sought him out. They'd preyed on him, knowing that he had no other option but to become their minion.

Well, he was done being under their thumb.

"Yes, yes. I know," Facilier answered. "I know I have just a few more days before the payment is due." He held up a hand. "However, I have a proposition for you fine gentlemen. I recognize that Tiana's soul was part of our deal, but what if I get you a different soul? I have a few options—"

A stiff wind blew, strong enough to knock him to the ground. He steadied himself on his hands and knees, bracing against the fierce gust of air.

"Okay." Facilier held his hand up to his face. "I . . . I . . . I understand. I will get you hers. When have I ever let you all down?"

Another blast of wind. It sent him crashing into the wall. Jars and bottles toppled from the shelves above him, shattering into thousands of pieces as they landed on the hard floor.

And as quickly as his friends from the other side had appeared, they were gone.

Everything was silent. The temperature in the room returned to the normal chilliness of late February. Facilier remained on the floor, his chest heaving with each breath he took.

They were becoming more impatient, more violent. Their insatiable appetite for mayhem grew stronger with each passing day.

He pushed himself up from the floor and searched through the documents that had scattered around the room, seeking the contract he'd *thought* he was signing on Tiana's behalf last year. Once he found it, he tucked it underneath his arm, grabbed his cane and top hat, and stormed out of his emporium.

He considered going straight to LaBouff's sugar mill and snatching that stupid prince by his perfect hair. He could drag Naveen to Tiana's restaurant so that he could torture him in front of her. But those goons working in LaBouff's mill would likely try to stop him.

Instead, he took off for Tremé. He'd used his illusions on Tiana successfully before; he could use them again.

Facilier spent the entire walk devising a creditable lie about Naveen's whereabouts, but when he arrived at the restaurant, the waitress informed him that Tiana wasn't there.

Facilier could barely control his rage.

"Where is she?" he growled.

The waitress looked him up and down as if he were a

foul bug she wanted to squash with her shoe. How dare this little peon treat him this way!

He stepped closer to her. *"Where is she?"* he repeated slowly.

"Is there a problem here?"

Facilier stepped back as James walked through the swinging door. A red-and-white checkered towel was thrown across one burly shoulder. He was strong and healthy, and had no idea just how much he owed Facilier for being here.

"Can I help you?" the man asked. By the tone of his voice, Facilier could tell that he had an opinion of him. One that was not good.

"I was looking for the owner of this restaurant," Facilier answered.

"Well, I'm one of the owners."

Thanks to me.

He should tell him that right now. What would his reaction be? What would James say if he learned that an artillery shell meant for his heart had, instead, embedded itself in a tree in Belgrade? All because Facilier had petitioned for it to happen that way on his behalf. Had paid for it, possibly with his own soul.

"It's a young woman who introduced herself to me as the owner," Facilier said. "She wanted to talk to me about possibly being an entertainer for the guests." He pulled out a deck of cards and did quick work, flipping them and fanning them out.

"Tiana never mentioned that. . . ." James pulled the towel from his shoulder and wiped his hands with it. "She had some business to tend to—a friend called on her for help. She'll be gone overnight, but should be back some time tomorrow. I'll tell her you stopped in."

"Great," Facilier said. He tipped his hat to the man and gave the waitress, who still stared at him suspiciously, a stern look. "You can count on my return."

As he walked away from the restaurant, Facilier clutched the handle of his cane so hard he nearly broke it. He couldn't sit around waiting for Tiana to show up. Time was running out.

Where could she have gone?

Facilier retreated to the French Quarter. He prowled around the market, searching stalls where he'd noticed her shopping in the past. Maybe she'd stopped to make a few purchases before traveling to this supposed friend in need.

When he didn't see her anywhere, he took off for the pier, hoping to find her looking at all the freshly caught seafood being sold along the banks of the Mississippi. He slipped several times on the slimy green algae clawing its way up the dock.

There was something pernicious happening here—the

never-ending fog, the peculiar algae growing on the water. He'd asked around about the bugs Tiana had accused him of summoning and discovered that a swarm of giant mosquitoes had attacked those at Congo Square after he'd left that morning.

He didn't know what had caused any of it, but he knew it was supernatural, and malevolent at that.

And he wasn't the one behind it.

"Can I help you, fella?" a fisherman asked.

Facilier turned his nose up at his foul stench, but the man didn't seem to notice.

"Yes," he said. "I'm looking for a colored girl. Not too long out of high school. A little bit skinny."

"Oh, you talking 'bout the one with that restaurant over in Tremé? She comes by to get fish every so often."

"That's her," Facilier said. "Have you seen her around today?"

"Sure did. She came by looking to rent a boat, but I sent her over to old Pete, because none of my boats are good for trawling around the bayou."

"The bayou?" Facilier asked, his mouth going dry.

"That's what she said," the man replied. "I thought maybe she's gonna try her hand at frogging. Fry up some frog legs to serve in that restaurant of hers."

Facilier rubbed his jaw. "Maybe you're right," he said.

But the old fisherman had it all wrong.

There was only one reason Tiana would take off for a last-minute trip on the bayou. Only one person she could be on her way to see.

Things had just become infinitely worse for him.

29

Naveen

The boat made a low puttering sound as it sloughed through the swamp waters. Louis relaxed against the starboard side and twirled his trumpet on his finger. Charlotte had declared that the rocking was making her both seasick and sleepy. She was currently curled up toward the front on the boat's knobby bench, with one of Tiana's bags of provisions serving as her pillow.

Naveen returned his attention to Tiana. She was focused, her eyes constantly roaming from left to right. She had refused his offer to take over driving duties, proudly declaring that she could steer the boat just fine on her own. All he wanted was to give her a little time to rest.

As he stared at her profile, Naveen wondered what had spawned her need to constantly be in pursuit of something. As if taking a moment to just relax was some kind of invisible mark against her.

"Are you sure you do not want me to take over?" he tried again. "Just for a little while, so that you can stretch your neck."

Is that the right phrase? Stretch your neck?

"I've got it," she answered. "The canals are getting narrower the deeper we get into the bayou. I've gotta take care to stay in the center of the waterway. Last thing we need is to have the propeller get caught up in a bunch of weeds."

After a few minutes, their tranquil surroundings were polluted with a loud snore. Naveen looked over his shoulder and chuckled at the sight of Louis and Charlotte now sharing the same bag as a pillow.

"So much for help from those two, eh?" he said.

Tiana glanced over her shoulder and smiled. "It's probably for the best. Easier to concentrate on where we're going."

Naveen thought it best as well. He liked the idea of not having to share Tiana's attention with their other boatmates.

Although it was not as if she was paying all that much attention to him. After her earlier teasing about his interesting dance moves, she had gone back to manning the boat and had not spoken much.

"Do you find it odd that the heavy fog is no longer with us?" Naveen asked, deciding the weather was a safe subject to start with. "I would have thought it would be worse here in this soupy swamp, no?"

"I don't know what to make of that fog," she said, but then she sat up straighter. "Actually, I just had a thought! Maybe it's because we're no longer in N'awlins, and it's the city that's—" She stopped. Her mouth pulled into a frown. "I'm not sure," she said. "I just hope it lets up soon back home."

A bug whizzed past Tiana's head and she flapped her hand around, waving it away. "Ugh! I don't particularly like these stowaways. Especially after Congo Square." She shifted toward the side of the boat, then ran her fingers through the water.

Naveen's breath quickened as he was struck with a strange sense of familiarity. It was as if he had already seen her do that very thing.

"Have I . . . have we been here before?" he asked.

Tiana looked at him, her big brown eyes narrowed with suspicion. "What do you mean? In this boat?"

"Yes." He nodded. "I remember you talking about your dislike of bugs. You did not want to eat one."

Her eyes widened with dismay.

"What am I talking about?" Naveen nervously laughed. "That was a ridiculous thing to say. Why would there be talk about you eating a bug?" Although he was certain there had been. Well, almost certain. He shook his head. Maybe the heat was getting to him. "And, of course, we have not been here before. *We* have not been anywhere before." He huffed out a regretful sigh. "You practically run whenever I am near you."

The moment he said the words, Naveen wished he could take them back. They revealed too much. He was afraid if Tiana knew just how much she captivated him, she would pull away even more.

"It's not you," she said.

His eyes shot to hers. "It's not?"

"Forget I said that," she said quickly.

"No. No, please." He leaned toward her. "What did you mean?"

"Really, it's nothing." She hesitated for a moment before continuing. "It's like I said before: I'm very busy with my restaurant." She glanced away from the water just long enough to grace him with a subtle grin. "But I guess it wouldn't hurt to occasionally sit and talk with you and Lottie when y'all are at the supper club."

"I would like that very much," Naveen said.

He would like it even more if it were just the two of them, without Charlotte, but that would come eventually. He would take baby steps with Tiana.

They returned to that companionable silence again, but Naveen no longer felt the impulse to fill it with chatter. He had achieved what he had set out to accomplish: he had managed to get Tiana to smile at him. Talk to him. She had even agreed not to scurry away when he approached her.

"Naveen?"

Tiana's soft voice pierced his musings.

"Yes?"

"I actually am getting a little tired. Would you mind taking over for a minute?"

"Of course not." He stood so quickly that he caused the boat to wobble just a bit.

Charlotte woke up with a start. "What's going on?"

"It's nothing, Lottie," Tiana said. "Naveen is going to drive the boat for a while. Go back to sleep."

"Oh. Okay," Charlotte said, then put her head down again.

"Sorry about that," Naveen replied. He moved closer to the motor and grabbed hold of the wooden handle used to steer it. As Tiana released her hold on the handle, her hand brushed against his.

It felt as if a bolt of electricity flashed through him. The air around them was heavy with something Naveen could not describe as they stared at each other for several moments, neither moving their hands.

"I . . . I'm going to get a pear," Tiana said. "Do you want anything?"

"Not a pear," Naveen said without thinking. He mentally scolded himself over his forwardness.

But Tiana did not chastise him. Instead, a blush formed on her delicate cheeks.

Achidanza! She was so lovely; she took his breath away.

She finally slipped her hand away from his and moved to the front end of the boat. Naveen could hear her shushing Charlotte in a soothing voice. A few minutes later she returned, claiming the spot where he had sat for much of their journey.

"So, Tiana, where exactly are we headed again?"

She took a bite of her pear and chewed excruciatingly slowly, so slow that Naveen was sure she had done so on purpose. After a moment, she said, "There's a lady who lives down on the bayou. She's special. She has . . . umm . . . special powers." She chuckled. "I know this may sound crazy to you, but—"

"No," he said, cutting her off. "If you need to see a bayou lady with special powers, who am I to judge?"

He almost asked if she had ever mentioned Mama Odie to him before, but after his statement about the bug, he thought it best to not say anything.

She smiled that smile at him again. The one that made Naveen think that maybe he really *was* starting to make some progress.

"I was a bit surprised that you wanted to drive the boat at all," Tiana said. "You're not one for manual labor. At least you didn't use to be. You've changed."

"How do *you* know that I have changed?"

"Umm . . . because . . . well, you made quite the splash when you first came to N'awlins. Your reputation for being a laissez-faire playboy was well known throughout the city."

"Yeah, well, that was last year."

"It doesn't seem all that long ago," she remarked in a wistful voice.

"No," Naveen said. "No, it does not." He tipped his head to the side. "Yet, in many ways, it feels like a lifetime."

"Really? How so?"

He shrugged. "I just feel like a different person. I cannot explain it." Naveen chuckled. "I often think about what my parents would say if they saw their . . . what was that phrase you just used?"

"Laissez-faire? It means carefree," she said around another bite of her pear.

"Yes, yes! Their laissez-faire son. My father would probably say, 'Why did it take you coming to America to learn the value of a hard day's work?'" He mimicked his father's voice.

Although he was not so sure about that anymore. Based on that letter he had received from his parents, they no longer cared about his lack of a work ethic.

But *he* cared.

He did not want to be seen as that lazy, carefree playboy anymore, especially by Tiana.

"How do you know so much about my reputation?" Naveen peered at her from his side of the boat. "It sounds as if you were paying more attention to me than you like to let on, Ms. Tiana."

She pulled her bottom lip between her teeth, a demure smile playing at her lips. "Don't flatter yourself," she said, but the words didn't hold much censure.

It was almost as if she was . . . *teasing* him.

Was she teasing him? It would be a very good thing if that was the case. Teasing was one step closer to . . . to . . . well, to not running away from him.

Tiana reached over and pulled a leaf from a low-hanging branch. She twirled it between her fingers.

"Can I ask you something?" she asked.

"Anything," Naveen quickly answered.

"Do you ever think about going back home to . . . where is it you're from again?"

He sent her a sly smile. "Come now, Tiana. Would you have me to believe that you don't know where I am from?"

"Fine." She rolled her beautiful brown eyes. "Maldonia. Do you ever think of going back home to Maldonia, Mr. Prince?"

Naveen decided to be honest.

"Sometimes," he answered. "But I'm not sure I would go back to stay. I miss my parents and the rest of my family, but I want to show them all that I can move about the world without our family's money. That I can make it on my own. And, well, maybe I want to show myself that, too."

"Do they know you're working in a sugar mill?"

"What's wrong with working in a sugar mill?"

"Nothing," she said. "You just don't see that many princes doing it."

"Well, it is nice to be the first at something in my family," he said with a grin.

They relaxed again into one of those comfortable silences. This time, Naveen did not interrupt it. He welcomed the sound of the birds chirping and the toads croaking. There was something peaceful about the unseen inhabitants of the swamp going about their day. He glanced over at Tiana and caught her yawning. It was the prettiest yawn he had ever seen.

"You can go to sleep if you would like," he told her. "You can trust me to man the boat."

"I don't think so," she said with a laugh. She yawned again.

This one was, by far, the prettiest yawn he had ever seen.

"I'll stay up and keep you company," she said. "Just keep us steady. Don't veer off course for a second."

"You have a lot of demands, you know that?"

"So I've been told," she said.

He peered out over the water again. "I don't know why, but I cannot shake the feeling that I've been here before," Naveen remarked. "There is something about this swamp that seems very familiar to me. The smell, I think. I cannot explain it."

"Well . . ." Tiana started, then stopped.

"Well, what?" Naveen inquired.

"Well, maybe some of the men who work at the sugar mill are from around here. You've probably smelled it on their clothes. It's not easy to get rid of this scent once it's in your skin."

"So are you telling me I will smell like this stinky swamp forever?"

She laughed. "It'll wear off eventually."

"You have a lovely laugh," Naveen said. "So beautiful, so rare."

"I laugh all the time," she countered.

"You should laugh more often when you are around *me*. I would like very much to make you laugh, Tiana."

Naveen could not be sure, but he thought he saw a faint spark of interest in her gaze before she broke eye contact. She fiddled with the kerosene lamp she'd brought.

"Should I light this?" she asked.

He sighed. Just when he thought they were bonding, she pulled away.

"I can see just fine right now," Naveen answered. "Why don't you save it in case it gets murkier?"

"Okay," she said. Then she yawned again, with her whole body this time, stretching her balled fist in the air.

"Actually, I think I will take that nap. You'll wake me if you need me?" she asked.

There was much he would still have liked to say, but Naveen feared they would go right back to the way things had been, when she had seemed put off by his very presence. So instead, he said, "I have it from here, Tiana.

"Get some rest."

30
Tiana

As the boat bobbed along the bayou, Tiana tried her best to get some sleep. It should have been easy enough after her eventful morning, but her mind was too keyed up to allow her body to get the rest she needed.

Facilier's threat consumed her.

What if he made good on his promise to harm her family? Was he sending those shadowy figures to hurt her daddy right now? Was her mother safe? Would he do something to the restaurant, like set it on fire, the way he'd most likely done to Rudy Davis's band's instruments?

And what about Mr. Salvaggio? He still hadn't turned

up, and Tiana couldn't help wondering if Facilier was behind the disappearance.

The unknown was as frightening as the little she *did* know when it came to what that awful con man could do. Who knew what else he had up his sleeve, or how long he planned to torment her with his requests? He could very well demand she be at his beck and call for the rest of her life.

She said a fervent prayer that Mama Odie would help her find a solution to this mess she'd gotten herself into.

Tiana gave up on the idea of getting any sleep, but kept her eyes closed. It was safer to make Naveen think she was resting so he wouldn't turn that charismatic charm on her again.

She had been through this before with him, nestled in the coziness of this very same bayou. She remembered all too well what it was like to listen to his soothing voice as he talked about anything and everything.

It was where she'd fallen in love with him.

Talking with him earlier had brought back such fond memories—memories she was afraid for a moment that he'd also remembered. But it had also called to mind what she'd been forced to give up when she agreed to the conditions of Facilier's deal last year.

For just a moment, Tiana allowed her mind to wander

to that ideal fantasy world. A world where she had her restaurant, her daddy, *and* Naveen. Where she didn't have to
worry about any harm coming to her family. Where she
could live out her days cooking scrumptious meals for the
people of New Orleans and dancing to sweet jazz music in
Naveen's arms.

The world she currently lived in was far from that ideal
fantasy she so often conjured up in her dreams. In *this*
world, everything came at a cost.

Despite the troubling thoughts that continued to invade
her mind, Tiana managed to drift into a fitful slumber. She
couldn't have been sleeping for more than a half hour when
a disquieting sensation rushed through her.

She woke up with a start and found Louis manning
the boat.

Oh, no!

"Louis." Tiana spoke through clenched teeth. "What
are you doing driving?" She looked around. "And where
are we? This doesn't look familiar to me at all."

"He said he knew a shortcut," Naveen said from the
starboard side of the boat.

"A shortcut?" Tiana asked.

Why, why, *why* had she let them talk her into allowing
them to come along? She should have stuck with her original
plan and taken this boat out by herself. She had certain

milestones she'd remembered that would have guided her directly to Mama Odie's. She had no idea where they were now. They could be heading back toward New Orleans for all she could tell.

"Louis, tell me you know what you're doing," Tiana pleaded.

"I do," he replied. "I know this bayou like the back of my hand." He gave her a toothy grin. "Just trust me."

Her brow pinched as she cast a quick glance over their surroundings. Something wasn't right about this. Whatever canal Louis had guided them into was much too narrow for their boat. She could practically reach out and touch the banks of the bayou.

"Louis, I'm not sure about this," Tiana warned. "It's too narrow." She looked over the side of the boat. "And this water is too shallow."

"Oh, it's not that bad," Louis said. "I promise, I know what I'm—"

The sound of the boat suddenly crashing against an embankment rang out loudly in the quiet stillness of the bayou.

31

Tiana

"Louis! Ahhhh!" Tiana pitched forward in the boat, nearly tumbling over the side. Lottie rolled off the bench where she'd been sleeping.

"What happened!" Charlotte screamed. "Why aren't we moving? And why is it so dark here? Goodness, Tia, why did I let you talk me into this?"

Tiana whirled around. "Me? *You're* the one who decided to tag along, Lottie. I would have been just fine by myself."

"Really? Does this look fine to you!"

"Let us all calm down," Naveen said, "and see what kind of damage has been done. It may not be so bad, eh."

They all climbed out of the boat. As Charlotte took Naveen's hand, she slipped and fell into a putrid patch of slimy mud.

"I'm never doing this again," Charlotte said, looking down at her trousers, which were now streaked with sludge.

"Let's hope we never have to," Tiana said. She looked over at Lottie. "Sorry I snapped at you."

"Don't worry about it, sugar. Stress brings out the worst in me, too. You hear that, swamp creatures?" Charlotte called out as she gingerly navigated the soupy shoreline. "Don't test me! You stay away from me and I'll do the same!"

Tiana rounded the side of the boat to stand with Naveen and Louis, who were both studying the bow. She had no idea how Louis had managed to wedge the vessel inside the cluster of gnarled branches and prickly brambles. Some of the vines had thick thorns that were at least two inches long.

Naveen scratched the back of his head. "This looks . . . uh . . . pretty sticky."

Tiana took a step closer, grateful she'd worn boots but regretting that they were her good leather ones and not the plastic rain boots. They squished as her feet sank into the mud. She just knew they would be completely ruined before all was said and done.

She braced her hands against the hull and tried to give it a push. The boat didn't move a single inch.

"We tried that," Naveen said.

"Well, I'm sure you did," she returned. "I just wanted to see how stuck we were."

"We are pretty stuck," he said.

She peered at the thicket from several angles. "If we can find a few branches that are thin enough to maneuver through these vines, but sturdy enough to give a little leverage, I believe we can pry the boat out. Let me see what I can find."

She backed away from the boat. She started to flail in the mud, but before she could tumble backward, a set of strong arms braced around her.

"I have you," Naveen said. He was so close she could feel his warm breath against her ear. Tiana did her best to ignore the goose bumps pebbling up and down her skin, but she would have had a better chance of ignoring a fireworks display taking place on her front porch.

"Thank you," she said. She disengaged herself from his hold and moved several feet away. It still didn't feel far enough. She could have moved clear to the other side of this bayou and it still wouldn't have left enough room between them.

She dusted her hands off on her coveralls. "I'm going to search for something to dislodge the boat."

"I think me and Louis can do that," Naveen said.

"We'll all do our part," Tiana replied. "I'm not just going to stand here twiddling my thumbs while the big strong men go in search of something to get us out of this mess."

Tiana took a gander at Charlotte, who was brooding as she sat on a downed cypress tree. She walked over and pulled her friend up by her arm, then pointed to the left side of the bayou's shoreline.

"You and Louis can go that way, and Lottie and I will search this way," Tiana said, pointing in the opposite direction.

"We will?" Charlotte asked with a horrified shriek.

"Yep, we sure will," Tiana said. She plopped a hand on her hip. "Let's see who can find the best branch."

"Ah, it is a competition, then?" Naveen asked, his brow arched, a small smile playing at the corners of his mouth.

Oh, goodness, was he flirting with her again? Was *she* flirting with *him*?

This was *not* the time.

It was never the time to flirt with Naveen. Doing so would only lead to the heartache of realizing that they could never be together.

Tiana made the decision then and there to end this ill-advised teasing between them. Not only was it foolhardy, it was dangerous.

Electing not to respond to his question, she looked up at the sky and said, "Let's go. Before dusk settles and we're stuck here in the dark."

32

Tiana

Tiana dodged thatches of thick vegetation that protruded from the earth as she led the way opposite where Naveen and Louis had traveled.

"You doing okay, Lottie?" she called over her shoulder.

"What do you think?" came Charlotte's retort.

Despite the direness of their situation, Tiana had to laugh. "If it makes you feel any better, I'm proud of the way you're holding up. You haven't complained nearly as much as I thought you would."

"Just give me time," Charlotte replied.

The deeper they journeyed into the copse of

algae-covered trees and tall reeds, the more pungent the briny, stagnant air became. The humidity wrapped itself around them like a damp, dank cloak, its saturating presence bordering on unbearable, despite the fact that it was not quite spring. It signaled a scorching summer ahead of them.

Something swooped down just over their heads, emitting a loud caw. Charlotte yelped.

"What was that?" she cried. "Oh, goodness, Tia, I just know we're gonna get eaten by some horrible swamp creature."

"The animals here are more afraid of you than you are of them," Tiana said.

Except for the gators, but she wouldn't mention those.

"That's hogwash," Charlotte said. She slipped and reached out for a nearby tree to steady herself. "Eww! Eww! Eww!"

"What now?" Tiana asked.

Charlotte pointed to a horde of bugs crawling along the tree bark where she'd just had her hands.

Tiana held up both of hers. "I can't help you. You know how I feel about bugs."

She took a step back and caught her foot on a broken stump protruding from the ground. Tiana flailed, her arms windmilling in the air. She overcorrected herself and pitched forward, barreling into Charlotte.

They both landed against the bug-covered tree.

"Ewwww!" Tiana and Charlotte screeched simultaneously.

"Move, move, move," Charlotte said, pushing at Tiana.

Tiana scrambled into a standing position. She slapped at her arms, even though she hadn't been against the tree long enough for any of the bugs to get to her. Charlotte, on the other hand . . .

"I am officially complaining," Charlotte said as she peeled a slimy slug off her sleeve and flung it on the ground. She pointed in the area where she'd thrown the creature. "What's that?"

Tiana looked down. The brooch Ms. Rose had given her lay among the foliage.

"Oh, it must have slipped out of my pocket when I fell," she said. Tiana retrieved the brooch and, this time, pinned it inside her coveralls. "Come on," she said, reaching for Charlotte's arm. "We can't let Naveen and Louis win."

"So it *is* a competition," Charlotte drawled.

"A friendly one," Tiana quipped.

"Hmm. You know, Tia, I've been wondering . . . how friendly *do* you feel toward Naveen?"

"Don't start, Lottie."

"I just think if you gave him half a chance—"

"Don't," Tiana reiterated.

Charlotte threw her hands up. "Fine. I won't say how perfect I think you are for each other. You're driven, and he's so carefree. You balance each other out!"

Tiana marched ahead, ignoring Lottie.

"But you two *are* perfect for each other," her friend called.

Tiana ignored that, too.

They happened upon an area of fallen tree limbs ripe for the picking. Both she and Charlotte searched the timber pile.

"Okay, what about this one?" Charlotte asked, holding up a scrawny pole that didn't look as if it could hold the weight of a one-pound catfish.

"I don't think that one will be strong enough."

"We've been poking through these sticks for twenty minutes already," Charlotte said.

"Just be patient," Tiana said. "We'll eventually find the perfect branch."

"In case you hadn't noticed, patience isn't one of my virtues."

"You don't say?" Tiana laughed.

"You, on the other hand, have the patience of a saint, Tia. Always have." Charlotte tossed a stubby branch over her shoulder. "Take the other day at Maison Blanche, for instance. I don't know how you kept your cool when that saleswoman stopped you from trying on that hat."

Tiana paused in the middle of lifting a rotted-out tree limb from the pile. "Lottie, you do realize such things happen to me all the time, don't you?"

"What?" Charlotte recoiled, her face a mask of confusion. "Tia, what are you talking about? That lady was absolutely horrible to you. You're saying she's been that way to you before? Why didn't you tell me? I would have suggested we go to another store."

"It wouldn't have mattered," Tiana said as gently as possible. "It would have been the same way at any of those department stores." This was neither the time nor the place to have this conversation. Though, in all honesty, Tiana wasn't sure when would be a good time to have this conversation. There were some things that were just better left unsaid, especially when dealing with her well-meaning but often oblivious friend.

"Don't worry about it," Tiana said.

She turned her focus to a pile of reeds, twigs, and tree limbs that had collected at the base of a nearby cypress tree.

Despite the damp earth muffling the sound of Charlotte's footsteps, Tiana could hear the sucking sound of her feet sinking with each step she took through the mud.

"Tia?" Charlotte's voice was quiet. "Tia, please talk to me. How can I know how to fix this if you won't even talk to me?"

"There's nothing for you to fix."

"It sounds as if there is."

"This is bigger than you, Lottie. It's . . . complicated." Tiana blew out a weary breath. "Besides, we have other things to worry about right now."

"But what makes it so complicated?"

"Because we're different! Don't you get it, Lottie? We're different. How can you not see that?"

Tiana covered her face with her hands. One part of her wanted to shield her friend from this truth. It was just easier to let Lottie live in her perfect little world where everything was black and white, and those murky shades of gray didn't exist.

Yet Tiana had been forced to face these facts ever since she was a little girl. She had known how different their worlds were from the moment she stepped into the LaBouff mansion and realized the entirety of the little house her family lived in could fit in their grand entryway.

She'd known as she watched her mother sew dress after dress for Charlotte, using the kind of soft, silky fabrics Tiana could only dream of wearing. Fabrics so much more luxurious than the rough cotton her own dresses were made of.

Those differences—the stark reality of the existence she lived compared to Charlotte's—had been part of Tiana's life for as long as she could remember. Her mama had told her a long time ago that it wasn't proper to mention the LaBouffs' money, but just because she couldn't *talk* about it, that didn't mean Tiana hadn't noticed.

It hadn't occurred to her until years later, when they were both in their teens, that Charlotte had never fully grasped that Tiana didn't have all the privileges she had. And here they were, both on the cusp of turning twenty years old, and Lottie still didn't seem to understand.

"Even though we live in the same city, it's as if we come from two different worlds," Tiana told her now. "I don't know if you understand just *how* different our worlds are."

"I'm not as naive as you assume, Tia. I know Big Daddy's money allows me to live a . . . well, a charmed life."

"It's not just about the money. It's about everything, about our lives in general," Tiana said. "What happened at the department store is a perfect example."

"What happened at Maison Blanche was *not* right. And they will never get another red cent from me."

"I know it wasn't right, but I also know it's the way things are. It's the world that *I* have to live in, Lottie." Several uncomfortable seconds ticked by before Tiana asked in a quiet voice, "Do you want to know how I got roped in with the Shadow Man?"

"I have no idea why you'd ever get caught up with the likes of him," she answered.

"It's because, at first, he offered to give me my restaurant," Tiana said. "I turned him down, but I was tempted, Lottie. I was tempted because I spent years working at Duke's Cafe and Cal's Restaurant. I socked away every penny I earned, and it was barely enough for the down payment on that old rundown sugar mill."

"But you *did* buy your own restaurant!"

"But look at how long it took. And as grateful as I am that Daddy and I were able to afford that building in Tremé, it still isn't the place I had my heart set on. Of course, it's not as if the Fenner brothers would have sold it to me anyway," she continued with a sarcastic snort. "They'd already decided that I wasn't fit to run a restaurant like that."

"What gives them the right to decide what you can and can't do?"

"It's done all the time," Tiana answered. "People assume I'm a maid because that's usually the only type of work a colored woman can get in this town. It's the only type of work we've been allowed to do, save for those who have skills that can't be denied, like Mama. People are often surprised to hear that I'm a chef who owns her own restaurant."

"Well, at least you've shown those Fenner brothers that you *can* run a restaurant. And I'm sure you'll eventually earn enough to buy that building you really want."

Tiana leveled her gaze at Charlotte. "How long have we known each other, Lottie?"

"Well, Tia, you know we've been knowing each other since we were both in knee-highs."

"And how long have I talked about opening a restaurant?"

"For as long as I've known you," Charlotte said with a laugh. "All you've ever talked about was making your daddy's gumbo and selling it in your restaurant one day." She put her hand on Tiana's shoulder and squeezed it encouragingly. "That's why I'm so happy to see you finally getting that chance now. You made it happen."

"Tell me something, Charlotte. In all that time, did you ever think to ask Mr. LaBouff to help me?"

Charlotte froze. "Well . . . well, no. You're so proud, Tiana. You would never have taken charity from Big Daddy."

"You're right, I wouldn't have accepted charity from him, but do you ever wonder why it never crossed your mind to offer to help me, Lottie?" Tiana swallowed past the knot of disappointment clogging her throat. "Your daddy is the richest man in the city, and one of the most influential. There are more ways he could have had an impact than just with his money. Like vouching for me with the Fenner brothers, or talking with the councilmen about my venture. Or even hiring me to cater his company parties."

"Are you saying all of this my fault?" Charlotte asked.

"Of course not," Tiana said. She hated feeling this way. She hated the sadness in Charlotte's eyes. In a way, she understood why it had never occurred to Charlotte to offer help. She'd had everything handed to her, sometimes on an actual silver platter. She was the product of her daddy's overexuberant affection.

If you lived your entire life never wanting for anything, why would you ever look at someone else's lot in life and compare yours to it? It just wasn't in her friend's nature.

"I'm not blaming you for anything, Lottie," Tiana said. "But I need you to understand that the world sees us differently." Tiana shrugged her shoulders. "It's not fair; it's the way things are."

Charlotte glanced at her, nodding slowly. "Well, I say we start to change the way things are. I say we raise a ruckus until things change." She held her hand out to Tiana.

Tiana paused, then took the hand and shook it. It wasn't as easy as that. But it was a start.

"I say you've got yourself a deal." She sighed. "But before we can change the world, we have to figure out how to get that boat out of those brambles. And look here," Tiana said, picking up a slim but sturdy-looking branch. "I think we've found a winner!"

She started back toward the boat, but before she could take more than a couple of steps, Charlotte grabbed her hand again, halting her progress. Tiana looked at their clasped hands and then up at her friend's face. The look in her eyes was so humble and full of understanding—Tiana wasn't sure if she'd ever seen such a look from Charlotte in all the years she'd known her.

"I meant what I said." Her tone was earnest. Heartfelt. "I know that I can be selfish and stubborn, but I want to be a good friend to you. The *best* kind of friend. Because that's the kind of friend you have always been to me."

"Oh, Lottie." Tiana dropped the branch and wrapped her arms around her.

"I'm glad you're here."

33
Tiana

"There y'all are!" Louis's boisterous voice greeted them as soon as they cleared the thicket of trees.

Tiana held up the branch she'd carried back. "This is the best we could find. How did y'all do?"

"About the same," Naveen answered, motioning to a long pole that looked to be thin enough to fit between the bottom of the boat and the gnarled vines. Tiana just hoped it was strong enough to withstand the amount of effort it would take to dislodge the vessel. "You'd think there would be a better selection of sticks out here in . . . well . . . in the sticks. But they were either too fat or too skinny or too short. Very frustrating."

"We'll make do with what we have," Tiana said. She looked up at the sky. "I can't believe I'm about to say this, but I think we should wait until morning."

"Are you sure?" Naveen asked.

She nodded and hooked her thumb back toward where she and Charlotte had just returned from. "I spotted a bit of a clearing back there. It wasn't a large space, but it seemed big enough for us all to stretch out for the night."

"Are you saying we have to sleep on the ground?" Charlotte asked. "Why can't we sleep on the boat?"

"You can take your chances on the boat if you want to," Tiana said. "But if it happens to dislodge while you're asleep and drifts away . . ." She shrugged her shoulders.

"Fine, I'll sleep on the ground," Charlotte groused. "I swear, once we get back to N'awlins I'm gonna have Big Daddy treat us to a full day of pampering. We deserve it."

"I do have a blanket, if that makes you feel any better," Tiana told her. She looked apologetically over at Naveen and Louis. "Unfortunately, that's all I have. I only packed it in case I got chilly while on the boat. At the time, I thought I would be the only one out here."

"Not a problem," Naveen said. He clamped a hand on Louis's shoulder. "We can rough it, right, my friend?"

"Rough it? Man, this feels like home to me." Louis grinned.

"You sleep on the ground when you are at home?" Naveen balked. "Tiana, maybe you should consider paying my friend here a little more when he plays at the supper club, eh? At least enough for him to afford a proper bed."

"Louis gets paid handsomely," Tiana said. She narrowed her eyes at Louis. "He just likes the great outdoors." She turned to the boat. "Let's get the food. I'll get started on dinner as soon as we set up camp."

They grabbed the bags out of the boat and, with Tiana leading the way, marched in single file toward the clearing.

"Tia, look over there," Charlotte called. She pointed toward the bank of the bayou. "Are those palmetto leaves near the shoreline? Maybe we can lay those out on the ground as some kind of cover."

"Good thinking, Lottie," Tiana said. "Let's get these to the clearing. Then we can come back for the palmettos."

The area Tiana had spotted earlier turned out to be larger than she'd first thought. There was more than enough room for them all to spread out, and there was even a large tree stump with a smooth top, as if someone had made a table for them.

"This is going to do just fine," Tiana said.

They set their supplies near the tree stump and returned

to the bayou's edge to pick palmettos. In no time at all, they had several dozen stacked along the bank.

"I reckon this is enough," Tiana said. She glanced up at the ominous gray cloud that had drifted overhead. "The rain is coming. We need to get back and find ourselves a tree to settle in under before it starts to pour."

Charlotte pulled another palmetto from the marshy area. "Maybe just a few more. I like a plush bed—" She paused and pointed at the water. "What's that ripple?"

Tiana whipped around. Her stomach dropped.

"Lottie, get back!" Tiana screamed just as a large alligator lurched forward, its massive body splashing against the shore.

Naveen reached over and grabbed Lottie by the waist, jerking her away from the water.

"Everybody, run!" he yelled, carrying Lottie in his arms and galloping through the reeds, palms, and cattails.

Instead of running away from the shore, Louis started toward it.

"Louis, what are you doing? Don't go near the water!" Tiana cried.

"Don't worry," he said. "I know how to handle these gators." He turned to the huge reptile, his hands raised in entreaty. "It's okay, fella. We're just getting a few of these palms. Nothing to worry about. Just give us a—"

The gator launched itself at him.

"Louis!" Tiana yelled.

Louis hightailed it away from the bayou, running toward Tiana at full speed. His eyes were wide with fear and confusion and hurt.

"Are you okay?" Tiana asked him.

He shook his head as he gulped down air with huge, lung-filling breaths. He rested his hands on his thighs. After a moment, he took Tiana by the arm, moving several yards away from where Naveen and Charlotte stood.

"You don't understand, Tiana," Louis whispered. "That was Henry. We grew up together. It was as if he didn't even know me."

The sadness in his eyes broke her heart. "I—I don't think he does, Louis," she reminded him in a soft voice. "You're not one of them anymore."

Tiana stood by silently, offering her friend comfort as he digested her words. She could see the reality sinking in as myriad emotions moved across his face, the realization that he could not straddle both worlds. Now that he was human, his old life here on the bayou truly was over.

A pang of guilt shot through Tiana. Even though she had done what she had thought Louis wanted, what she had thought would keep him safe, she wondered if it had been right to bring him into her deal with Dr. Facilier at all.

Placing a hand on his rough arm, she looked over at the other two and called, "Let's get our palm fronds and get back to camp before the rain comes."

A loud crack of thunder rang out, like an exclamation point on her statement.

Charlotte stood as the lookout while Tiana, Louis, and Naveen quickly gathered up the palm fronds they'd already collected.

Once back at the clearing, the mood was subdued. They went about setting things up for the night, the encounter with the gator bringing the dangers they faced out here in the bayou into stark relief.

Thunder rent the air, and sheets of heavy rain poured down like a curtain all around them. But, oddly, the area where they'd set up their camp remained dry, as if an invisible dome covered them.

"Does this rainstorm seem peculiar to you, or is it just me?" Naveen asked.

Tiana couldn't explain it, so she simply shrugged.

She made a paste with the sardines and spread it over the loaves of fresh bread she'd bought at the market before they left. She set it out, along with some of the fruit and shelled pecans.

She continued to observe Louis out of the corner of her eye as she nibbled on her meager dinner. His forlorn mien was so contrary to his usual cheery disposition, it was as if he was an entirely different person.

Because he was. That was the issue. He was a person. She wondered . . . after a full year as a human, was he starting to regret the change?

After finishing up her meal, Tiana dusted off her hands and went over to him. She quietly approached, giving Louis space to decline her company if he chose. Relief washed over her when he patted the ground next to him.

"You didn't eat much," she said, gesturing to his half-eaten bread.

"I don't have much of an appetite."

"You know, Louis," Tiana started in a lowered voice. "When I made that deal with the Shadow Man, I included you in it because I knew how much you'd dreamed of becoming human. But I shouldn't have assumed I knew what you might want or need. I'm so sorry." She paused. "If we can figure out a way to change the deal . . . would you want to go back to the way things were?"

He shrugged. "I like playing with the Crawfish Crooners, but I do miss my family sometimes." He looked over at her. "I'm not sure I'll fit in with them anymore, not after what happened tonight with Henry."

"Henry didn't recognize you as you are now, but I'm sure he would if you return to your former state. Maybe

Mama Odie could help with that, too." She covered his fore-arm and gave it a squeeze. "I would miss you, but I want you to be happy."

"I would miss you, too. And Charlotte and Naveen. And the guys in the band." His expression was full of remorse.

"You decide which would make you happier. The choice is up to you." She looked him in the eye. "It should've *always* been up to you."

Louis shot her a shaky smile, and she left her friend to his thoughts, pushing up from the ground and returning to the tree stump to clean up the remnants of their dinner—only to discover Naveen and Lottie putting things away.

"I was going to do that," Tiana said.

"You fixed the meal," Charlotte pointed out. "The least we could do is clean up. You don't have to do everything yourself, Tia."

Tiana stood there, uncertain what to do with herself.

"See, we can be useful," Lottie said once they were done. She stretched her arms above her head and released a yawn. "But today has been a lot. I'm going to bed. At least I hope I can get some beauty sleep out here."

She grabbed the blanket and went over to the bed of palmettos they'd spread over the ground.

Meanwhile, Naveen motioned for Tiana to come with

him. She followed him to one of the big cypress trees that surrounded their camp, and they both slid to the ground, sitting with their backs against the tree's trunk.

"Is he okay?" Naveen pointed at Louis, who remained in the spot where Tiana had left him, on the other side of the clearing.

"I think so," Tiana said. "He just misses his family."

"I can understand that," Naveen remarked.

Tiana studied his profile, realizing he was in a similar situation, even if his wasn't magically motivated. "It's been a year since you've seen them," she said.

"Back on the boat, you asked if I ever think about going back." He picked up a small twig and twirled it around. "My parents have invited me to return home."

Tiana was shocked by the sudden, profound anguish that instantly swept over her just at the thought of him leaving. Of course, she'd considered it numerous times this past year, telling herself it would be better for her if he *did* return to his homeland. Yet hearing those words sent a sharp pain straight to her chest.

She swallowed past the lump of emotion clogging her throat before asking in a quiet voice, "Will you?"

Naveen brought his knees up and rested his elbows on them. He continued to twirl the stem between his fingers, a contemplative look on his face. After several moments ticked by, he looked over at her and said, "Not if I have a reason to stay . . . Say, from you?"

Her breath caught. "Me?"

"Yes. You," he said softly. "There are many things in America that I have come to enjoy, but I can find those things back in Maldonia. There is only *one* thing here that I cannot find anywhere else. That is you, Tiana." He turned to her. "I want the chance to get to know you better. Will I get that chance if I remain here in America?"

"Oh, Naveen." The words came out in a raw whisper. Despair over what she knew could never be threatened to shatter what little control she still held over her emotions.

"I am simply asking for a chance," he said.

She didn't have the heart to tell him that there was *no* chance, not if she wanted to keep him safe.

Instead, Tiana reached over and took his hand. She threaded their fingers together and tilted her head to the side, until it rested on his shoulder. "Let's get some sleep. We've got a long day tomorrow."

Tiana sensed he wanted to say more, but he didn't. Pretty soon the driving rain and the low hum of buzzing insects were the only sounds on the bayou.

34
Tiana

The Louisiana Bayou
Sunday, February 1927
Two days before Mardi Gras

"Up and at 'em!" Tiana clapped her hands as she walked around the makeshift camp they'd set up last night, rousing her crew. She nudged Charlotte with the toe of her boot. "Wake up, Lottie. We're already behind, and we still have to pry the boat loose."

Naveen stood from where he'd slept, slumped against a tree trunk. He stretched his arms up in the air, moving his neck from side to side as if working out kinks. "Eh, not the best sleep of my life, but not the worst, either."

"I'll have an order of flapjacks with maple syrup," Louis said as he twisted underneath his palm-frond blanket.

Tiana poked him with a branch. "This isn't a diner, Louis. Wake up. We need to get going."

She rolled up her blanket, tying it with twine and looping it over her shoulder.

"Grab those poles," she instructed Naveen and Louis. "And pray that we can dislodge this boat." She looked to the sky. "The rain passed us by last night, but that doesn't mean we'll be so lucky today."

Ten minutes later, they were trudging through the mud, on their way back to the boat.

"Are you sure this is the right way?" Lottie asked. "It's easy to become disoriented when every tree and shrub looks the same."

"It's the right way." Tiana pointed to a cypress tree that canted to the left, its branches nearly touching the ground. "See this tree, the one bending over like a gentleman taking a bow? I made note of it last night as we were searching for a place to camp out. There's another one a few yards away that looks as if someone carved a portrait of a cat in the bark."

They continued their trek through the marsh. The area

around their campsite had been spared from last night's conspicuous rainstorm, but judging by the saturated grounds, this part of the bayou had gotten a good soaking.

"There it is!" Lottie pointed at the cat ears etched into the tree bark. "Dang, Tia, you sure are good at this camping-around-the-bayou business. I still don't get it. How'd you even come to know about all of this?"

"Maybe I can explain it to you one day," Tiana told her. She still wasn't sure how to address the questions Lottie would undoubtedly have about Mama Odie, and wondered if maybe she should give her friend a little insight into what had happened the year before.

But how would she even broach the subject?

You don't know this, Lottie, but Naveen and I were both turned into frogs at your Mardi Gras ball last year. Oh, and Louis? We met him while traveling through this bayou. He was a gator at the time.

Lottie would fall away in a dead faint.

It was probably better to keep things as vague as possible when it came to discussing her prior dealings with these bayous and the quirky lady who lived there.

Naveen and Louis had traveled ahead and were already at the boat when she and Lottie arrived. Tiana quickly joined them, adding her muscle, but the boat remained rooted in the tangled branches.

She walked around to assess the situation from the other side. Tall shoots of cattail cradled that side of the vessel, their fluffy brown ends thwacking against the wooden hull. She leaned in closer, shoving the stalks to the side with her elbow, but there were so many that most flapped right back into place.

"If I can just . . . get these . . . out of the—" The tall plants parted. She looked over her shoulder to find Naveen holding the cattails at bay with a branch. "Way," Tiana finished.

His eyes brimmed with infectious humor and the familiar kindness she'd come to associate with him.

"Thank you." Tiana acknowledged his help with a gentle smile.

He shrugged. "Hey, that's what friends do for each other, eh?"

Was he her friend?

It was starting to feel that way, particularly after their conversations yesterday. Their playful banter had been a delight, harkening back to the time they'd spent together on this very bayou almost exactly one year earlier. Maybe, once they returned to New Orleans and she put all this horrible business with the Shadow Man behind her, the Fates would take pity on them and allow a semblance of friendship between her and Naveen. It wasn't part of the deal, but given the way she'd unswervingly held up her end of the bargain, there should be room for a few concessions.

She sighed.

You knew what you were signing up for.

As far as her relationship with Naveen was concerned, at least. It was the other thing that she hadn't signed up for—the looming threats that had served as the catalyst for this trip—that she should be focused on.

No more daydreams. She needed to get to Mama Odie.

While Louis and Naveen tried their hardest to lift the boat's bow, Tiana worked her branch underneath it. She did the same with the stick they'd brought back, wedging it as far as she could. Unfortunately, it wasn't very far at all. There was no way this would give them the leverage they needed to push the boat free.

"Lottie, over here," Tiana called over her shoulder.

"Me?" Charlotte yelped.

"Your clothes are already dirty," Tiana said. "A little more mud won't kill you. Put all your weight on that edge of the stick."

Despite the effort she put into each thrust, neither she nor Charlotte had the muscle required to move the boat.

"As much as I hate to admit this, I think we need more manpower on this end," Tiana said.

"Just remember you're the one who said it," Naveen

told her as he grabbed onto the end of the branch she held. Louis joined Lottie.

"On the count of three," Naveen said. "One . . . two . . . three." They pushed down on their respective branches and the boat moved a smidgen. "Yes! Again," Naveen called. "Again."

"It's working," Tiana said excitedly.

"Yes, it is," Naveen said. "Uh . . . the only problem is that, at this rate, I fear it will take us about three days to get the boat free."

"You're right." Her shoulders slumped.

"No giving up just yet," Naveen said. He approached the front of the boat again and peered at it from several angles. "Ah, yes. There's a little more room here. If I can get my hand on the front of the boat, maybe I can push."

"Be careful," Tiana called.

He looked back at her, one brow cocked in inquiry. "You are concerned about my welfare, eh? That's good to know."

Goodness, is he capable of turning that charm off for even a second?

"Just push the boat," Tiana said.

He winked at her before turning his attention back to his task.

She watched as he maneuvered his hand through a small

gap in the vines and branches. It was just wide enough for him to sneak in there. Tiana wasn't sure he would be able to do much with just that one hand, and there certainly wasn't enough space for him to get a second palm on that boat.

Still, he pushed and pushed and pushed.

"Maybe if I switch hands, I can—"

"Watch out for that—"

"*Ooowww!*" Naveen bellowed as a sharp piece of wood scored his flesh.

He jerked his hand free and clutched it against his chest. Tiana could see blood seeping through the fingers covering his injured hand. She let go of the stick and ran to him.

"What happened?" Lottie asked, coming up along-side her.

"Let me see it," Tiana said. He pulled back when she reached for his hand, but she refused to back down. "I need to see how bad it is."

He finally relented, slowly letting his uninjured hand fall away.

"Ugh!" Lottie screeched, skittering back to where she'd come from. "I hate blood!"

"I'll stay over here." Louis put a hand to his stomach. "Blood makes me squeamish."

Tiana rolled her eyes at the two of them. She winced as she studied the nasty, jagged gash marring Naveen's previously unblemished skin. The flesh around the cut puckered.

"Give me just a minute," she said.

She walked over to the side of the boat and retrieved the bag that held the remaining food. She searched inside for the handkerchief she'd used to wrap up some biscuits, sticking it in the front pocket of her coveralls before making her way back to Naveen.

"Give it here," she said again. Holding his hand, she grabbed the edge of his shirt and began dabbing at the cut. "I hope this wasn't your favorite shirt."

"In fact, it was," he said. Her eyes flew to his. Before she could apologize, he smiled and said, "I'm only kidding."

"You," she growled, trying to hide her smile. How could he be both endearing and insufferable at the same time?

She concentrated on clearing the small particles of wood from his hand.

"Ow," Naveen said, slightly jerking his hand away.

"I'm sorry," Tiana whispered. "It's a pretty nasty gash. I'm sure it stings like the dickens."

"I'm not sure what the dickens are, but if they feel like fire, then yes, it stings like the dickens."

She cleaned the cut as best she could, but it still didn't look good.

"I wish I had some iodine or something to put on it,"

she said. "I'm afraid this will become infected, especially out here in these swamps. Who knows what kind of parasites are lurking here?"

"Well, that is very discomforting, Tiana. I would have rather you not mentioned that at all."

"I'm sorry," she murmured again. She reached for the handkerchief in her breast pocket, scratching her own knuckle on Ms. Rose's brooch as she retrieved it. She shook out the handkerchief, making sure there were no crumbs from the biscuits that could stick to the cut. She wrapped the cloth around his injury, then pulled the ribbon holding her hair in place and used it to secure the dressing.

"There you go," Tiana said. She shook out her hair, letting it fall to her shoulders.

When she looked up at him, Naveen was staring back at her, a compelling spark of wonder in his eyes. In that moment, it felt as if they were alone, just the two of them in this quiet, cozy corner of the world.

"This is the second time you have tended to my wounds," he said. "Thank you." His voice was low and soft, like a feather brushing across her skin.

"You're welcome," Tiana whispered, still staring into his eyes.

She told herself to look away. The feelings swirling through her as she continued to stare at him were dangerous.

But these feelings were too potent—too irresistible—for her not to indulge them for just a moment longer. She stared into Naveen's hazel-colored eyes and tumbled headfirst into the fantasy of what it would be like if she had never agreed to Facilier's demands.

What if, after getting off the boat from Maldonia, Naveen had walked through the doors of Duke's Cafe for a cup of coffee, taken one look at her, and decided she was the one for him? How magical would it have been if he had whisked her away and pledged his love for her? She would have had everything she'd ever wanted: Naveen, her restaurant, her daddy . . .

No!

No, her daddy would be dead. And who knew if she would have had her restaurant at all? It was easy to constantly harp on what the Shadow Man had cost her, but she should never forget what she'd gained from their deal.

Tiana cut her eyes away from Naveen's and dropped his hand.

"We need to get this boat dislodged and be on our way," she said. She turned back toward the stick she'd found and gripped the end of it. "Come on, Lottie. You'll need to put some muscle in it."

Tiana could see Naveen walking toward her out of the

corner of her eye. "You can stand over there," she threw out over her shoulder. "We don't need you injuring your hand even more."

"But, Tiana—"

"We've got this," she said.

She sensed his despondency, but she couldn't concern herself with Naveen's feelings right then. Dabbling in those games of what-ifs was foolhardy. More than that, it was dangerous. It caused her to forget what was at stake, and how deadly things could turn out for all those she loved if she wasn't careful.

Naveen's love was something that could never be hers. It had only taken a split second to weigh the pros and cons, and she'd decided his safety—and the safety of her family, and having her daddy back in her life—was worth the cost. She couldn't forget that now.

"Louis, why don't you get in the boat and start the engine? Maybe the motor's power, along with our own elbow grease, will be just the thing we need."

"I can do that!" Louis said.

He climbed aboard the boat and settled at the stern. Tiana had hoped his weight would help pop the boat's bow out of the branches, but it didn't.

"Ready?" Louis asked.

"Ready," Tiana called back. He revved the motor and, to her utter relief, the boat began to inch back. "Yes! It's working, Louis! Hit it again."

The motor whirled, and she and Lottie pushed harder.

"Uh . . . Tiana," Naveen said.

"Not now," Tiana told him. "Again, Louis!"

The motor roared again.

"Tiana, you may want to—" Naveen started, but Tiana stopped him.

"Wait," she said. She sniffed. "What's that smell?" She looked up and noticed a plume of gray smoke coming from the back of the boat. "Oh, no! Louis! Louis, stop!"

But it was too late. Tiana knew the moment she heard the motor rev one last time, then sputter, that they were in trouble. Her entire body slumped as her spirits deflated like a popped balloon.

"That did not sound good," Naveen said.

"What happened?" Louis asked.

"I think the motor burned out," Tiana said.

"What? I didn't . . . I didn't mean to."

"No, Louis. It's not your fault. It's . . . it's just my luck," Tiana said. She wondered for a moment if this was the Shadow Man. Could whatever dark powers he held reach her all the way out here?

"I did it!" Charlotte yelled.

The three of them turned to find Charlotte kneeling in the mud. More important, the bow of the boat was now free from the brambles.

"Wow, Lottie!" Tiana said. "Great job!"

"Except now we can't move the boat with no motor."

"Yes, we can," Tiana said. "There are oars. We're gonna have to paddle our way to Mama Odie's, but we'll get there. Let's get moving!"

She took over the driving duties again, not trusting anyone else to get her to her destination. She was once again in control of her own destiny.

"Almost there," Tiana whispered.

35

Naveen

Naveen sat at the rear of the boat, feeling useless as Tiana, Louis, and even Charlotte worked in tandem to paddle the boat onward. He'd picked up one of the wooden oars with the intention of doing his share of the work, but had to drop it seconds later. His hand still throbbed from his attempt to help.

If he had still been in Maldonia, it would never have even occurred to him that he should contribute to the effort to row the boat. But he was no longer the person he'd been back in his parents' kingdom. Even if he considered taking them up on their offer to return home—a decision that continued to confound and frustrate him—he would be returning as a different man. A better man. A man determined to prove that he had something to contribute to the world.

This fierce need to be useful was still new to him, but it was strong. And the feeling grew even stronger whenever he was around Tiana.

Witnessing the effort she put into making her restaurant a success inspired him; it pushed him to seek the same for himself. He wanted her to see him as someone who took pride in putting in a hard day's work.

Naveen cradled his head in his good hand, releasing an exasperated sigh.

He was not sure *how* Tiana saw him now. He was in a perpetual state of confusion when it came to her.

He had been so sure he was making progress, given the laughs they'd shared yesterday. Yet this morning, Tiana was right back to avoiding him. Remembering how she'd reacted after bandaging his hand, as if she could not get away from him quick enough, caused a sharp ache to pierce his chest.

If only he could figure out why she treated him that way. What more could he do to make her like him?

Except she *did* like him. He was sure of it.

The way she had laughed at his silly jokes and teased him. The way she had tended to his injured hand, taking care not to hurt him, as if hurting him was the absolute worst thing that could ever happen. The way she had stared into his eyes as they had stood so close to each other.

She cared about him, but for some reason, she was still hesitant to show it.

Naveen tried to flex his hand, but the moment he did, he felt the skin crack open again, and blood seeped through the handkerchief Tiana had wrapped around his wound.

"Oh, Naveen, you're bleeding," Charlotte said.

"It is nothing," Naveen said to Charlotte, but he was looking at Tiana. He wanted to know if she had heard, and if she was worried.

He saw her back stiffen, but she did not turn.

"Are you sure? Your entire hand is red now," Charlotte said.

"Is it hot to the touch?" Tiana asked, although she kept her eyes straight ahead.

Naveen ran his fingers over his injured hand. "I . . . uh . . . I can't really tell. Strange, eh?"

"Not if you're feverish," Tiana said. "Lottie, touch his hand and see if it's warm, or if it hurts when you touch it."

"I don't wanna touch it," Charlotte cried.

"His hand won't bite you," Tiana said. "Just press on the flesh surrounding the cut. But be gentle."

Naveen held his hand out to Charlotte, who approached

it with the same caution one would take when encountering a venomous snake. She gingerly poked at the back of his hand with her finger. At first, Naveen had intended to jerk it back as a joke, but there was no joking about it. Her touch sent a flash of intense pain shooting through his hand. He yelped.

"Yep, I'd say it hurts when I touch it, all right," Charlotte called.

"I knew it," Tiana said. She shook her head. "Infection is setting in."

"What does that mean?" Naveen asked, trepidation slithering down his spine at the foreboding he heard in her voice.

"Oh, I know," Louis said. "You're gonna have to chop off your whole hand if you don't wanna lose your arm. I saw it happen before."

"What!" Naveen screeched.

"Louis, you are not helping," Tiana hissed. "You're not going to lose your hand," she said. "I'm sure Mama Odie will be able to help. She can do anything."

"How much longer before we're there?" Naveen asked.

"It won't be long," Tiana said.

Finally, she turned to him, glancing over her shoulder and looking him directly in the eyes.

"You'll be okay. I promise you, Naveen."

There it was again. That concern for him that she could not mask, despite how often she tried to hide it. What was she so afraid of?

He needed to figure out a way to break past the barrier Tiana had erected against her feelings for him. If only he knew *why* she continued to do so, it would be so much easier for them to get past it. He just did not understand. Tiana's behavior was the opposite of what he was used to.

He wasn't arrogant enough to think that every woman he encountered would just fall at his feet—well, okay, maybe he had been that arrogant in the past. Mainly because it was true. Women *did* fall at his feet. He was a prince, after all.

Yet the one person he felt the deepest connection to was the only one who appeared immune to his charms.

Still, it was more apparent to him than ever that the magnetic pull between them wasn't just a figment of his imagination. It thrummed through the air whenever they were near.

He just hoped it, and *he*, was enough.

36

Facilier

Facilier cut around the corner of the old Cabildo, holding his hat against the fierce breeze that blew in from the river. The fog had grown thicker despite the wind. It swirled around like a dust cloud, cloaking the entire city in a dense, blinding mist that made it difficult to see more than three feet in front of him. The green algae had reached the French Market. It swathed the open-air stalls in grimy, viscous muck, forcing the vendors to abandon their wares.

Facilier's heart raced. Blood pounded in his ears as he tried to do the impossible: outrun the Shadows.

He bumped into people as he dashed in and out of

storefronts, muttering curses and warning them to stay out of his way. He needed to get away from here, to find somewhere to hide.

Maybe that was the key—he should just leave New Orleans. Head to Chicago or Detroit, as so many of the people who once lived here had done.

An anguished howl tore from his lips at the realization that it wouldn't matter. There was no escape for him. No matter where he fled.

Still, he ran as fast as he could, darting around corners as he made his way through the French Quarter. He had been trying to outrun these demons for years. Their grip on him, on his very life, was like a vise. Constantly squeezing. Forever demanding.

Even if they collected Tiana's soul instead of his own, would he ever be free?

He slipped into a narrow alley a few blocks away from his home. His eyes roamed the crumbling brick walls of the century-year-old buildings in search of the telltale nebulous blobs that had been chasing him. When he didn't see any sign of them, he released an unsteady but calming breath.

He turned to exit the alley, and, without warning, three dark shadows slithered up to him. He startled, dropping his cane and then scrambling to retrieve it. Fear snatched the breath from his lungs as he took several steps back.

"Gentle . . . gentlemen," he croaked. "How are you? It's been a while."

The three shapeless forms swirled around him, moaning and groaning in displeasure, reminding him what would happen on Mardi Gras night.

"Don't you worry. I haven't forgotten about you," he assured them.

The moans grew louder, coming in a rush that made it difficult for him to decipher exactly what they were saying, but he heard the most important words. He was down to his final days.

"I'm working on it, gentlemen. Tiana will sign that contract. You'll get your soul. I promise." He held his hands out. "You know you can always count on me."

The three Shadows roared. One of them whipped around him and knocked his top hat off his head. It swooped in again, jolting Facilier with a solid blow to his back. He stumbled to the ground and braced himself for another strike.

He remained in that crouched position long after the Shadows had disappeared, his body shaking with lingering panic and fear. In the decades since he'd first partnered with them, he had never witnessed such a virulent attack. Their rage was palpable.

Facilier finally stood and straightened his clothing. He

dusted off the dirt that clung to his pants and jacket and looked around to make sure no one had witnessed his humiliation. Fortunately, the alley was empty.

Except . . .

Facilier squinted as he tried to make out the small figure he saw outlined in the murky fog. He took one step forward, then another. And another. The closer he got, the clearer the shape became.

It was a small child. He stood next to a filthy pile of garbage, just outside the back door of one of the Quarter's eating establishments. The young boy's ashen face was gaunt, his cheeks hollow and smudged with dirt. He picked through the trash, examining the rotting vegetables and table scraps with hungry eyes.

This little miscreant was one of hundreds who roamed about the city. Abandoned by parents who could no longer afford to feed them. Ignored by the countless people who walked past them begging in the streets.

And he'd just borne witness to the indignity Facilier had suffered.

Facilier took another step toward him. A loud crack rang out from the broken glass he'd unknowingly stepped on.

The young boy's head popped up. He looked toward the sound, and their gazes connected across the mere three feet that now separated them. His wide, terrified eyes conveyed his panic. Facilier reached out and grabbed the child by the arm before he could run.

"Not so fast," he said.

When that frightened gaze settled on him, Facilier was struck with an unpleasant sense of familiarity. It was uncomfortable. Unwanted.

As he stared into the depths of the filthy child's dark brown eyes, he couldn't help seeing another child. The child sat at his mother's knee as she prepared a poultice for a sick neighbor. Even though she barely had enough to feed her own family, she had nursed the neighbor back to good health with medicinal herbs, bowls of vegetable stock, and help from the generations of ancestors who had come before her.

His mind's eye catapulted him several years into the future, to when that same young child had grown into a scrawny kid who ran the streets, getting into trouble. So angry with the universe for taking his mother away far too early, he'd rebelled, opting for two-bit hustles in order to get ahead instead of learning the Vodou traditions his mother had practiced and tried to teach him.

And ever since, he'd been digging himself deeper and deeper into debt with his *friends*.

Facilier's head snapped back. He shook himself out of his reverie and relinquished his hold on the young boy. But before the boy could scramble away, Facilier caught him by the arm again. With his free hand, Facilier reached into his pocket and pulled out several coins. He placed them in the boy's palm and closed his tiny dirt-streaked fingers around the money.

"Go and get yourself something to eat," Facilier told him. "Find a warm bed tonight. That's what this money is for, you hear me?"

The boy nodded, his eyes still wild with fear. Then he took off down the alley, his small body quickly disappearing in the dense mist.

Facilier's lips twisted in a frown as he continued to stare off into the distance. This sudden awakening of his conscience was most inconvenient. What did he care about a homeless delinquent, especially when he should have been focused entirely on finding Tiana?

Facilier tilted the brim of his hat to shield his eyes and steadied himself on his cane. Moving out of the alley, he returned to the hustle and bustle of the city, easily swiping the wallet of a man in a tailored suit walking in the opposite direction.

That was more like it.

It was time for Facilier to continue his search.

He would find Tiana.

And he would make her pay what was due.

37

Tiana

An excited buzz hummed through Tiana's entire body as their boat's bow cut through the murky swamp water, fevered anticipation building up in her bloodstream.

They were close! She could feel it!

She'd spotted a weirdly shaped cypress tree a few minutes earlier and instantly recognized it as one she'd seen the last time she was here. Mama Odie's house would appear soon. Just a few more minutes and they would see it.

She paddled with renewed vigor now that they were so close to their destination. Yet, despite her excitement, Tiana could not fend off the trepidation that tingled at the back of her neck at the thought of approaching Mama Odie for help once again. She was intimidated by the quirky Vodou lady who talked in riddles and kept a snake as a pet. The one who always seemed to know exactly what she was thinking.

But she has a good heart.

The reminder assuaged a bit of her worry. Mama Odie had been willing to help both Tiana and Naveen the year before. Hopefully, she would be willing to do so again.

Please. Please. Please.

The strangeness of having to rely on someone else for help struck Tiana anew. She knew she was independent to a fault. She had lost count of how many times she had wasted hours—sometimes even *days*—toiling away at some task or another, refusing to ask for help.

But Tiana would not pretend that she could get out of this mess with Facilier on her own.

"I don't think my arms can take much more of this," Charlotte cried.

"Just a little further, Lottie," Tiana said.

"Are you sure?" Charlotte asked.

"I am, I promise. It should be right—" she started, but Naveen cut her off.

"There it is!"

Tiana's eyes grew wide as the boat broke through a

curtain of moss that hung like delicate lace from the spindly branches of two trees. There in the middle of the swamp grew the biggest tree Tiana had ever seen. Hundreds of steps were carved into its massive trunk. They wound their way up to the rickety fishing boat that sat nestled between a cluster of gnarly branches.

"Yes!" Tiana said. It took all she had not to cry tears of joy.

"That's not a house," Charlotte said. "That's a ship-wreck. It looks as if it was blown there by a hurricane."

Tiana wouldn't have been surprised if that was exactly how Mama Odie had come to reside in that tree.

"There's a lot more to that little boat than meets the eye," she told Charlotte. "Everything is going to be okay now. Just watch. Mama Odie will know what to do about the Shadow Man."

They paddled up to the humongous cypress. Tiana lifted the heavy rope from the boat and tossed it over a chunky tree stump near the base of the tree.

Once she'd secured their boat, she plunked her hands on her hips and released a deep, satisfied breath.

"Well, we made it," she said. A sense of foreboding sneaked its way into her head, but she tamped it down. There was no reason for her to be afraid.

She gingerly climbed out of the boat, doing her best to find purchase on the tree's lumpy roots that protruded from the water.

"Is that safe?" Charlotte asked.

"Of course it is." She reached a hand out to help Charlotte. "Come on." Her foot slipped, and she had to fight to keep her balance.

"Umm . . . I think I'm going to stay on the boat," Charlotte said. A moment later, a huge bug zigzagged around her head. She yelped and scrambled out of the boat. "On the other hand, maybe I should join you."

"Ah . . . this brings back memories," Louis said as he hefted his huge body off the starboard side.

"Yes, it does," Naveen said, climbing out after Louis. Once out of the boat, he stood with his fist perched on his hips and looked around. "*Why* does it bring back memories?"

"Oh, well, you know," Tiana hedged as she started up the steps. "You're probably remembering some other house in the swamp that you've visited. Once you've visited one swamp house, you've visited them all."

"But I've never—"

"We'd better get up there," Tiana interrupted.

The carved steps squeaked loudly in the quiet bayou, so loudly Tiana wondered if it wasn't by design. It was an

ingenious way to alert whoever was in the house that someone was on their way up the steps.

"You're going too fast, Tia!" Charlotte called.

"Yeah, I'm gonna take it slow," Louis puffed.

Tiana looked back to make sure both were okay, then
continued up the steps. She was ready to make her case to
Mama Odie and hopefully gain the old lady's help. Despite
her excitement, she slowed as she approached the door to
the boat house. The rusty hinges looked as if they were
ready to fall off.

"Who's there?" an unfamiliar voice called from the
other side of the door.

Tiana jumped. "Mama Odie?"

The door opened a few inches and the sliver of a face
appeared through the slit.

"I said, 'Who's there?'"

It opened a little more. Tiana couldn't make out any
of the features, not with the way the person stood in the
shadow of the doorway, but she could tell by the shape that
this was *not* Mama Odie.

Could they be at the wrong house?

No, this was definitely the house. Weren't any other old
fishing boats sitting in big cypress trees around these parts.

"I came to see Mama Odie," Tiana said.

The door opened a bit wider and a young woman

walked out into the dimmed sunlight. Her golden brown skin was several shades lighter than Tiana's, and she had a red-and-black checkered kerchief tied around her head. Her eyes were a color Tiana had never seen before: a mixture of green and hazel and gray. She was strikingly pretty.

"She's not here," the young woman said.

It felt as if someone had struck Tiana directly in the chest. She shook her head, unwilling to let the words sink in. There was no way she had gone through all this trouble only for Mama Odie to not be there.

"What do you mean she's not here?" Tiana asked. "She *has* to be here! This is her home."

"I know this is her home," the girl said. "But she's not here. Auntie Odie is in New Iberia, visiting her sister. My mama, Clairee."

"No," Tiana whispered. This was the one thing she had not considered. She took a step back, as if she could physically distance herself from the bad news. If not for Naveen catching her by the arm, she would have fallen off the steep wooden step.

"What happened to you?" the girl at the door asked, jutting her chin toward Naveen's hand.

"Ah . . . I came out on the losing end of a fight with an angry tree branch," he said.

"He cut it on a log while trying to dislodge our boat from some brambles," Tiana murmured, her mind still reeling.

"It don't look good," the girl said. "The way it's puffed up like that means infection is setting in." She looked them both up and down, her face a mask of distrust. But then she backed into the house and held the door open. "Come on in."

Both Tiana and Naveen remained outside.

"Well, come on," the girl said. "You need to get some salve on that hand before you lose it. I'll whip up something." She tilted her head, indicating that they were to follow her.

Once they were alone, Tiana looked to Naveen. "What do you think?" she whispered.

"I am a bit frightened," he admitted. "But my hand, it hurts like . . . what was that you said? The dickens?"

Tiana sighed. "I guess we should go in. You need to let her see about it. She can't do any more damage."

The moment they entered the house, Naveen's footsteps halted. He stood just past the entryway, his eyes taking in every nook and cranny of the room.

"I've been here before," he said.

Tiana frowned. She wasn't sure what was happening. Naveen wasn't supposed to have any recollection of anything that happened during their time as frogs, but ever since they had taken off on the bayou, Tiana could tell that memories were beginning to return.

She released a nervous laugh. "Don't be ridiculous."

"No, no. I have," Naveen insisted. "I don't know when, but I've been here." He rubbed his chin with his fingers. "There was a snake. It was a peculiar snake." He put a hand to his head. "It makes no sense, but I *know* it is true."

Just then, the girl returned. She held several colorful glass jars and bottles against her chest. "Come on in the kitchen," she said. "I'm Lisette, by the way," she threw out over her shoulder.

"I'm Tiana, and this here is Naveen. My friends Lottie and Louis are still making their way up the staircase."

"Navigating those stairs takes a lil getting used to," Lisette said.

Tiana followed her into the room where she'd helped Mama Odie whip up a pot of gumbo the last time she had been in this house. She held her breath, waiting for Naveen to mention how familiar this room was, too. But he was uncharacteristically quiet.

There was a large mortar and pestle sitting on the table. The bowl's smooth interior was scored with marks, likely from years of use.

"So, what is it you folks want with Auntie Odie?" Lisette

asked. "If you need her to put a spell on someone, I'll tell you now that she don't use her knowledge for stuff like that."

"No, that's not it at all," Tiana said. "I've been here before, and Mama Odie lent her assistance. I was hoping she'd be willing to do it again. You see, I've gotten myself into a bit of a . . . situation." She wondered how much she should divulge, but what more was there to lose?

Tiana leaned a little closer and said, "I got involved with a Vodou man back in N'awlins."

Lisette's eyes lit up. "Oh, y'all came from N'awlins? I love it there."

Tiana thought for a moment. If this young woman was related to Mama Odie . . . "We really could use some help. But since Mama Odie isn't here, maybe you—"

"I can't do what Auntie Odie can," the young woman said simply. "That's not my gift."

"But—"

"Hey, Mama Odie," Louis's overexcited voice interrupted her. He lumbered inside, Charlotte trailing behind him, out of breath. "You not Mama Odie," he said, looking at Tiana but hooking a thumb toward Lisette. "Who this?"

"Mama Odie is visiting family out of town," Tiana explained. She couldn't stop her shoulders from wilting with disappointment. She wondered if she could wait for the older woman's return.

Charlotte swooped gracefully into a wicker chair as Tiana moved closer to the table. Watching Lisette add several leaves and berries to the mortar, Tiana was struck by the girl's efficiency and how competent she appeared as she measured each ingredient. Her baby-soft skin made her look so young—she couldn't have been more than fifteen years old.

She uncorked a slim bottle, not unlike those Tiana had spotted in Facilier's workshop. The moment the cork was out, a putrid smell rose from the container.

"*Faldi faldonza,*" Naveen said, waving his uninjured hand in front of his nose.

"It's the valerian root," Lisette said. "It has a foul odor, but it will soothe the sting while the ribwort fights the infection."

She sprinkled several of the fragrant leaves into the mortar, then used the pestle to grind it all into a dark green paste.

"If you don't mind my asking, how'd you learn to do this?" Tiana asked.

"My mama taught me," Lisette said. "She's an herbalist, too. I'm still an apprentice, but there's nothing complicated about making a salve to stop infection."

"Your mama and Mama Odie are sisters?"

"Auntie Odie is my mama's older sister. I came to take

care of Auntie's house while she visits Mama. She left a few days ago, but she'll be back in about a month's time."

"A month!" Tiana said. "That's way too long." She studied Lisette's face. "Are you sure you don't have any of Mama Odie's special powers?"

Lisette rolled her eyes. "They're not special powers," she lamented. "Do you know anything about Vodou?"

"Not really," Tiana admitted. "I just know that the Shadow Man is causing some awful things to happen around the city with it. And I know that Mama Odie used her . . . gifts to help me last year."

"I don't know what this Shadow Man is all about, but sounds to me like whatever he's involved in is a lot different from what Auntie Odie and the rest of my family practices. We call on the *Lwa*, the spirits of our ancestors that offer healing and protection from harm. It's used for good, not for evil."

"That's exactly what I need," Tiana said.

"Well, unless you can make it to New Iberia to fetch Auntie Odie, you'll have to wait. And even if you went there to fetch her, I don't think she would come back here until she's done with her visit. She still treats Mama like a little girl, spoiling her rotten."

Lisette stuck her fingers in the concoction she'd made and rubbed the paste between her thumb and forefinger.

She brought it to her nose and sniffed, not reacting at all to the pungent aroma.

"I think this will do. Send your boyfriend over here," she said to Tiana.

"He's not—*we're* not . . . He's not my boyfriend!" Tiana stammered, her face growing hot.

The young girl's brow arched in a way that told Tiana she was not fooling her one bit.

Lisette took Naveen's injured hand in her own and slathered a thick layer of the grainy salve over it. Naveen pinched his face, but as more of the salve went on, his expression turned from one of concern to relief.

"Feel better?" Tiana asked him.

"Yes, it does," he said, a bit of wonder in his voice. "It does."

"I have a scrape from when I fell getting out of the boat," Charlotte said. "Is there a chance I can get some of that smelly green stuff, too?"

"As soon as I'm done with this one here, I'll take care of yours," Lisette said. She lifted a square of cloth from the table and ripped it down the middle, then tore it several more times until there were six narrow strips of fabric. She gently but efficiently wrapped four strips of cloth around Naveen's injured hand. Once she got to the end, she reached under the kerchief covering her head, pulled out a hairpin, and used it to secure the dressing.

"Wow," Naveen said, moving his wrist back and forth as he stared at his hand. "This is impressive," he said. He looked up at Lisette and smiled. "I am very impressed."

"It *is* impressive," Tiana said. "That's a great skill."

Lisette shrugged her shoulder as if making a concoction that would save Naveen from possibly losing his hand wasn't a big deal.

"We all have our part to play in this world," she said. "Being an herbalist is mine." She brought the mortar over to Charlotte and rubbed some of the salve on Lottie's tiny scrape. "It won't take long for this one to heal. I'll jar some of this up so that you can take it back with you."

Take it with them?

It suddenly occurred to Tiana that she would be on her way back to New Orleans without Mama Odie's help.

Without *any*one's help.

She was on her own. And, it was becoming increasingly evident, in way over her head.

38

Tiana

Tiana's mind swirled with worry as the reality of her situation began to sink in. She paced back and forth in front of the bathtub-shaped cauldron in the middle of the room, the angst building in her bloodstream with each second that passed.

There had to be a way out of this. Maybe if she—? It was possible she could—?

There was nothing!

Once again, she found herself facing a problem she could not solve using her own devices. Putting in extra hours or working harder than anyone else would do her no good when it came to Facilier and his friends on the other side. She was dealing with powers outside of her realm of control.

She stopped walking, a sudden sense of doom crashing over her.

"I can't do this alone," Tiana said in a strained voice. She covered her face in her hands. It felt as if these walls were closing in on her, squeezing her lungs. She hated this feeling. She *never* allowed herself to give up, but she couldn't see a way out.

"Tia?"

Her shoulders stiffened at the sound of Charlotte's voice, but Tiana didn't look at her. She couldn't bear to see Lottie's look of pity staring back at her.

"Umm . . . Tiana?" came Naveen's sweet voice.

Her hands fell from her face. She was unable to ignore him, no matter how much she wanted to. It wasn't just Naveen and Charlotte, but Louis and even Lisette had come to see about her. They didn't look at her with pity; it was genuine concern on their faces. It made Tiana want to burst into tears.

"What exactly did you need from Auntie Odie?" Lisette asked. "Maybe I *can* help."

"Not if you don't have her powers—"

"*Knowledge*," Lisette corrected. "And even though

I don't have the knowledge Auntie Odie has about such things, there are others who do. Now, tell me about this fella you've gotten yourself mixed up with. Maybe we can figure out a way to get you out of this."

A combination of hope and optimism began to coalesce in her blood.

Tiana stared at the curious faces staring back at her and wondered how much she should say. The less they knew about her dealings with the Shadow Man, the safer they would be.

Then again, they had all come this far with her. She couldn't keep them completely in the dark any longer.

She sniffed, wiping her nose on the sleeve of her filthy shirt. She directed her attention to Lisette but spoke loudly enough so that they would all hear her.

"His name is Dr. Facilier," Tiana started. "People around the neighborhood always warned us kids to stay away from him. They say he deals in bad magic, and nothing good can come from it."

"I gather the energy he deals in isn't good at all," Lisette said. "Healing energy is at the center of the Vodou my mama and Auntie Odie grew up practicing in Haiti. It's filled with goodness and light and blessings from the ancestors who have gone before us.

"But there are others who choose to use their knowledge

for the wrong thing," Lisette said, her voice whisper soft, as if she were afraid someone beyond these walls would hear her. "I've been warned away from those people, too."

"I knew better," Tiana said. "But . . ." She glanced over at Naveen. "I found myself in a desperate situation. The Shadow Man offered to provide things I had only hoped for in my dreams, something I thought I could never have again." She sucked in a deep breath. "And then he threatened to hurt the people I love."

"He threatened you?" Naveen asked. His brow furrowed with displeasure, and Tiana couldn't deny that it felt nice to see how angry he was on her behalf.

"It felt as if I had no other choice but to take the deal," Tiana said. "I made the choice I thought would give me that thing I really wanted while keeping my loved ones safe.

"But Facilier changed the rules. A few days ago, he demanded I make a new deal. When I told him I wouldn't, he started to make good on his threats. He's caused all kinds of horrible things to happen. But I'm afraid if I give in to his demands this time, he will continue to ask for more and more, and I'll never get out from under his thumb."

Lisette nodded. "Yes, I'm sure he will. You give people like that an inch and they'll take a whole mile. You can't trust this Facilier fella to do the right thing."

"No, I can't," Tiana said. "That's why I came seeking

Mama Odie's help. She's the only person I can think of who would know what to do."

Lisette crossed her arms over her chest, a contemplative frown on her face. After a moment, she said, "There's a possibility there's someone else who can help. She's an old friend of Mama and Auntie Odie. They all grew up together in Port-au-Prince."

"Who is she? *Where* is she?" Tiana asked. "Does she live out here on the bayou?"

Lisette shook her head. "She's back in N'awlins. She lives in the French Quarter."

Tiana threw her head back and sighed up at the ceiling. They'd come all this way when the answer was right at home?

"What's her name?" Tiana asked again. "And can you give us directions to exactly where she lives in the Quarter?"

Lisette screwed up her lips, a confused look on her face. After a minute, she shook her head. "Sorry, but I just don't know enough about N'awlins to tell you how to get there."

Tiana's shoulders wilted.

"But I can *show* you," Lisette piped up. "I may not recall the street names, but I've been to Tee Lande's home with Mama and Auntie several times. I'm pretty sure I'll remember the way once I'm there and can see it for myself."

Tiana was almost afraid to hope. "You're willing to come back with us?"

"You sound like you need the help," she said. "My mama and auntie always taught me to help good people who are in need." She looked Tiana up and down. "You seem like good people."

"I am good people," Tiana rushed out. "I promise I am. Please, Lisette. If Mama Odie can't help me, then I must go to her friend to see if she's willing to do so."

Lisette walked back over to the table where the ingredients she'd used to make the salve still sat. She picked up one of the jars and replaced the cap, slowly tightening it.

"Well, I *have* been wanting to go back to N'awlins for quite a while," she finally spoke. "All the tall buildings and streetlights and cars. It's just so dreamy compared to the bayou." Her excitement seemed to build the more she talked. Her eyes lit up as her lips curved in a smile. "Oh, and I want to go to a speakeasy and listen to music. And dance! It's been *so* long since I went out dancing."

She spun in a circle, the hem of her rough ankle-length denim skirt twirling about her legs. She let out a giggle that reminded Tiana that she was still a girl, despite seeming so wise beyond her years.

"I'll make you a deal," Tiana said. "If you come back with us and bring me to . . . what's her name again?"

"Tee Lande," Lisette said. "She's not my real auntie, but she's always felt like one to me."

"Okay, if you can bring me to your Tee Lande's home in the French Quarter, you can come over to my restaurant and dance your heart out. And then I'll make sure to get you back here to Mama Odie's. Maybe Louis can bring you?" Tiana said, looking to him. "You think so, Louis?"

"Wait," Lisette said before he could answer. "Isn't it almost Mardi Gras?"

"Yes." Tiana nodded. "This coming Tuesday."

"Hmm . . ." Lisette pulled her bottom lip between her teeth. "I'm supposed to be here taking care of Auntie Odie's house, but I can't go to N'awlins this close to Mardi Gras and then leave before the big day."

Tiana looked to her with cautious hope. "Does that mean you're coming with us?"

Lisette paused for a moment before nodding. "Yeah, I'll take you all to Tee Lande's. And you can take me back after Mardi Gras."

"Oh, thank you!" Tiana launched herself at her, gathering her in a hug. She felt the girl stiffen in her arms. She quickly released her and stepped back. "I'm sorry. I'm just so grateful."

"Yeah, I can tell," Lisette said. She took several steps back and held up her hands. "Here's what we'll do. Y'all will help me get everything in order here at the boat house. I have to make sure all is secure if I'm going to leave Auntie Odie's place for several days. Then, first thing in the morning, we'll set out for N'awlins. It shouldn't take us more than a couple of hours to get there."

"A couple of hours?" Tiana balked. She wasn't so sure Lisette would be able to lead her to this Lande woman's home after all, not if she thought it would only take two hours to make it back to the city.

"I can see what you're thinking," Lisette said. "Don't you worry." That cagey smile returned to her lips, and then she winked. "I know a shortcut."

39

Naveen

The Louisiana Bayou
Monday, February 1927
One day before Mardi Gras

Naveen changed position on the bench at the bow of the ship, leaning first on his left elbow, then on his right. He could not find a comfortable position. Most likely because there was no way to get comfortable while he sat here doing nothing but looking out over the murky swamp ahead.

He'd been banished to lookout duty, and he was still brooding over it.

Both Tiana and this Lisette girl—who happened to be just as strong-willed as Tiana—had quickly shot down his offer to help row the boat, even though he assured them that his hand caused him very little discomfort. It stung a little, but that stinky green salve had worked like magic. He could flex all five of his fingers without flinching.

The only thing still making him flinch was his bruised ego. It was difficult to sit here while the others pulled his weight—literally.

Naveen glanced over his shoulder at the others rowing in unison to the tune of Hoagy Carmichael's "Riverboat Shuffle," which Louis hummed.

"Psst . . ." Naveen whispered at Charlotte as he slid over to where she puffed out labored breaths with each rotation of her oar. "Here, let me do that," he said, reaching for the long handle. "I insist."

"Oh, thank you," Charlotte said with a grateful sigh.

"Naveen?"

He looked at Tiana. The normally smooth skin of her forehead creased with a frown.

"Please, Tiana. I cannot just sit here and do nothing. You must allow me to row. Just for a little while, eh?"

She stared at him for a moment before a delicate smile curled up one corner of her mouth.

So now she found him funny? Her reactions continued to confound him.

"Why are you smiling?" Naveen asked with much suspicion.

"You don't even realize how much you've changed, do you?" she asked.

He peered at her. "Is it such a big deal that I want to row a boat down a bayou?"

She answered with that musical laugh of hers. "It is a *very* big deal. When I first met you, the idea of you begging to do such menial labor is something I could not fathom."

"Yeah, well, do not hit me in the head with an acorn this time, eh!"

Tiana's eyes widened. "What did you say?"

Naveen frowned. "I . . . I recall you pitching an acorn. It hit me." He pointed to the top of his head. "Right here. We were in the swamp. I see it so clearly."

"Are you sure?" Charlotte asked.

"Yes!" Naveen said. "But . . . but that makes no sense." He searched Tiana's face. "Does it?"

"No," she said quickly. "I've never been in the swamp with you before." She gestured at the oar. "You can row for the next ten minutes, and then you're back on navigation duty."

His scalp still prickling with unease, Naveen shook his head, trying to put the disturbing episode from his mind. Had he lost more blood than he had thought?

"And be careful," Tiana added. "I don't want you reinjuring that hand."

"Ah, but as long as I have some of Lisette's wonderful smelly paste, my hand will be just fine."

"The next bit will cost you two nickels and a plate of beignets," Lisette called from just behind him.

"You drive a hard bargain," Naveen responded. "But it is worth it. Seriously, you should sell that stuff. It is marvelous."

"He's right, you know," Tiana told her. "All those factory workers who get hurt while dealing with that machinery would pay good money for your concoctions."

"They would," Naveen said with an enthusiastic nod. "Believe me, I have seen my share of injuries at the sugar mill. If you have one specifically for burns, you could be one of the richest women in New Orleans. It is something to think about. I can even help."

It suddenly occurred to him that those were not just empty words; he actually *could* help her. This past year of working for Mr. LaBouff had not only established that he was a pretty good salesman, but also that he *liked* it. And he was good at it.

Maybe he could use that skill to help others.

"Ow!" Naveen howled. He looked down to discover the dressing covering his wound had begun to unravel, and the wood from the oar was rubbing against his cut.

"See," Tiana said. "I knew something like this would happen." She handed her oar to Charlotte and quickly made her way to his side.

"Here," Lisette said, handing Tiana a stout jar. "Put a little more of the salve on it."

Tiana balanced the jar on her leg and used both hands to unravel the remaining strips of cloth from around his hand. Naveen could barely believe his eyes. The cut looked as if it had been healing for days instead of just overnight.

"Wow," Tiana said. "Naveen's right. You really should bottle this stuff up. I have a friend who has a stall in the French Market. I should introduce you to her. I'll bet she'd sell your salve for you." She looked up at him and grinned. "Not to take the business away from you, but you seem to have your hands full selling sugar."

She returned her attention to his hand. Naveen studied her as she concentrated on smoothing the paste across the wound.

Even the streak of dirt across her cheek could not detract from her beauty. Her hair flew wildly now that it was no longer bound by that ribbon, and he decided he liked it this way.

His eyes were drawn to her mouth as she pulled her bottom lip between her teeth. He had caught her doing the same thing while at the restaurant. He now recognized it as something she did when she was focused on completing a task.

Naveen wondered what she would say if he told her that he was falling in love with her. Maybe she would throw him off the side of the boat.

But, then again, maybe she would tell him that she felt the same way.

There was something about being on this bayou with her, something about their surroundings that conjured a feeling of . . . what did that French fellow call it? Déjà vu. It felt as if they had been here before, as if this was not the first time he had cruised these canals, talking to her, falling for her.

Tiana looked up at him. Their gazes caught and held.

Naveen's breaths became shallow as something potent and intense flashed between them. Only a few inches separated them, an expanse barely the length of his hand. His eyes still locked with hers, Naveen leaned forward.

The boat collided with a wave and bounced up in the air.

Tiana's head snapped back. "Umm . . . where's the hairpin Lisette used to secure the bandage?" she asked.

It took a moment for her question to register. He was still entranced by their near kiss, his mind caught somewhere in those breath-stealing seconds when his most fervent fantasy had nearly become a reality.

"Naveen?" she called softly.

"Yes?"

"The hairpin? Where is it?"

"I'm not sure," he said, looking to either side of him. "Maybe it slipped down to the deck?"

"Oh, wait! I have something even better." She reached into the front pocket of her coveralls and, after some twisting around, came up with a rose-shaped bauble of some sort. She turned it over in her hand to show him the pin on the back. "This'll keep it in place even better than the hairpin."

"It is a bit fancy for the swamp, but it's not as if I haven't been accused of being overdressed before," Naveen said.

She laughed, the reaction he'd hoped for.

Just as she released the pin from the back of the brooch, they hit another rough patch of water and the piece of jewelry sailed out of her hand and over the side of the boat.

"Oh, no!" Tiana said. She peered over the edge, but there was nothing but foaming green water. "That was a gift from Ms. Rose," she said.

"Uh-oh," Charlotte said.

"What?" Naveen asked.

She held her palm out. "Did you feel that?"

"Feel what, Lottie?" Tiana asked.

A deafening crack of thunder pierced the tranquil swamp just as the skies opened and a deluge poured down. The five of them released simultaneous screams.

"Keep rowing," Tiana called. "Maybe we can outrun the storm."

They rowed as fast as the murky waters would allow, but it seemed as if the storm cloud was following them.

"Uh, Tiana, I know we need to get back, but we will have to stop," Naveen called over the roar of the pelting rain.

"We can't," she said. "We're not all that far from the city. Maybe another hour."

"But we can hardly see in front of us. The bayou is so twisty; we may run into the bank again if we aren't careful."

"He's right," Lisette shouted. She pointed to their left. "Look over there. We can tie the boat to that tree stump and find some cover. Hopefully it won't last too much longer."

The rain continued to drench them, and a brisk wind blew as they waited for Tiana's answer.

"Okay," she said. "But if this rain doesn't let up in a half hour, I say we just fight through it."

"Deal," Naveen said.

They rowed toward the tree stump Lisette had pointed out. There was a cavity that looked as if it had been cut out especially for their boat. Once they had secured it, they all ran into a thicket of trees just a few yards away and huddled together underneath a canopy of leafy branches.

The boat rocked violently from side to side as the howling wind whipped up the water. Streaks of lightning stabbed the ground, like a mighty javelin lunging from above.

"Where did this storm even come from?" Tiana asked. "Everything was calm just a few minutes ago."

"Is there anything else that can go wrong on this cursed trip?" Charlotte groused.

"Don't borrow trouble," Tiana told.

"That was supposed to be a joke, Tia. I honestly don't think there *is* anything else that can—"

"The boat!" Lisette cried. "It broke loose!"

"*No!*" Tiana screamed.

Naveen sprang into action, taking off for the shoreline. That boat was their only way home; he could not let the current drag it down the bayou. He raced toward it, but a second later, Louis whizzed past him.

"I got it!" Louis called before diving into the water. He cut through it like a knife, swimming out to the boat and catching the rope in both of his hands.

"When did Louis learn to swim like that?" Charlotte asked as she caught up with Naveen.

"Come on," Tiana called. "We need to help him pull the boat in."

They all waited on the bank of the canal for Louis to arrive back with the boat.

"Good job, my friend," Naveen said as he gave him a hearty pat on the back. "You swam out there like you've been doing it all your life."

"We got lots of ponds up there in Shreveport," Louis said. He and Tiana shared a smile, which, again, confused Naveen. But he had no time to ponder what that meant.

The rain still poured, but it had let up enough for them to see.

"Tiana had the right idea," Naveen said. "If we hang around here, the boat will just collect rainwater. I say we continue now that the rain isn't coming down as hard."

"Let's get on with it," Tiana said.

They all climbed back in the boat and started paddling up the canal, but it only took a few moments for Naveen to sense that something was very, very wrong.

"Are we . . . sinking?" Charlotte asked, putting voice to Naveen's fear.

"What did you say about this trip being cursed?" Lisette asked. She pointed at her feet, where water gurgled up from a puncture in the boat's flat bottom. "I think you may be right."

40

Facilier

Facilier paced back and forth, nearly slipping several times along the algae-covered dock that lined the bank of the Mississippi River. The briny, viscid seaweed had invaded the city, climbing up from the river and clawing its way across the piers, railroad, and market and into the Quarter. The city workers with their shovels and rakes were no match for the slimy invasion.

Facilier had long before stopped trying to shield his nose from the pungent odor of fish, shrimp, and whatever other sea creatures the dirty men hauled in big nets from their fishing boats. Every so often one would ask him if he wanted to buy a bucket of trout, or oysters, or catfish, but they mainly left him alone, which was exactly how he liked it.

He didn't want to involve anyone else in this business he had with Tiana. He didn't need any nosy people coming to her rescue, as if she were a damsel in distress. They didn't realize just how crafty she was. But he knew.

Facilier pulled out his pocket watch to check the time.

Where is that girl?

He had only one day left. If he didn't get her signature on that contract before sundown tomorrow, he was done for.

That father of hers had been adamant that she would be back by now.

Unless she *was* back and he had missed her.

Facilier had been so sure she and that motley crew she ran with would be easy to spot among all these fishermen, but seeing how busy this dock was—combined with the fog that had grown so thick he could barely see anything more than two yards away—they could have slipped past him without his taking notice. Especially if Tiana had seen him first.

Damn her!

His heart began to race as he intensified his search, going up to various fishmongers and boat captains, asking if they'd seen a girl traveling with several other young people. If Tiana and her friends had returned, someone would have noticed. LaBouff's prissy daughter would stick out like a sore thumb among these mangy, hardened fishermen.

He sprinted from one boat to another until he was sure he'd talked to every fisherman here. No one had seen anyone resembling Tiana or any of the others.

Well, he was done waiting.

"I'm going to do what I should have done from the very beginning," Facilier snarled.

His topcoat whipped around him as he turned and headed for the crowded gangway that bridged the dock to the market. He headed straight for the streetcar on St. Charles Avenue and rode it until they reached his destination uptown.

Yes, he'd wanted to do this the elegant way—the way that guaranteed less mess, less risk.

But the time for keeping things close to the vest was over.

He stepped off in front of the white mansion he'd looked at from afar so many times over the years. He dusted the dirt from his coat and straightened his top hat. Then he stalked up the walkway as if he owned the place.

Because, if he played his cards right, soon, he would.

41

Tiana

Tiana wasn't sure she'd ever felt more relieved than when their boat rounded the shaded bend and the egress of the bayou came into view. She could see the white dome that sat atop the twenty-plus stories of the Hibernia Bank Building, the tallest building in the city.

But that was all she could see.

A corpulent greenish cloud shrouded the city. It even obscured the spires that sat atop the cathedral. Tiana had never seen anything like it.

"That doesn't look good," Naveen said from over her shoulder.

"No, it doesn't," Tiana said. "But at least we're almost there. I don't know how much longer that tarp will hold the water out."

Tiana still wasn't sure why Lisette had packed a tarp for a couple of days in the city, but she wasn't questioning her. Stuffing the hole in the bottom of their boat had saved them.

A troubling thought suddenly occurred to her as they neared the approach to the Mississippi River.

"Guys, I don't think we can paddle this boat against the current of the river, especially with that thick algae covering it. It's been hard enough rowing along the bayou, and those waters were relatively calm."

"I think you're right," Lisette said.

"Wait a minute." Tiana held up a hand. She pointed to a rickety pier that had seen better days. "See those railroad tracks just beyond this old pier? They lead to the main docks. I think we should tie the boat here and find the fisherman that rented it to us. Maybe he can get someone to come out with a motored boat and pull it back to the dock."

Tiana shuddered at the thought of what it would cost to cover the damage that had been done. She wouldn't be surprised if it depleted what little savings she had been able to amass since buying their building in Tremé. But it would be worth it if this Lande woman Lisette spoke of could provide the help Tiana needed to finally defeat Facilier.

They navigated their boat to the pier. The dark green sludge that coated the entire structure made it a thousand times more difficult to tie the boat down, but they were able to secure it with double knots to one of the wooden beams. With the way her luck had been going since that big rainstorm hit, the entire beam would probably break away and send the boat sailing back down the canal before the fisherman could get back here to pick it up.

Once out of the boat, the five of them started down the train tracks that ran along the shore's edge. They arrived at the main dock twenty minutes later.

"My goodness," Tiana cried with a gasp. The sludge was even thicker there. It covered every surface, its moldy, putrid smell permeating the air.

Tiana searched through the miasma of imposing fog, algae, and confused people, hunting for the old man with the scar on his face from whom she'd rented the boat. She found him in the same spot where he'd been two days earlier.

"You're back," the fisherman greeted. He looked around. "Where's my boat?"

"About the boat," Tiana started. She quickly explained the trouble they'd encountered and how they'd burned up the motor. "But I will cover the cost of all repairs," Tiana assured him.

The fisherman huffed out an aggravated breath. "That's

one of my best," he said. Then he shrugged his bony shoulders. "Though I know the bayou can be brutal. You say it's down at the old pier just before Arabi?"

She nodded. "We tied it to one of the beams. I'll go back and get it, but it will have to wait until later this afternoon."

The man was shaking his head. "I'm gonna need it before then." He gestured to the other boats leaving the dock, bobbing along the choppy, scum-covered water. "This here is selling time, and you're already late bringing it back."

"I know, sir!" Tiana said. "But—"

"There's no buts about it. I need my boat, girlie. Now, you get it or I'm gonna have to call the authorities."

"Tiana." Naveen put his hand on her shoulder. Tiana whipped around to face him. "I can go back for the boat. Louis, you'll come with me, eh?" he asked.

"Yeah. Sure I can," Louis said.

Naveen turned back to her, his penetrating eyes pleading with her to accept his help. "You don't have to do this all on your own. We're here for you. *I'm* here for you."

Tiana hesitated as a blend of uncertainty and gratitude converged. This was her mess. She'd pulled them all into this; she shouldn't expect her friends to get her out of it.

But Naveen was right: she didn't have to do this alone. She couldn't.

"Okay," Tiana answered.

The shame she thought she would feel didn't materialize. All she felt was overwhelming relief at knowing she didn't have to rely solely on herself.

An embarrassed flush raced across the fisherman's craggy face. "Well, maybe I can go out there with you two," he said, contriteness suffusing his voice.

Tiana turned to him. "I meant what I said about covering the cost of repairs. I pay my debts," she said.

The old man waved her off. But then his eyes narrowed.

"Hey, wait a minute. You're the one with that supper club in Tremé, aren't ya?"

Tiana nodded.

He snapped his fingers. "Thought so. There was a fella here asking about ya not long ago."

An unwelcome sense of dread washed over her. "Someone asking about me?" Tiana asked.

"Yep. Tall skinny fella." He plopped a hand on top of his head. "Had on a big ol' hat. One of those fancy kinds."

Facilier.

"Thank you for letting me know," she said. "And thanks for being so understanding."

Naveen clamped his hands on her shoulders and turned her to look at him. "It is him, is it not? That Shadow guy."

She nodded. There was no need to withhold the truth.

"I am coming with you," Naveen said.

She shook her head. "No. Please, just help him to get his boat back." She released a deep breath. "I'll take care of the Shadow Man."

"Are you sure?" he asked. The concern in his voice wrapped around her, providing comfort she hadn't realized she so desperately needed.

"Yes, I'm sure," Tiana answered. "Thank you, but I can handle this."

Naveen seemed reluctant to let go of her shoulders, but after several seconds passed, he finally did.

"Tia, you sure you're okay, sugar?" Charlotte asked.

"I will be once I talk with this woman Lisette is taking me to see," she said.

"Okay. Well, in that case, I'm catching a taxicab home," Charlotte said. "I need to burn these clothes and spend the next three hours in a nice hot bubble bath."

Tiana walked over to her and wrapped her in a hug. "Thanks for all your help out on the bayou, Lottie. You really stepped up."

"Well, what did you expect—that I would let my best friend down?" she replied. "I will always be here when you need me, Tia. Remember that." She pulled back slightly and narrowed her eyes. "Unless you need me right now, because I am serious about that bath."

"Go clean up," Tiana said. "Get ready for tonight."

"Tonight?"

"Yes," Tiana said. "It's Shrove Monday. I'm not letting the Shadow Man ruin the big day-before-Mardi-Gras celebration."

Tiana turned to Lisette.

"Take me to your Tee Lande."

42

Tiana

Tiana and Lisette took off for the French Quarter.

As they made it past the dock, Tiana had a difficult time comprehending what she was seeing. It looked like something out of a nightmare. The fetid vegetation that covered the river and dock had invaded the city, climbing across the train tracks and over the stalls of the French Market. The slimy growth covered the abandoned baskets of the vendor's wares, as if people had dropped everything and scurried away with all haste.

Her horror only escalated as they marched on. The

algae had made its way into the French Quarter; it had climbed up the exterior walls and wrought iron galleries of the structures that lined Decatur Street.

As they waited on the other side of the street while a line of cars passed, Tiana cringed at the nauseating sound the Model Ts made rolling over the boggy substance with their tires. She would probably hear the sickening squish in her sleep for years to come.

"It's this way." Lisette motioned for her to follow. "Down this promenade."

"You sure you remember?" Tiana asked as they made their way along the walkway between Jackson Square and the Pontalba Townhouses.

"I'm sure," Lisette said. "She lives in this big red building. There's a courtyard that has a stone fountain in the middle of it, and the fountain has a bunch of little naked babies carved into the sides of it."

"Cherubs?"

"Whatever they're called," Lisette said with a shrug. "They're naked and holding musical instruments. Tee Lande is on the second floor. I can't remember which place exactly, but I know she's there."

Lisette gasped when they arrived at the end of the promenade. She pointed to their left. "Look at that!"

Tiana pressed her fist to her mouth as she tried to make sense of what was happening. The algae undulated, rolling toward the steps of St. Louis Cathedral, then retreating just as quickly, as if an invisible force fought to keep it at bay. An odd but undeniably radiant energy resonated from the area surrounding the church. Its creamy alabaster-colored facade remained pristine while everything around it was overrun by the dark green sludge.

What kind of terror had Facilier unleashed?

"I don't know what's going on, but I have to stop it," Tiana said.

"Let's hurry and get to Tee Lande's," Lisette said. "She'll know what to do."

"What if she's moved since the last time you were here?" Tiana called after her.

"She's lived in that building as long as I've been alive. She's there. Trust me."

It wasn't easy to put her faith in a teenage girl who didn't really know the city, but what choice did she have?

They hurried beyond the cathedral and the convent.

"Here it is," Lisette said, stopping at the gate of a deep red brick building with pretty flower baskets hanging from ornate wrought iron galleries. "See, I told you," she said, looking back at Tiana and smiling as if guiding her to a random building in the Quarter proved anything. They entered the gate and found their way to the courtyard. The fountain etched with cherubs sat in the center of it, just as Lisette claimed it would.

Tiana surveyed the area, hoping for any telltale sign that would indicate which of these apartments housed a Vodou lady from Haiti.

"I think you're looking for me."

She whipped around.

A tall, stunningly gorgeous woman stood a few feet away, a wicker basket overflowing with stems of fragrant lavender hooked on the crook of her arm. She wore a gauzy, flowing caftan. Colorful embroidered flowers ran along the neckline and hem of the pale peach dress.

Tiana stopped short. Something about her eyes seemed familiar.

"I've been expecting you," the woman said.

"Tee Roselande!" Lisette ran to her, enveloping her in a hug.

Shock rooted Tiana where she stood. She wasn't hunched over, and she was no longer wearing layers and layers of clothes, but . . .

"Ms. Rose?" she whispered.

"Wait, you already know my Tee Lande?" Lisette asked.

"I know *Rose* the flower vendor," Tiana said.

"Hello, Tiana," the woman replied. She wrapped an

arm around Lisette, who continued to stare up at her with worshipful eyes. "Your trip to Odie's place took longer than I anticipated it would."

"How do you know where I went? What . . . what is happening?"

"I gather you lost the brooch I gave you," Ms. Rose said as her gaze traveled from the tip of Tiana's feet to the top of her head.

Tiana knew she looked a fright, with her tattered, mud-stained clothes.

"But," the woman continued, "I trust it provided at least some protection for you while on your journey. I'm sorry that I could not do more, but my giving you the brooch very likely tested the limits of what is allowed."

"Allowed?"

"By the universe," Ms. Rose said. "Much has been imposed upon it already because of your involvement with Facilier."

Tiana released a shocked gasp. She took several steps back. "What do you know about Facilier?"

"I know much more about him than you do, which is why you need to listen to what I have to say. The universe is not at all pleased."

The woman was talking in riddles with her vague assertions about the universe. It compounded Tiana's bewilderment over discovering that the old flower monger apparently knew more about her than she'd first thought. Her head was swirling.

"You've . . . you've been lying," Tiana said. "You've been lying to me . . . manipulating me . . . this entire time." The hurt and confusion clogging her throat made it difficult to get the words out.

"I have not," Ms. Rose said.

"Can someone explain what's going on?" Lisette asked.

Ms. Rose turned to the girl. "I just made a batch of those tea cakes you love. Why don't you go up and have some? We'll be right there."

Tiana was shaking her head. "No, *we* won't," she said, backing away.

"Tiana." The woman's voice was stern. Uncompromising. "There is no time for you to be upset with me. There are powerful forces at play here, much more powerful than you or I. More powerful than the Shadow Man. Facilier doesn't have the powers you think he has. *He's* the one who has been manipulating you." She hitched her head toward the staircase Lisette had climbed up. "Follow me. I'll explain everything."

"No!" Tiana stated more forcefully. The woman's brows shot up. "I don't know who you are," Tiana said. "With your flowers and your paintings and all your other gifts. What was that about?"

"I will explain," Ms. Rose said, her tone even harder than before.

Tiana refused to be intimidated. She'd been lied to, manipulated. Again. What kind of game was this woman playing with her? "I'm supposed to just trust you?"

"Yes," Ms. Rose stated. "I'm the only one who can help. And at this point, I'm not sure how much. There is no time to waste."

Tiana backed away, not wanting to turn for fear of what the woman would do.

She didn't know what to think. Or whom to trust.

"I've put up with enough lies from the Shadow Man," Tiana said. "As far as I'm concerned, you're no better than he is."

She turned on her heel and raced out of the courtyard, past the gate, and to the only sanctuary she could think of.

43

Tiana

Tiana was out of breath by the time she reached Tremé. Still, a cry of relief broke free as the supper club came into view.

She *needed* to be there. Even though the thought of having to get through an entire dinner service—cooking, entertaining patrons, cleaning up after all was done—made her want to collapse, she needed the comfort of the place she and her daddy had built.

She cut through the alley that led to the back entrance of the supper club, but before she entered, Tiana took a moment to collect herself.

A jagged, painful sense of betrayal threatened to over-whelm her at the thought of Ms. Rose—Roselande—lying to her all this time. She'd considered the woman something of a friend. Had Ms. Rose been pretending during their neigh-borly chats? Was Tiana just a pawn in some game between Roselande and Facilier? A game she'd never agreed to play in the first place?

Maybe she should have stuck around and demanded the woman explain herself. Ms. Rose owed her at least that much after months of deceiving her.

She swiped at the angry tears that she hadn't even real-ized had started to fall.

It was imperative she not show any sign that anything was amiss. Given the time of day, her daddy was likely in there preparing for that night's dinner service. If he had an inkling of what was going on, Tiana wasn't sure what he would do. Or what Facilier would do in retaliation.

"Just get through tonight," she told herself. *Take this prep time to think things through, to find another solution.*

She would figure out how to take care of the Shadow Man on her own, without Roselande's help.

When she walked inside, she spotted her daddy stand-ing at the prep station. Her dark mood immediately lifted at the sight of him.

"Hey there, baby girl," he called, his ever-present smile

as warm as a comforting hug. "You back from seeing your friend? How is she?"

"Hey, Daddy," Tiana answered, then walked over and gave him a kiss on the cheek. "Yes, I am. My friend . . . well." She waved that off. "It's not important. It's so good to see you, Daddy."

"You saw me the day before yesterday." He laughed as he expertly diced bell peppers into uniform pieces.

"But it's *always* good to see you," Tiana said. "It's something I've learned to never take for granted."

"That's a good lesson to learn," he said. He glanced over at her and frowned. "You get caught up in a storm or something, baby girl?"

Tiana looked down at her filthy clothes. Maybe she should have gone home first; maybe Charlotte had had the right idea. She needed a bath.

"I did," she said. "The rain caught me on my way back to N'awlins. I'll go get cleaned up soon." She walked over to where her apron hung on a hook near the rear of the kitchen. "But I should start on the gumbo before I do. Once it's cooking, Addie Mae can watch it while I run home and bathe."

"If she ever shows up," her daddy said. "I haven't seen or heard from her all day."

Tiana's fingers fumbled in the middle of tying the apron around her waist. That didn't sound like Addie Mae.

"I wonder if she fell ill," she murmured. She wished Addie Mae had a telephone, but Southern Bell's service was still a rarity in most households in the city. "Let me get to this gumbo, and then I'll see if I can find Lil Johnny Taylor to go check on her."

She scrubbed the dirt from her hands and underneath her nails, then filled her daddy's big gumbo pot with water. Together they took it over to the stove. She then made quick work of chopping up the remaining vegetables and adding them to the pot, along with chicken and andouille sausage.

A now-familiar sense of dread climbed up Tiana's spine as she walked over to the pantry and moved the jar of green beans to the side. There behind it stood the small vial filled with the potion Facilier had given her, next to the larger one he'd shoved upon her at the market. The potion meant to keep her Daddy alive, next to the one he wanted her to put into all her dishes to keep their deal going.

Facilier doesn't have the powers you think he has. He's the one who has been manipulating you.

Roselande's earlier assertion pried at a question that had puzzled Tiana since Thursday night, when Facilier had suddenly changed the rules of their deal. She'd balked at the flimsy excuse he'd given her as to why she needed to start adding the larger potion to all of her dishes. It hadn't made sense, and he had never explained the reasoning behind it.

"*He doesn't have the powers you think he has,*" Tiana whispered as she continued to stare at the vials. Could it be? Could that be one thing Roselande had been honest about? For months, had Facilier used whatever was in that small bottle to control *her*, not her daddy? Had he convinced her to do his bidding, not with magic, but with his words, his illusions?

He *was* a master manipulator.

She slid the beans back into place and left the potions—both of them—where they were. This batch would not include Facilier's contribution.

"You okay in there, baby girl?"

Tiana cleared her throat. "Yeah, Daddy. I'll be right out."

She left the pantry and returned to her gumbo, trying her hardest to quell her unease. She could very well risk everything she loved with the decision she'd just made, but this was more than just a gut feeling.

She knew that Facilier had deceived her more than once with his mind games, tricking her into thinking she was standing in the restaurant of her dreams or that he'd harmed her parents.

Well, her daddy was right there in the kitchen, alive and healthy.

Tiana went over to the stove and lowered the fire under the pot.

"Daddy, I'm gonna let this simmer for a bit while I look for Lil Johnny. I'll send him to check on Addie Mae."

She lucked out and found Lil Johnny Taylor just a couple of blocks away from the restaurant. Tiana paid him a nickel to run over to Addie Mae's house and return with word about why she had not shown up for work.

When she returned to the restaurant, she found her daddy standing over the gumbo pot.

"It isn't burning, is it?" Tiana asked.

He looked over his shoulder, a sheepish grin on his handsome face. "No, you caught me stealing a taste."

Tiana burst out laughing, something she couldn't imagine herself doing just an hour before.

James sipped the brown liquid from a big cooking spoon. "Mmm . . . that's a good gumbo." He took another sip, then broke out in an awful, body-racking cough.

Panic sent her running. "Daddy!"

Tiana grabbed the spoon from him and tossed it aside.

What had she done? Why had she taken a chance with that potion?

"I'm fine." Her daddy pounded his chest, his smile returning. "Gumbo just went down the wrong pipe is all. That's what I get for sneaking a taste before it's done."

Relief made her muscles weak. Her hand trembled as she covered her forehead with her palm. "You scared me."

"Everything's okay. Don't get yourself so worked up, baby girl." He gestured toward the dining room. "Why don't you go out there and get the tables ready for tonight? And then you can head home to wash off and dress for the big Shrove Monday dinner crowd. I'll do the same once Carol Anne and Jodie get here to watch the kitchen."

Tiana nodded, but her entire body still hummed with anxiety. Something wasn't right. She felt it in her bones.

She entered the dining room and went about straightening the tablecloths and centerpieces. Her hurt and anger came roaring back at the sight of the flowers Ms. Rose—Roselande—had given her for the restaurant. As she picked up some petals that had fallen onto the table, she had a mind to toss all the flowers away. Same with all the paintings hanging up around here.

She looked over at the most recent one the woman had gifted her and blinked in confusion. She dropped the flower petals and raced to it, her mind unwilling to register what her eyes were clearly seeing.

Or *not* seeing.

Nearly all the people were gone. Of the half dozen colorfully outfitted Mardi Gras Indians in the original portrait, only one remained.

Tiana slowly shook her head as she backed away from

the painting. This couldn't be right. Someone was playing tricks on her again.

"Miss Tiana! Miss Tiana!" Lil Johnny Taylor rushed through the restaurant's front entrance. "Miss Addie Mae is gone," he said.

Icy fear wrapped around her heart like a fist.

"What do you mean she's gone? Was her mother at home?"

Lil Johnny nodded. "She was. Miss Phyllis said Addie Mae went to fetch some things at the market and was supposed to bring them back home before leaving for work, but she never did. I went to the market, but nobody's there on account of that green stuff growing everywhere."

Tiana's rising panic refused to subside. "Thanks, Lil Johnny," Tiana told the boy, slipping him another nickel.

Facilier was behind all of this. She had no doubt about it.

"Daddy," Tiana called as she entered the kitchen. But she found Carol Anne and Jodie there instead.

"Mr. James just left," Carol Anne said. "He said he'll be back in time for the dinner service."

Tiana nodded. "Have either of you talked to Addie Mae?"

Both girls shook their heads.

"Tia! Tia!" Charlotte burst through the swinging door and into the kitchen. "Oh, Tia!"

"Lottie, what's the matter?" Tiana captured her friend by her shoulders. She was still wearing her mud-stained trousers. "What's going on?"

"It's Big Daddy! He's missing!"

Tiana's entire body went rigid, while Lottie's shook like a leaf in the middle of a hurricane.

"What do you mean? What makes you think he's missing?"

"He's not home."

"Maybe he's at the mill."

"He's not." Lottie was shaking her head. "I just came from there. No one at the mill has seen him, either." She walked back into the dining room, cradling her head in her hands. "Oh, Tia, I don't know what to do."

Just then, Naveen and Louis arrived, both looking as if they actually had come through a hurricane. Their clothes were covered in muck, and they reeked of dank, smelly rot.

Naveen hooked a thumb toward the door. "I don't know what's going on out there, but it looks as if the swamp followed us back here. That slimy green sludge is everywhere."

"And the fog is worse than ever," Louis piped up.

Charlotte turned to them. "Naveen, have you seen Big Daddy?"

"Mr. LaBouff?"

"Yes. No one knows where he is, not even his closest

friends. Big Daddy would never just up and leave without telling a single soul where he was going. Alfred said he's been gone since this morning. It isn't like Big Daddy to leave without saying anything to anybody."

"Don't get yourself worked up," Tiana told her, running her hand up and down her friend's arm to soothe her, even though her own nerves felt as though they were twisting and tying into knots.

"What's that?" Charlotte pointed to tiny specks of dirt that dotted the tablecloth. Tiana went to dust them away, and dozens of bugs took flight.

She screeched, running away from the table. But the bugs were suddenly everywhere, swarming around in the same way the mosquitoes had attacked on Saturday.

Ms. Rose's flowers! The winged insects flew out of the center of each bud and whizzed around the dining room like a tornado. Terror shot through Tiana as she thought about the mosquitoes at Congo Square.

She scrambled into the kitchen.

"Shut everything off!" Tiana called out to Carol Anne and Jodie. "Just shut off the stove and leave that food there. Get out! *Get out!*"

44
Tiana

"Tiana! Tiana, where you going?"

She could hear Louis hustling to keep up with her, but she had no time to waste. "I've got something I need to do," she called over her shoulder. "Go and see about Lottie."

"Naveen is taking care of Charlotte. I'm coming with you."

"No," Tiana said, hastening her steps.

"You're going to the Shadow Man, aren't you?"

Tiana stopped and turned to him. "Please, Louis, I have to do this alone."

"Let me join you, Tiana."

Tiana shook him off, determined not to endanger the life of another loved one. "No."

Louis flinched. He stepped back, his face a mask of hurt.

"I'm sorry," Tiana said. "I know you want to help, but please, Louis, just listen to me. I will handle this."

He didn't say another word—simply nodded, turned, and walked back the way they'd come.

Tiana started to go after him, but she needed to get to Facilier. She would smooth things over with Louis later. She pivoted and continued on her mission. The fog was so thick she could only see a couple of feet in front of her, but she didn't let it deter her. She once again had a sense that something was following close behind.

She moved so fast down the sidewalk she was practically running in her haste to get to the French Quarter and Facilier's dark, creepy emporium. Her skin crawled at the thought of crossing the threshold of that purple door. There was a sinister weight to the air inside Facilier's home, as if evil was not only allowed, but welcomed.

Tiana's feet stopped short.

She didn't have to bother with going to his home, because he was right there, three feet away from her. The fog obscured his facial features, but she would have known that top hat anywhere.

He sat at a small wooden table on the street corner near

Jackson Square, an array of playing cards spread out before him. He riffled the rest of the deck, shuffling them with one hand. He called out to a gentleman passing by and gestured to the cards, but the man shook his head and continued walking.

His eyes still focused on the man who had just shunned him, Facilier said, "I wondered when you would show up, Tiana."

The blood drained from her face as the sound of her own heartbeat pounded in her ears.

"Where are Addie Mae and Mr. LaBouff?" Tiana hissed. "And where is Mr. Salvaggio? I know you're behind their disappearances." Facilier continued to shuffle the cards. "Well, are you gonna answer me?" Tiana asked.

"I warned you," was his answer. He slowly turned to face her. A sinister smile played at the corners of his lips. "You're the one who decided not to heed my warning."

"And I warned *you* that you'd best leave my family and friends out of this!"

"Some friend you are," Facilier snarled. "I'll bet you haven't noticed those other two were even gone."

Tiana frowned, but then she remembered Maddy coming up to her on Saturday. "You have Georgia and Eugene!"

"Oh, *now* you remember them?"

She shoved hard, toppling his table and sending the

playing cards flying into the air. "Where are they!" she yelled.

Facilier righted the table, then perched himself on its corner. He studied his fingernails for a moment before buffing them on the collar of his vest.

"You let them go, you hear me? Let them go right now!"

Like a deadly lion pouncing on its prey, he launched himself at her, his sneering grimace stopping only inches from her face.

"Or what, Tiana? What is it you *think* you can do to me? You have no power. *I'm* the one who holds all the cards here."

Just then, a stiff wind blew, and the playing cards that had scattered on the ground whirled around like a cyclone. Tiana watched in fascinated horror as, one by one, the cards flew into Facilier's waiting hand. His maniacal laugh echoed around her.

"I warned you not to trifle with me, little girl. The consequences of your actions go far beyond just you."

Without warning, Ms. Rose's words slammed into her brain.

The drum is beaten in the grass, but it is at home that it comes to dance.

Her actions had repercussions for her entire family. She had brought this upon everyone.

Facilier reached into the inside pocket of his vest and produced that blasted contract. "Now, for the last time, sign this!"

She shoved his hand away. "I'm not signing anything," Tiana said. "You can't make me, because you have no real power. Just tricks. Roselande told me so."

His body stiffened in shock, his eyes bulging with instant rage. Tiana took an unconscious step back.

"Watch it, Tiana. You're playing the wrong hand. Bring Roselande into this, and you'll be sorry."

"Tiana! Tiana!"

She turned at the sound of Louis's panicked voice. "Louis, I told you not to follow me!"

"It's Mr. James," Louis called from down the street.

His words snatched the breath from Tiana's lungs. She took off running, hearing Facilier's deep, rumbling laugh behind her.

Tiana caught up with her friend, reaching her arms out as if to buoy herself. "What's going on? What's happened?"

"It's your daddy, Tiana," Louis puffed out. "You need to get to the house—now!"

45

Tiana

Tiana rushed through the front door and stopped, dread rooting her where she stood. She pressed a hand to her chest at the sight of her father's huge body sprawled on the sofa, his head cradled in her mother's lap. His skin was ashen and wrinkled. He looked years older than he had when she'd seen him at the restaurant just an hour before.

"I'll be right back," she heard Louis say, but all her focus was on her parents. Tiana hurried to their side. She knelt down on the floor next to them and took her father's hand in hers. His fingers were gnarled, the skin papery thin.

"What's going on, Mama?"

"I don't know," she answered. Her mother looked up at her and Tiana saw true fear in her eyes. "He was just fine when he came home. He went into the bathroom to wash up and get ready for the big night at the supper club. When he came out, his hands had wrinkled up like a dried prune. I thought maybe he'd soaked in the tub too long, but then I noticed the gray hair at his temples."

The gray was no longer just at his temple. More than half of her daddy's beautiful dark brown hair was now peppered with wiry gray strands.

"Hey, baby girl," he called, his voice a thready whisper. He peered up at her with rheumy eyes. "I don't think I can make it to the supper club tonight." He coughed. "I don't know why I'm so tired."

"Don't worry about the restaurant," Tiana said. "We won't be opening tonight anyway." She wouldn't explain about the bugs or the food they'd left abandoned. None of that was important at the moment.

The restaurant.

The vials were there. Tiana wondered—if she gave the usual potion to him now, would his illness be reversed?

"Mama, I have something that may help. I'll be back as soon as I can."

She raced from the house, making it to the supper club

and back home in record time. She hastened to her father's side and uncapped the smaller vial.

"Here, Daddy," Tiana said, putting the vial up to his lips. "Drink this."

"What's that you're giving him?" her mother asked in a panicked voice.

"Just give it a few minutes, Mama. Trust me."

But could she trust Facilier to have been telling the truth? She still didn't trust the new larger concoction, but what about the one she'd been using these past months? Did this tincture really have any effect whatsoever on her father's fate?

Tiana could hear her heartbeat thumping in her ears as the seconds ticked by. She zeroed in on the gray hairs on her father's head, willing them to start turning back to their dark brown color. She studied the wrinkles creasing his once-smooth skin, praying they would even out.

"Come on, come on, come on," Tiana murmured. But after several minutes had passed, it was clear the potion she'd been adding to her gumbo all this time was truly worth nothing. It had all been a charade.

That damn Shadow Man.

There was a knock at the door.

"You expecting somebody?" Tiana asked her mother. Eudora shook her head.

She walked over to the front door and opened it. Lisette stood outside on the porch. "Tee Lande told me where to find you," she said.

Tiana's first instinct was to turn her away, but Lisette had done nothing wrong. In fact, she'd helped when she had no incentive to do so.

"Come in," Tiana said, moving out of the way so that she could enter. "Mama. Daddy. This is my friend, Lisette. Lisette, this is my mother, Eudora, and my father, James."

"Hello," Lisette said. Her eyes immediately zeroed in on James. "He isn't well."

"No, he isn't," Eudora said. As if to punctuate her statement, James coughed again. It was hoarse and brittle and sent a chill down Tiana's spine.

"He's very weak," Eudora continued.

Lisette walked over to the sofa and went to touch James's forehead, but Eudora pushed her hand away.

"You don't have to worry, Mama. Lisette is an herbalist. She's a healer. If anybody can help Daddy, she can."

Lisette laid the back of her hand to James's forehead, then along his forearms. She used her fingertips to gently press against his glands, starting behind his ears and traveling down his neck until she reached his chin.

Tiana stood back and watched as the young girl went through a methodical assessment of her father's symptoms.

"He isn't feverish," Lisette said. "But that cough doesn't sound good at all."

There was another knock on the door. Before Tiana could answer it, Naveen and Louis walked in.

"I brought Naveen to see if he could help," Louis said.

"Thank you, Louis," Tiana said. "And I'm sorry. You know, for earlier." She owed him that apology for being so cross, but in true Louis fashion, he seemed to have no ill will toward her.

"It's okay, Tiana," he said.

Naveen came to stand behind her. He put one hand on her shoulder and gave it another of those reassuring squeezes. Despite all the months she'd spent avoiding him, Tiana could not have been more grateful to have him near her right now.

"Where's Lottie?" she asked.

"She's at home, waiting for her father to return," he answered.

Tiana's stomach flipped as she remembered the conversation with Dr. Facilier. He had Mr. LaBouff and all the rest; she had no doubts about that. Tiana was determined to find them, but she had to figure out what was ailing her father, too.

"I don't understand what's happening," Tiana said,

looking down at him. "He was just cooking with me at the restaurant. How did he become so frail, so quickly?"

"I'm not sure what it is, either," Lisette said. "But I can whip up a tincture to help build up his strength and get rid of that cough."

She gathered her skirts around her and pushed herself up from where she'd knelt next to the sofa.

"Here's what I'll need." She listed a number of herbs, many of which Tiana fortunately had in the kitchen.

"I don't know where we're going to get ivy leaves," Tiana said.

"There are several herbalists in the French Quarter. You may have to ask around, but I'm sure someone has some."

"I'll go to the Quarter," Louis volunteered.

"Bring back as much as you can," Lisette told him. She looked down at Tiana's father. "At the very least, it'll keep him comfortable."

"What can I do?" Tiana asked. She couldn't just stand there while her father suffered.

"You can show me to the kitchen and help me get started. We'll have to grind the thyme and elderflower into a powder. If we get started now, we can be done by the time the scaly one is back with the ivy leaves."

Tiana kissed her daddy on the forehead, then led Lisette

to the kitchen. They spent the next half hour collecting and preparing the ingredients for the medicinal syrup, and once Louis returned with the ivy leaves, Lisette was able to complete the final steps. The young girl also made a broth with the marrow from chicken bones Tiana had set aside for soup stock.

"Okay," Lisette said, carrying a coffee mug filled with the concoction into the living room where Tiana's father lay. "Try to get him to drink at least half of this."

After handing the mug to Eudora, Lisette joined Tiana, Naveen, and Louis, who all stood by, nervously watching James sip the steaming liquid.

In just the hour since she'd returned home, her father seemed to have aged another ten years. Spots dotted his hands and forearms, and the skin around his mouth and eyes had wrinkled even more.

Tiana placed a hand on Lisette's forearm. "Thank you."

"Now it's just rest and prayers," Lisette said with a shrug. "I wish I could do more. Maybe Tee Lande can help."

Tiana hesitated.

"Tee Lande isn't a bad person, and I don't like you thinking she is," Lisette said, as if she could read Tiana's mind.

"Ms. Rose—Roselande—lied to me," Tiana said.

"If she did, then she had good reason." Lisette jutted

her chin toward James. "Let's just watch over your daddy for now."

And that was exactly what they did all night long. Tiana, her mother, Lisette, Naveen, and even Louis sat in the tiny living room, keeping vigil over her father's steadily weakening body.

46
Tiana

The Ninth Ward, New Orleans
Tuesday, February 1927
Mardi Gras

Tiana awoke the next morning with a crick in her neck, courtesy of the uncomfortable chair she'd slept in. The moment she opened her eyes, she looked to the sofa. Her father remained motionless, his head still in her mother's lap.

Tiana pushed herself up from the chair and quietly made her way over to them, even though Louis's snores would mask any noise she made. He, Lisette, and Naveen were all still asleep.

"How is he?" Tiana asked as she neared the sofa.

Once there, she gasped.

His hair had gone completely white, and the wrinkles on his face had deepened. He looked like an old man.

Her mother glanced up at her with tears in her eyes. "I don't know what's happening to him, Tiana."

"Go to Roselande." Tiana jumped at the sound of Lisette's voice from just behind her. She turned to face her. "Go to her. Now."

Tiana swallowed deeply and nodded. "I'm going."

"Who is Roselande?" Eudora asked.

"She's someone I'm hoping can help," Tiana said. She pulled her bottom lip between her teeth to prevent it from trembling. "Because Daddy needs help, and I don't know what to do."

She kissed her mother's forehead, then her father's. Tiana's stomach twisted at how wrinkly his smooth skin had become. He was aging before their eyes, becoming an old, brittle man. How much longer before . . .

She didn't want think about what could possibly come of this.

They'd been through this before. She'd made a deal

with the proverbial devil to erase what had happened to her father. She would not lose him again.

"I'll be back soon, Daddy," Tiana whispered to him. "I'm gonna figure out how to help you."

She grabbed her purse from the hook near the door, then bounded down the porch steps. She went to the expense of hailing a taxicab instead of waiting for the street-car to arrive. She would not pinch pennies. Time was of the essence.

Tiana instructed the cab driver to take her to the corner of Royal and St. Ann Streets in the French Quarter. That would put her exactly where she needed to be.

Navigating through the thick fog made the drive more harrowing than Tiana's frayed nerves could withstand. The green sludge had reached the edges of the Ninth Ward. Pretty soon, it would take over the entire city.

By the time the cab driver pulled up to the building, her hands were shaking.

She still wasn't sure if she could trust Roselande. The flower monger had kept so much from Tiana, had perhaps even known who Tiana was before ever introducing herself. Remembering their encounters over the past few months, and how Ms. Rose would share all those gifts and her little drops of wisdom, Tiana now wondered if it had all been orchestrated. And to what end?

Couple that with the infestation that had sprung from the Mardi Gras flowers the woman had given her, and the shifting imagery in the painting hanging on the wall at her restaurant, and Tiana wasn't sure Ms. Rose was any better than Facilier.

Had Roselande put some kind of curse on her supper club? Was that the point of her gifts?

No, she couldn't trust Roselande. . . .

But her father's life was now at stake. And she had no one else to turn to.

Tiana opened the gate of the red brick building and walked down the short colonnade that led to the courtyard. She spotted Roselande standing before a row of planters filled with colorful blossoms, a watering can in her hand. It suddenly occurred to Tiana that the courtyard had somehow escaped the dense fog that encompassed the rest of the city.

The dazzling pink roses, saffron freesia, and deep purple violets overflowing from the planters were a stark contrast to the drabness shrouding New Orleans. The air was redolent with the soft scent of lavender and sweet, tangy aroma of primrose. How had the woman managed to maintain such a beautiful garden in the midst of all this gray?

"You're back." Tiana jumped as Roselande turned and faced her. A serene smile played about her lips. "Happy Mardi Gras."

She hadn't even considered that it was Mardi Gras day. All the plans she'd made for the big celebration seemed so insignificant now.

"Something's wrong with my daddy," Tiana said. "I came hoping that you could help him. Help *me* help him."

"Why don't we go inside?" Roselande suggested. "We can have tea and talk for a bit."

"I don't have time for tea!" Tiana said.

"Yes, you do," the woman stated in a firm voice that brooked no argument. She set the watering can on the ground and started up a nearby flight of stairs, not bothering to look back to see if Tiana followed.

When Tiana entered the small apartment, she wasn't surprised to find it as colorful as the dress worn by the woman who lived there. The walls were painted a vibrant red, and curtains of sparkling beads hung in the doorways.

"Please, have a seat." Roselande motioned to a chair at a large round table that was covered with a bright yellow tablecloth.

Tiana balked. She would not just sit here and socialize while her daddy was growing into an old man. They were wasting time.

"I don't—" Tiana started, but quickly quieted when Roselande turned to her.

"Please. Sit," the woman said. Then she smiled. "There is always time for tea."

Tiana reluctantly fell into the chair. She fidgeted as she watched the woman walk over to the basket of flowers she'd been carrying when Tiana and Lisette arrived yesterday. She broke off several of the lavender stems and placed them in a pot on the stove. Then she added water first to that pot, next to a teakettle, lighting fires underneath both.

"Does the lavender keep away evil spirits?" Tiana asked.

"No."

"So why are you using it?" she asked.

The woman looked at her with one shapely eyebrow hitched. "Because of the pleasant scent, of course."

She retrieved a tin from the counter and walked over to the table.

"There's nothing magical about these flowers, either," Roselande said as she scooped up a heaping teaspoon of dried flowers and placed them in two of the delicate teacups that sat on the table. "But we have a lot to discuss. And it is always best over a nice cup of tea."

Tiana jumped at the piercing sound of a loud whistle and felt like a complete fool when she realized it was only the teakettle.

Roselande carried the brass teakettle back to the table, poured the steaming water over the dried flowers, and then took the seat across from Tiana. A delicately floral scent permeated the air. Using a teaspoon, Roselande swirled the flowers around her teacup until the water turned a color that matched the caftan she wore, then brought it to her mouth and took a sip.

She looked Tiana directly in the eye. "Do you understand what is happening, Tiana?"

"No. That's why I'm here."

But she *did* know. At least she knew *why* this was all happening.

Roselande looked at Tiana expectantly.

"It's my fault," Tiana went on, her throat tight. "Dr. Facilier warned me what would happen if I didn't do what he asked, but I thought he was bluffing. And now my daddy is dying. He's growing older and older. He's aged at least thirty years since last night."

"Is that so?" Roselande asked. "You know, when I was a young girl, my mother would always say, *tan ale; li pa tounen*. Time goes; it does not return. It's another way of saying that one can never return to the past. But maybe it is better to say that one *shouldn't* return to the past. Nothing good will come of that."

"I know that now," Tiana said. "I never should have made that deal with Facilier. Look what's happening to the city."

Roselande shook her head. "But he doesn't have the power to facilitate what is happening right now. This isn't between you and Facilier. Well, it isn't *only* between the two of you," she amended. "The universe is sending a message. I'm afraid it is very, very unhappy."

"With me, or with Facilier?" Tiana asked.

"With you both, because you have both caused this disruption. My mother had another saying: *Pye chat dous men zong li move.* The paw of a cat is sweet, but its claws are nasty." She set down her teacup. "You saw the sweetness of Facilier's deal without considering the consequences that could follow."

"He left me no choice," Tiana said.

"There is always a choice. The manner of pestilence that has been unleashed on this city conveys just how upset the universe is with the deal that was made. The fog. That awful green sludge that is everywhere. The swarm of insects—"

"You mean like the ones from your flowers?" Tiana asked, unable to keep the accusation out of her voice.

"You are talking about the marigolds and lavender?"

"Yes. Thousands of bugs flew out of the flowers last night. For all I know, they're still in my restaurant."

Roselande released a sigh. "I was hoping the flowers would provide a level of protection, along with the paintings.

They were supposed to look over you, to shield you. But the forces are stronger than I anticipated."

"Is that why the Mardi Gras Indians in the painting keep disappearing?"

Roselande's brow creased in confusion, but then understanding dawned in her eyes. "So my calls for protection were not completely ignored. The disordering of the painting is a message, likely sent from the *Lwa*. Beware, Tiana. I wouldn't be surprised if those around you start to go missing."

"People *have* gone missing," Tiana said. She ran down the list of all who had disappeared over the past few days.

"By removing the people from the painting, the spirits were trying to alert you as to what was happening. Unfortunately, you did not understand how to receive their message."

Tiana shook her head, unsure what to make of any of this.

"Can you please tell me what I need to do to fix it?" Tiana asked. She was growing impatient.

But Roselande simply took another sip of her tea before setting the teacup back on the saucer and folding her hands on the table.

"You see, Tiana, there are things that happen in this world that are beyond what many people can comprehend.

There are powerful forces at play. Most are good and cause no harm, but there are others that seek to wreak havoc. Unfortunately, Facilier chose to follow *those* forces, and now he has dragged you into it."

She pinched her lips together, a pensive look clouding her eyes. "I knew there was something sinister here from the moment I arrived in New Orleans."

"It's Facilier," Tiana said. "People in the neighborhood always would warn us about the Shadow Man and his Vod—"

"No." Roselande stopped her. "Do not associate what Facilier practices with Vodou. Vodou delivers peace and goodness into the world. It offers healing to those who are sick and solace to those who are hurting. It is about bringing joy into the heart, not misery and despair. Never confuse that which Facilier practices with the religion of my homeland." She let out a sigh. "Facilier could have done much good in the world if he had taken the time to learn the ways of our people, but he decided he wanted to go the easy way." She rubbed her thumb and fingers together. "Easy money."

"He wants more than money," Tiana said.

"Yes, he wants power. Always has. Facilier wants to control the city of New Orleans, and he believes if he can control those in power, then everything he has ever wanted will just fall into his lap. That is where you come in."

"But I have no power over this city," Tiana said. "All I have is my restaurant."

"You have very powerful people who dine at your restaurant, Tiana. Facilier sees you as his ticket to get to those people."

"Mr. LaBouff," Tiana whispered.

The woman nodded. She tilted her head to the side. "How did you get mixed up with the Shadow Man in the first place? That's the one thing I haven't figured out."

Tiana hesitated for a moment, but reasoned that she could not hold anything back from Roselande if she wanted the woman's help. She gave her a detailed account of what had transpired at Mardi Gras the year before, and in the year since.

"All right. It is making sense now," Roselande said once Tiana was finished. "His next payment is due."

"Payment?" Tiana asked. "So it *is* about money?"

"Not that kind of payment," Roselande answered. "In order to provide the things he promised when the two of you made that deal, Facilier had to call upon malevolent forces. And now those forces are demanding payment. I can't imagine their price for bringing someone back from the dead. Whatever it was, you can be assured it was very steep."

Tiana thought for a moment. "Would those forces happen to look like shadows?"

Again, Roselande nodded. "They can take many forms."

"I think they've been following me," Tiana said.

"I wouldn't be surprised. They'd want to keep an eye on you. Facilier has no knowledge of how to call upon the *Lwa*, so he must rely on these shadows instead."

"So what do I do?" Tiana asked. "How do I defeat Facilier? And what can I do to help my father? How do I stop him from growing old so fast?"

The pitying look that instantly clouded Roselande's face turned Tiana's blood cold.

Her voice trembled as she asked, "There *is* something I can do, isn't there?"

"Here's what I know." Roselande sucked in a deep, cleansing breath, then slowly released it. Folding her hands on the table, she looked Tiana directly in the eyes. "There is a symmetry to everything. You bargained for extra time with your father that he should have never been given, so I believe the universe is taking that time back.

"I've only heard of this happening once before, but those affected did not physically age. They were stripped of their memories, and they—"

"Ms. Margery," Tiana said with a gasp.

"I don't follow," Roselande said with a frown.

"Ms. Margery and Buford and Mr. Smith at the fabric

shop. Something is going on with their memory," Tiana explained.

"And you've had dealings with all of these people, either now or in the past?'"

"Yes, all of them," Tiana said.

"It makes sense," Roselande said. "The universe is extracting the time you took from it by snatching up memories from those around you."

Tiana tried to wrap her head around all of this. It was still so much more than she could handle right now.

"So are you saying that whatever is going on with my daddy and the others is because the universe is upset with me? It isn't because I didn't put Facilier's potion in the gumbo I made yesterday?"

Roselande shook her head. "Whatever Facilier gave you has nothing to do with this. *That's* most likely some sort of con on his part. I told you already, Tiana. This—the fog, the algae, your father's woes—is far beyond anything he can do."

"So why is this happening now? I made that deal with Facilier a year ago!"

"I think you just answered your own question," Roselande replied. "You're approaching the one-year anniversary, which also happens to line up with Shrovetide, or Shrove Monday as they call it here. The Monday before the beginning of the Lenten season is a time of seeking absolution for the sins committed over the previous year."

"But what sin does my daddy need to seek forgiveness for? He's the most honest man I know."

Roselande brought her teacup to her mouth and took a very long, deliberate sip. "You are a very smart girl, Tiana. I think you already know."

It wasn't her daddy's sins. It was hers.

"It's because I brought him back, isn't it?" Her voice cracked.

"I'm afraid so," Roselande said. "Remember what I said about the symmetry of these events? It was one year ago today that you caused this disturbance in the universe by receiving something that never should have been. The deal you made with Facilier disrupted the order of things," she said. "To set things right, you must allow fate to continue as it first saw fit."

Apprehension skated along Tiana's skin, causing goose bumps to pebble up and down her arms.

"What are you saying?" she asked, although she feared she knew what Roselande was going to say before the woman spoke.

"*Kote ki gen dife a, gen dlo tou*. Where there's the fire, there's water, too," she said. "Every problem has a solution."

"What's the solution?" Tiana asked. She was near her breaking point.

"Your father," Roselande answered. "As much as you want him to remain with you and your family, it is not meant to be."

Tiana shook her head. She covered her mouth with her fist, trying and failing to mute the strangled cry that escaped her lips. Roselande reached across the table and gently placed her hand on Tiana's forearm. She gave it a firm squeeze.

"This extra time you've had with your father has been a blessing; it has been a gift. But it has come at a cost that is more than this world can bear. The longer you hold on to him, the more destruction and despair will be unleashed upon New Orleans and beyond. You must willingly relinquish your father to his rightful place in the universe, Tiana."

"Am I just supposed to let him die?" she cried.

"No," Roselande said. "Just letting him die isn't enough. You must give him *permission* to go. He is holding on because of you—because you brought him back here. Nothing will be right in this world until you make the choice to release him. That is what the universe demands. It's the only way to atone for the disruption you caused."

"So . . . so what do I do?" She released a hiccupping sob. "How do I give him permission to go?"

"In this world, all beginnings have an end. Or, as my people say, all prayers have an amen. *Tout laprivè gen amen.*"

"I don't understand."

"Your father has reached his end on this earth, Tiana. You are to offer these words until he passes on. Tout laprivè gen amen."

"Tout . . . tout la . . . la . . ."

"Laprivè gen amen," Roselande instructed.

"Tout laprivè gen amen." Tiana imagined saying the words to her father, watching him leave them once more. Forever. She shook her head. "I can't. I can't just sit by while he dies!"

"You must, Tiana. It is the only way.

"You must let him go."

47

Tiana

"I—I'm sorry," Tiana said, unsure whom she was talking to now, tears blurring her vision. She pushed her chair away from the table and stood abruptly. Then she ran out of the apartment and didn't look back.

She spent the entire cab ride home trying to discount Roselande's warnings. It was all too much for her to wrap her head around. How could a decision she had made a year before affect the entire universe? This fog? Buford and Ms. Margery and the others losing their memories? All of that was because of her? All because she wanted to have her daddy back?

She closed her eyes tight against the tears that began to stream down her face.

How was she supposed to willingly let go of her father when she'd just gotten him back? She wasn't ready to say goodbye to him.

But when would she *ever* be ready? a nagging voice asked. He could live to be a thousand years old and she still would not want to give him up. If she never willingly let him go, would he live forever?

It seemed impossible, but so did having her daddy back in the first place.

An onslaught of anguish assailed her, so intense it robbed her of breath.

The deal she'd made with Facilier had given her something most people only dreamed about—more time with a lost loved one. She had been granted an entire year that she never should have had with her daddy. Those long talks while sitting in the rocking chairs on the porch, picking vegetables in his garden, cooking together at the supper club; they were the most precious gifts. Ones she would cherish for the rest of her days.

But now her daddy seemed to be suffering.

She had asked Roselande for the way to fix the mess she'd put this city and all her loved ones through, and she'd gotten her answer. And deep down, she knew she couldn't brush it aside just because it wasn't the one she'd wanted.

Tiana braced herself for the wave of cold, hard truth. She would have had to say goodbye to her father at some point.

That day had just come all too quickly.

Tiana knew that things had taken a turn for the worse the moment the cab pulled up to her parents' home. Even through the dense fog, she could make out the herd of people from the neighborhood crowding the front porch. They stared at her with pity as she walked up the pathway to the porch steps, mournful expressions on their faces.

As she approached the front door, Mr. Miller from across the street put a hand on her shoulder. "It doesn't look good, Tiana. The doctor was just here. He says he's never seen anything like it." He gave her shoulder a gentle squeeze. "I'm sorry."

Tiana nodded, her throat aching as she entered the house. Her daddy lay in the same place she'd left him, his head cradled in her mother's lap.

Several of her mother's friends had arrived. A couple of them sat with her in the living room, while a few others were in the kitchen collecting meals that had been prepared by their neighbors. It was a ritual around these parts. Those in mourning did not have to worry about cooking or cleaning for at least a week after a death in the family. The entire community pulled together to offer support.

Tiana closed her eyes, remembering the last time she and her mother had gone through this. It seemed as if it had happened just yesterday.

Back when she'd agreed to Facilier's deal, she had not considered how difficult it would be to face this loss twice.

She looked over at Lisette, who stood near the sewing machine, away from those who crowded around the living room. Her solemn expression was filled with understanding.

Tiana nodded and mouthed a silent *thank you*.

"Every beginning has an end," she murmured to herself, voice shaking.

Tiana sucked in a deep breath before walking over to the sofa. Several of the women made room for her, clearing the space next to her parents.

She looked down at her father and could barely believe her eyes. His face was ashen, almost ghostlike. His body looked like an eighty-year-old man's. Tufts of gray hair grew from his ears. His age-spotted skin stretched over knobby, gnarled hands, which were folded atop his chest.

Someone brought over a chair and directed Tiana to take a seat. She did. And then she took her daddy's limp hand in her own and brought it up to her cheek.

Tiana closed her eyes and rubbed her cheek against his paper-thin skin. Her throat constricted as she tried to swallow past the knot of grief clogging it. With her free hand, she reached out and captured her mother's, lacing their fingers together.

Her daddy's eyes fluttered open. A tired smile drew across his lips.

"Hey, baby girl," he said. His voice was so weak, it was barely perceptible.

"Hey, Daddy." She gave his hand a gentle squeeze and tried to find the strength to say the words she needed to say. "You're tired, aren't you?" Tiana asked.

He nodded. His chest rose with the breath he struggled to take.

"I know," she whispered as tears once again began to stream down her cheeks. Her daddy tried to reach for her face, but he was too frail to lift his hand more than a few inches. The crushing realization brought even more tears to her eyes.

She straightened her shoulders, finding the resolve to press forward. She would not make it harder for her daddy to let go.

She soothingly rubbed her thumb back and forth across his wrinkled, fragile hand, offering comfort. Then Tiana closed her eyes and inhaled deeply, mentally preparing herself for what she must do next.

She managed to smile as she looked down at him and said, "Do you know how special it's been to be in that kitchen with you every day? It's been a dream come true, and I would not trade it for anything." Her lip trembled as her emotions threatened to overwhelm her. "But I don't think we will be cooking together any longer, Daddy. The time for that has passed."

"It's okay, baby girl," he said. "It's . . . going to be . . . okay."

"I'll miss it," she said. "I'll miss *you*."

"You'll see . . . me again."

"Yes," she said with an emphatic nod. "We'll see each other again one day." She swallowed past the anguish jammed up in her throat. "But, for now, it's time for us to say goodbye."

Tiana leaned forward and pressed her cheek against his. She took a deep breath. Now was the time. She had to make things right.

"Tout laprivè gen amen," she said softly, trying to channel all the beauty and care Roselande had in her words. "Tout laprivè gen amen."

She repeated the phrase quietly, over and over and over,

as tears streamed down her face and onto her father's wrinkled skin.

"It's okay to let go," she whispered in his ear. "We're going to be okay. I will take care of Mama, and she will take care of me." She kissed his wrinkled forehead. "I love you, Daddy."

They remained that way for untold minutes, with Tiana holding on to her daddy with one hand and to her mother with the other. She and her mother drew strength from each other as her daddy's breaths became shallower and shallower. Silent tears streamed down Tiana's face as she listened to her mother's quiet sobs. How she wished she could alleviate her pain.

But Tiana had come to learn that enduring this particular kind of pain was an unfortunate, but inescapable, part of life. She had gone to extraordinary measures to avoid the agony of losing her father only to end up in this exact place again. Her days of avoiding life's inevitable consequences were over.

She saw her daddy's chest heave one last time, and then he went still. Tiana was surprised by the unexpected sense of calm that washed over her amid her grief.

Murmurs drifted from near the front door.

"What is this?" someone asked.

"Have you ever seen anything like it?"

As people began to congregate around the door, Tiana made her way to the closest window. She gasped at the sight on the other side of the glass. The fog had thinned, but only in the area surrounding their house, and flower petals rained from the sky. They collected on the ground like a colorful snowfall.

Tiana closed her eyes, a gentle smile touching her lips. She was at peace, because her daddy was now at peace.

But she still had one last thing to do.

48

Tiana

Tiana started the now-familiar journey to Facilier's dark, dreadful home hidden within the depths of the French Quarter. The greenish fog remained here, as thick and suffocating as ever. Despite it, she could make out the ominous clouds hovering overhead. The last thing she needed at the moment was a downpour slowing her down, but she would not let it deter her. If she had to fight the elements along with the Shadow Man, that's just what she would have to do.

She didn't bother to knock when she arrived at his home. She marched right up to that purple door and barged in.

"Where are you, Shadow Man?" she called.

The place smelled of patchouli and peppermint, the pleasant aroma incongruent with the sinister charge that hummed through the air.

"So you've finally come to your senses," came Facilier's cold, menacing voice.

"I've come to put an end to this," Tiana said. "Now get out here! Don't hide from me."

Several moments passed before he stepped into the dimly lit room. Despite her determination to conquer him, Tiana still experienced that initial jolt of panic the Shadow Man evoked whenever he was near. She mentally pushed away her fear and stood up straight, clenching her fists at her sides.

He has no power.

"You've arrived just in time," Facilier said. He reached into his vest and pulled out a pocket watch. "There is only an hour left until sunset, which means you have an hour to sign your name to that contract."

"I'm not signing anything," Tiana said. "I will not live my life according to *your* rules. That was never part of the deal."

"That was *always* part of the deal," Facilier said, quickly closing the distance between them. He drew near, his face just inches from hers. "You've been playing by my rules all along, Tiana. You just didn't realize it."

"That's not how this works." She fought to keep her voice from trembling. She refused to let him see an ounce of fear. "You don't get to change the rules at your whim. But it doesn't matter, because I'm done."

"Are you now?" His brow arched as he stared her down, observing her as if she were a bug he wanted to crush with his shoe.

"That's right," Tiana said. "I fulfilled my obligation to you a long time ago. I don't want any part of any new deal, and there is nothing you can do to change my mind."

"Have you forgotten what's at stake? Or are you ready to see that dear father of yours perish?"

Tiana pulled in a deep breath and held her head up high.

"You're too late," she said. "My daddy is no longer here with us. He died just a little while ago."

As painful as it was to speak those words, Tiana took some satisfaction in the shock that registered on Facilier's face. His surprise was further evidence that the potion he'd given her had never controlled her father's fate.

"You're lying," he growled.

"I would *never* lie about that," Tiana said. "My father meant the world to me, but I've accepted what fate had in store for him." She straightened her shoulders, feeling empowered. "And now you can't hold his well-being over my head anymore. I'm done cowering before you, Shadow Man. I don't care what it costs—I'm willing to pay *any* price to be free of you!"

He glared at her, his nostrils flaring. "But are you willing to pay the *ultimate* price?"

Before Tiana knew what he was doing, he twisted around, his black coat arcing through the air. And just like that, he was gone, consumed by the darkness surrounding them.

She squinted, trying her best to see in front of her, but the faint light coming in from the open door didn't do much to illuminate the room. Her fists tightening in determination at her sides, Tiana pulled in a fortifying breath and stormed ahead.

She unclenched her hands and held them up in front of her, feeling around for the wall or a door. She let out a swift *oof* when she bumped into a piece of furniture of some sort, its pointed edge jabbing her hip.

Facilier's low, maniacal cackle reverberated around the room.

Tiana twisted around, searching for where the sound had come from. The more she searched, the more confused she became. The darkness disoriented her, making her head spin.

"Where are you?" she yelled.

A loud pop rang out. Tiana jerked. It rang out again, and then a puff of glittery purple smoke appeared before her. A moment later, Facilier materialized out of the smoky haze.

"You're running out of time, Tiana," he said in a sing-song voice. "The sun will soon sink below the horizon." He reached inside his vest again and produced that blasted contract. "Sign it," he hissed as he shoved it at her.

"No!" she yelled.

Summoning every drop of courage within her, she ran at him. Facilier struck out with his hand, and Tiana bounced backward as if she'd hit an invisible wall. She crashed to the floor, scrambling to find her footing. She pushed herself up and launched at him again, but he broke away and retreated deeper into the house.

Her heart thumping against her chest like a pack of wild horses, Tiana took off after Facilier. She heard a door slam shut and rushed toward the sound, running her hands along the wall until she encountered the door handle. She opened the door and stopped short.

It was pitch black.

She blinked several times, but couldn't make out even the faintest object.

"Enter at your own risk." Facilier's disembodied voice

came from somewhere in the empty abyss that stretched out before her.

Tiana paused at the threshold, her chest heaving with the swift breaths she sucked in. She closed her eyes.

This is for you, Daddy.

Then she charged into the darkness.

49

Tiana

The moment Tiana entered the room, she was suspended in the air, her arms flailing as her body spun in a dizzying circle. Facilier's laugh swirled around her. When she finally landed on solid ground, she found herself back in the heart of Lafayette Cemetery, where this had all started.

It was an illusion. It had to be.

"You're in my world now," Facilier said. "You should have taken the easy way out and signed the contract."

"Taking the easy way is what got me into this mess with you," she said.

"And I gave you what you wanted. I gave you your father."

"You didn't give me anything," she said. "It was your *friends* who did it. You don't have any power of your own, Facilier. You're nothing without your friends from the other side."

He shrugged his shoulders, as if she hadn't just ripped the veil off the fraud he'd been perpetuating all this time.

"You're right," he said. "But without me, you wouldn't have *access* to my friends from the other side. So you're nothing without me, Tiana." He pointed to his chest. "*I'm* the reason you were able to open that restaurant with your daddy. *I'm* the reason that little prince of yours isn't hopping around the bayou.

"You wouldn't have had any of the things you've enjoyed this past year if I had not summoned my friends from the other side on your behalf. *You owe me.* And them."

Her vision became hazy as her eyes fixed on a stone catacomb just over the Shadow Man's shoulder. A montage of scenes played across it, images of her cooking side by side with her daddy at the supper club. Of sitting at her restaurant watching Louis and his band play rousing jazz music. Of staring into Naveen's beautiful eyes as they drifted down the bayou together.

Tiana shook her head.

No.

She wouldn't fall for his antics again. He had a way of twisting his words around, of making her believe what he wanted her to. But he no longer had the upper hand.

Tiana had finally accepted that she didn't have to face her battles alone. After the pastor arrived at the house to sit with Mama, she'd returned to Roselande's to apologize and tell her what had happened. Then, together, they had come up with a plan to beat Facilier at his own game.

Tiana pressed a hand against her satchel, feeling for the vial tucked inside.

For this to work, he had to buy her bluff.

"If I wanted to make another deal with you, I would," Tiana started. "But I don't have to, because I have friends, too. And my friends can do everything your friends can do and more."

"That's not possible," Facilier said.

She arched her eyebrow in cynical amusement, just as he had done to her so many times.

"Oh, but it is," Tiana said. "And I have something you *don't* have. Something that will give you what you've been seeking all along: power."

She reached into her satchel and pulled out the large vial.

"You must take me for a fool," Facilier said. "I'm the one who concocted that potion. I know exactly what it can do. And what it can't."

"Except this isn't the potion *you* concocted," Tiana lied. "I got this one from my new friend—a Vodou priestess in the Quarter. She replaced the contents with something . . . a little more helpful."

His eyes narrowed. "You're talking about Roselande," he said. "A thorn in my side ever since she came to this city. I thought I warned you to stay away from her."

"And I told you that I'm done living by your rules. I explained to Roselande how you've been extorting me. She wasn't surprised by your dishonesty. I guess you have a reputation."

Facilier's nostrils flared.

"Now that Daddy has passed on, I've decided it's time I finally accept some help in getting the restaurant that I've always dreamed of." She shrugged, striving to keep her voice calm and relaxed. "As much as I love our little supper club in Tremé, you know that I've had my heart set on that gorgeous old sugar mill on the river." She held up the vial so that the color was slightly distorted. It looked more pink than purple. "And this will help me to get it."

"How's that?" Facilier asked.

"Roselande promised that if I drink this, it will give

me the insight I need in order to convince the wealthiest people in town to invest in my restaurant. She assured me that her gifts matched those of your friends on the other side, because they come from a noble place. Unlike yours."

She could tell the words affected him by the expression that flashed across his face.

Her heart raced within her chest as she considered her next move. She'd come to know Facilier well enough over the past year to anticipate what he would do.

She peered at the vial. "All I have to do is drink it, and everything I've always wanted will be mine. However"—she cocked her head to the side—"I'm willing to make a deal of my own."

"What do you want?" Facilier asked.

"You know more about how these things work than I do, but I was thinking that maybe if we split it, we can *both* get what we want."

His eyes narrowed. "Why should I believe you? You have nothing to gain by giving me half of Roselande's potion."

"Well, unlike *some* people, I don't do things simply for my own gain." She shrugged again. "It's like you said: you gave me an entire year with my father that I would have never had. Maybe I am a fool, or maybe I'm too loyal for my own good, but it feels as if I *do* owe you for providing such a precious gift."

"Yes, you do," Facilier said. He extended both hands, going for the vial. "Give it to me."

"Not so fast." Tiana jerked it out of his reach. She had to make him think she believed he was still in control. "If you want this, you have to reverse every awful thing you've set in motion over the last year. The fog, the green sludge—all of it! And you have to tell me where to find the missing people. Addie Mae, Georgia, and Eugene. And Mr. Salvaggio and Mr. LaBouff. "

"Fine," he hissed, his eyes never leaving the vial. "They're all tied up in one of the back rooms."

He snapped his fingers, and just like that, they were back in his house.

Damn him. She knew it had been an illusion.

"As for the fog," Facilier continued. "Well, that's up to my friends on the other side. The fog will lift when they get what they want."

"What do they want?" Tiana asked.

Facilier stared at her with an intense, piercing look. "Your soul."

Tiana sucked in a swift, terrified breath, thrown off. "My what?" she whispered.

"Well, it doesn't have to be *your* soul," he quickly added. "It can belong to anyone; my friends on the other side won't care. There are thousands of chumps around this city who no one would ever miss if they just disappeared."

Like the people you kidnapped? Tiana wanted to rail at him, but she shook her head to keep her cool. She had a part to play, and if she slipped up, Facilier would know that she was on to him.

"Are you sure about this?" she asked, adding extra suspicion in her voice just to throw him off.

"Yes," he said impatiently, his eyes never leaving the vial. "But you *must* sign your name to the contract," Facilier added. "None of the horrors will end if you don't."

"What would they do with the soul once they have it?" she asked.

"That's not my concern, and it shouldn't be yours," Facilier said. "Are you ready, Tiana? One last deal."

His willingness to sacrifice some innocent person's soul alleviated the last prickle of conscience she felt over what she was about to do. This snake in the grass deserved everything that was coming to him.

"Okay," Tiana said. "I'll sign it."

She followed him to a wooden desk that held a lamp, and grabbed hold of the fountain pen he held out to her.

Tiana bent over the contract, turning her back slightly as she scribbled across the bottom of the scroll.

"Okay, it's done," she said. She turned and held the vial out to him. "Now, you drink half, and I'll drink half."

His eyes were bright with triumph as he snatched the vial from her hand, wrenched the cork out of it, and gulped down the entire contents.

He threw his head back and let out a peal of laughter.

But his laughter quickly died as he clutched at his throat and staggered several steps back.

Tiana held out the contract to him, the words *Goodbye, Shadow Man* scrawled on the signature line.

His eyes grew wide with panic, and he began to gasp for air. He backed up against the wall and slumped to the floor, his face becoming mottled, bright red splotches appearing all over it.

Tiana had to fight the innate urge to reach out and offer assistance, but what could she do? This was *his* potion. She had no idea what was in it or how to mitigate its effects.

She looked on in horror as Facilier's eyes glazed over. For a moment, Tiana thought he was dead, but then he began to mumble words she could just barely make out.

"Are . . . you . . . ready?" he murmured, the words thick and slurred as they left his tongue. "Are you . . . ready, Tiana?"

"I think that's a question for you to answer, Shadow Man."

As she stood over him, Tiana noticed her silhouette shrinking as the sun dipped below the horizon. The air turned ice cold. The sound of faint, indiscernible groans rumbled behind her, growing louder with each passing second. Fear and shock rooted Tiana's feet to the floor as the dark shadows slithered along the walls and floors.

Her mouth hung open in dismay as the Shadows wrapped themselves around Facilier's limp body and carried him out of the room.

50
Tiana

Tiana wasn't sure how long she stood there, her body too exhausted for her to consider moving even a single limb.

Had that really just happened? Was she actually—*finally*—free of Facilier? Even though she'd seen it with her own eyes, it was still hard to believe she'd eradicated him from her life once and for all.

She spotted the rolled-up sheaf of papers on the floor. She picked it up and unfurled the tattered pages, taking a moment to read over it. Tiana's breath caught in her throat as she absorbed the words, her heart thumping wildly as the enormity of the fate she'd just escaped sank in. She could have very well signed away her soul.

She gripped each end of the contract and tore the document in two. Then she tore it again. And again. And again. Each rip was like music to her ears.

It sounded like freedom.

"Tia! There you are!"

Tiana swung around, surprise and happiness lifting her heart at the sight of her friends. Charlotte led the charge, followed by Naveen, Louis, and Lisette.

"What are you all doing here?" Tiana exclaimed. But her voice held no censure. She was so happy to see them all, grateful they hadn't heeded her command to stay away.

Charlotte wrapped her arms around her. "Oh, Tia, I was so afraid for you. I went to see you when I heard about your daddy, and Lisette told me you'd left. I realized you must've gone after that awful man."

"I'm okay, Lottie. And we don't have to worry about Facilier anymore."

Charlotte jerked her head back and regarded Tiana, concern etched across her furrowed brow. "What happened?" Charlotte asked.

"He got out-tricked," Tiana answered, leaving it at that. No one else needed to know what had taken place in this room.

Naveen walked up to her and gently cradled Tiana's cheek in his warm palm. He brushed his thumb over her cheekbone. "You have been hurt, *ma poupette*," he said.

Tiana was surprised by the bright red blood glistening on his thumb when he pulled it away from her face. She had no idea when she'd been cut.

"It's . . . it's nothing," she said. "I'll be fine."

"Are you sure? Lisette!" he called over his shoulder.

"No, really, I'm fine," Tiana said. She turned to Charlotte and grabbed her by the shoulders. "Lottie, your daddy is here somewhere—and others, too. We just have to find them."

"What?" her friend gasped. "Where?"

"I don't know. Fan out," Tiana called to the group. "Search every nook and cranny. Facilier told me they were hidden in a room somewhere in this house."

She pivoted on her heel, setting out for the door just to the right of them, but Naveen caught her arm and pulled her back to him.

"Tiana, are you sure you're okay?" he asked. "At least let Lisette take a look at those scrapes."

His concern touched her. She was struck once again by how different he was from that self-absorbed cad he'd been when she had met him a year earlier. Despite her best efforts not to, she'd fallen in love with him then. It would be so very easy to love this kinder, more considerate Naveen.

Tiana's breath caught in her throat, and her eyes grew wide as it suddenly occurred to her that there was nothing stopping them from being together anymore. Facilier was gone, and with him the barrier keeping her and Naveen apart.

Tiana beamed up at him.

"I promise you that I am just fine," Tiana reassured him. She cradled his face between her hands. "I will explain as much as I can very soon, but right now we need to find those folks the Shadow Man kidnapped."

She grabbed him by the hand and headed for the rear of the house. The structure was so much larger than it had seemed from the unassuming entrance, stretching back at least a half block or more. Before Tiana could turn the knob of the first door she came across, she heard Louis's rousing call from somewhere down the long hallway.

"I think they're in here!" Louis called.

Tiana and Naveen raced to where Louis stood. Naveen put his ear to the door.

"Mr. LaBouff?"

There was a pause, and then a cacophony of muffled cries clamored from just beyond the door.

"Yes, they are here," Naveen said excitedly. He tried the

door handle, but it was locked. No matter how violently he wrenched at it, it wouldn't budge. "Should we search for a key?"

"In this house?" Tiana asked. "That could take a lifetime. Who knows where the key to this door may be hidden?"

Or, even worse, what if Facilier had taken the key with him to the other side?

"Maybe we can knock it down?" Louis suggested.

"Outta my way," Lisette demanded, pushing her way through. She reached under the cloth covering her hair bun and retrieved a hairpin, then stuck the pin inside the lock and jiggled it. There was a click. She turned the knob and pushed the door open.

For a moment, no one moved. They were all stunned at the sight before them. Eli LaBouff, Addie Mae, Georgia, Eugene, and Mr. Salvaggio sat on the floor with their backs against the wall and their hands tied together with twine. Ragged pieces of cloth covered their mouths, preventing them from talking. And they were filthy, with dirt and grime streaking their faces.

"Big Daddy!"

Charlotte rushed into the room and threw her arms around her father.

"Let's get him untied first, Lottie," Tiana suggested.

She, Naveen, and Lisette made quick work of untangling the knots and setting the five of them loose from the bonds Facilier had used to imprison them.

"Where is he?" Mr. LaBouff said, scrabbling from the floor.

"It's okay, Daddy," Charlotte said. "You don't have to worry about him. Tiana took care of Facilier."

"That's right. No one has to worry about the Shadow Man again," Tiana said. She turned to Addie Mae and wrapped her friend up in a hug. She turned to Georgia and Eugene and did the same. "I am so, so sorry for what he did to all of you. It's over now."

But as she stood there with her arms around her loved ones, Tiana realized that it wasn't over. Her heartache was beginning anew as reality sank in. She would once again have to endure the pain of living in this world without her father.

As she waited for the soul-crushing grief to envelop her, an odd thing happened. The grief failed to materialize. Instead, she felt . . . joy. An overwhelming sense of peace weaved its way around her sadness.

Tiana knew she would always miss her daddy, but the hole his passing had left in her heart wasn't as hollow this time around. It was filled with memories of the past year—the laughs they'd shared, the meals they'd prepared together, and the all-encompassing love they'd experienced every single day. And a true goodbye.

Tiana closed her eyes tight, holding onto those memories. They would be with her always. Just as her daddy would be with her.

Always.

A muted rumble sounded from somewhere in the distance. Tiana tipped her head to the side to hear it better.

"What is that?" she asked. The growing noise quickly became clearer. It was the sound of a jazz band playing and the roar of a crowd.

"That's Mardi Gras you're hearing," Louis answered. "Time for me to get my horn and join in the parade!"

"I guess a little fog and green scum ain't enough to stop Mardi Gras," Charlotte said. "Come on, Lisette," she said, taking the girl by the arm. "We don't want to miss the floats!"

Tiana followed the others out of Facilier's home.

"The fog," Lisette said once outside. "It's gone."

"So is that nasty green stuff from the river," Charlotte remarked.

"Sure is," said a guy standing next to them on the sidewalk, bobbing his head to music from the band. "Most peculiar thing. Just as the sun went down, that fog rolled out as quickly as it rolled it. Same goes for the algae from the river."

Sundown?

"Symmetry," Tiana whispered.

"What was that?" Naveen asked.

"Nothing," she said. She looked up at him and smiled. Then she tipped her head toward where the others had wandered off, following the marching band and crowd of costumed revelers as they made their way through the French Quarter.

"What do you say?" Tiana asked. "You want to join the parade?"

Naveen's brow furrowed. "Are you sure you're not too tired?"

"Nope." She shook her head. "I've realized just how short life is. I think I should let my hair down for a change." She winked and held her hand out to him. "Let's go have some fun."

51

Naveen

The Kingdom of Maldonia
Three months later

Naveen could not hold back his smile as the car traveled along the tree-lined boulevard leading up to the grandiose entrance of the Grand Palace of Maldonia. The white marble dome atop the massive, two-hundred-room royal residence sparkled like a newly harvested pearl. After a three-week journey aboard a passenger ship and more than a year in America, the sight of his family's home brought more joy than he had anticipated.

The car rounded the reflection pool and fountain, coming to a stop before the twenty-foot, gold-plated doors.

"Ah, it's good to be home," Naveen said. He looked around at the other occupants in the car, who all sat in stunned silence. "What is wrong?" he asked.

"What *is* this place?" Lisette asked, her eyes wide with wonder as she stared out of the car's window.

Naveen shrugged. "It is home."

"This makes Big Daddy's house look like a shoebox," Charlotte said.

"I can't believe you grew up living in a place like this," Tiana said. She looked over at him. "Then again, yes I can."

Naveen threw his head back and guffawed at the car's ceiling.

"This looks like a place with really tasty food," Louis said.

"That it is." Naveen laughed again. "Come on. Let us go in. I'm sure my family is eager to see us, and if I know my mother, she has instructed the cooks to lay out a feast for the ages."

They were greeted by the king and queen the moment they walked into the palace. Naveen was staggered by the rush of emotion that hit him the minute he saw their faces. Formalities were brushed aside as he wrapped his mother and father in a hug.

"I've missed you," he said.

His younger siblings flooded the grand entrance, embracing him like a prodigal son returning. Which, he guessed, he was.

As Naveen predicted, his parents had ordered a grand celebration to mark their son's return home—temporary though it was. He'd informed them before he boarded the ship that he had chosen to make New Orleans his permanent home.

At Lisette's insistence, Naveen took their guests on a tour of the palace, including a drive around the hundred-acre estate. By the time they returned, more than fifty of his closest friends and family had arrived for the celebration.

Naveen felt conspicuous dressed in his traditional royal regalia, but one look at Tiana's face when he walked in the grand ballroom changed his mind. Following dinner, he immediately escorted her to the dance floor, where they waltzed until his father finally cut in.

Now, Naveen stood at the periphery of the dance floor, leaning against one of the marble columns and observing the guests enjoying themselves. His mother came up to him and patted his arm with her gloved hand.

"How are you, son?" she asked.

"I'm well, Mother," Naveen answered.

"You look well. And you look happy." She glanced over

at Tiana, who studied the traditional Maldonia folk dance his younger sisters were trying to teach her. "Does she have something to do with that?"

"She does," Naveen answered, unable to suppress the grin that drew across his lips. "I am in love with her, Mother. She is . . . my everything."

She arched a regal brow. "Now I understand why you turned down our invitation to return." She tipped her head to the side. "Should I expect a wedding and grandchildren soon?"

"Mother!" Naveen felt himself blush.

"You cannot fault me for asking." She looked over at Tiana again. "They will be lovely grandchildren." Her eyes lit up with excitement. "It will be fun to spoil them."

"Please do not speak of such things with Tiana," Naveen said. "We have only been together a few months. I have not brought up the subject of marriage."

"What are you waiting for? Get on with it."

He chuckled. "I will. Soon." Then he sobered. "You know, Mother, there are other reasons that I have chosen to remain in America. None more important than Tiana, of course."

"Of course," she said.

"But I like the person that I have become over this past year. I learned that I'm really good at selling things and helping others," he said with a laugh. "See Lisette over there? I just helped broker a deal for her to sell her homemade medicinals in the biggest department store in New Orleans.

"I like my job. It feels good to know that I can make my own way in this world, and do some good in it, too." Naveen shook his head. "I never thought I would say this, but I want to thank you and Father for cutting me off. It turns out that is exactly what I needed."

His mother cupped his cheek. "I am proud of you, son. I always knew you could accomplish anything once you discovered your heart's true desire. Well, at least I'd hoped that would be the case," she amended with a laugh. "Just know there is always a place for you here. You can always come home."

Naveen caught sight of a sparkling blue dress out of the corner of his eye. He looked over and saw Tiana walking toward them.

"I have found my home," Naveen said.

"Oh, yes." His mother patted his cheek. "My grand-children will be lovely."

She nodded and smiled at Tiana before drifting off to mingle with the other guests.

Naveen took Tiana by the hand and walked her out onto the balcony that overlooked the extensive ornamental gardens below.

"So are you enjoying your first night in the royal palace?" Naveen asked.

"What do you think?" she returned, a hint of sass in her voice.

"Well, I would hope you are, but I can also understand if it's a bit too much. My sisters can be a handful."

"They are lovely, and so are your parents, and that adorable little brother of yours. I think he has a crush on Lottie."

Naveen laughed. "He is a charmer, that one."

"I wonder where he gets that from?" She winked at him, then walked over to the marble balustrade and leaned against it. Looking up at the sky, she said, "Doesn't it amaze you that these stars we're staring at here in Maldonia are the same stars they're looking at back in N'awlins? It really puts things into perspective when you think about it."

"It does," Naveen said. "It tells me that no matter where I am, I can be connected to home if I just look up at the stars."

"And what a lovely home it is," Tiana said.

He shrugged. "It's okay."

"Okay? Do you want my honest opinion?"

"Of course. Always."

"I can't believe you would choose to live in that dusty little apartment in N'awlins when you could live here."

"It is not the apartment that is keeping me in New Orleans," Naveen said.

She turned to him, her smile demure, though there was a twinkle in her eye. "Is that so? What else is there that could even compare to this?"

"Come now, Tiana," Naveen said, taking her by the hands. The moon shone down on them, illuminating her beautiful face. "I don't have to tell you that I would give up all the money in the world to be with you."

"Would you really?" she asked.

"In a heartbeat," Naveen said. He leaned forward until his forehead met hers. Staring into her eyes, he said, "There is nothing that I would not do for you."

She regarded him with a devilish grin. "I'm gonna remind you of that when I make you wash dishes at the new restaurant."

Naveen frowned. "Did I say there was *nothing* I wouldn't do?"

"That's right," Tiana said. "And it's too late to take it back."

Then she claimed his lips in a sweet, tender kiss.

"I can't wait to see that new restaurant in action. *Your* palace," Naveen said when they broke apart.

Tiana grinned slowly. "Tiana's Palace—I like the sound of that."

Epilogue
Tiana

New Orleans, 1928
Mardi Gras

"How's it looking out there, Mama?"

"Like all the Mardi Gras revelers have converged on this place," Eudora said. "The line of people waiting for tables stretches all the way to the French Quarter. You'd better put on a second pot of gumbo, because you have a whole lot of hungry mouths to feed."

"That's just the way I like it," Tiana said as she added

a few dashes of Tabasco to the pot. Her daddy's dinged-up pot might not shine like the new copper and steel cookware in her gleaming kitchen, but Tiana refused to use anything else to cook her gumbo.

She could barely hear the band over the din of the noisy kitchen, but she found herself rocking to the faint sound of the traditional Mardi Gras song they were currently playing. She had requested their playlist include only the liveliest tunes. Tonight was a celebration, and she was determined to enjoy every single moment of it.

Tiana's Palace was filled to capacity yet again, just as it had been every single night for the past two weeks, ever since its grand opening. It truly was the place to be, with some of the city's most elite clamoring for a seat at one of her tables.

Just the day before, the newspaper had published a front-page story on the new restaurant that had everyone talking. Tiana's decision to employ an all-female staff—save for the Crawfish Crooners, who would always have a place on the bandstand—was the type of thing that made news from Baton Rouge to Mississippi. Some were skeptical, but many others applauded such a unique idea.

However, it was the food that had people lining up for a table. All her daddy's favorites were on the menu, and the people of this town couldn't seem to get enough. A reservation at Tiana's Palace was the most sought-after thing in all of New Orleans.

"Addie Mae, can you watch the gumbo while I go out to greet some of the guests?" Tiana asked her head chef.

"Sure thing, Tiana! You tell Mr. LaBouff that his oysters will be right up."

After suffering from nightmares for months following her rescue from the Shadow Man's dungeon, Addie Mae had taken some time to recuperate. She'd felt ready to return to work just as Tiana closed the deal to buy the old sugar mill she'd always dreamed of owning. The man the Fenner brothers had sold it to a couple of years before had decided to leave New Orleans—but not before enjoying an evening of good music and even better food at the supper club. When he'd learned it was Tiana who had put in an offer the very same day it went on the market, he'd sold it to her on the spot.

She'd never lost hope that the place would one day be hers. She'd felt it in her bones.

And now it was.

She would have pinched herself, but she already knew this wasn't a dream. This was real life, and she was embracing it all.

Tiana untied her apron from around her waist and went out into the grand dining room. It had taken a lot of blood, sweat, and tears to get it to this point, but with the help of her friends, her restaurant looked exactly as she had always imagined it would.

She was still a work in progress when it came to relying on others for help, but she was getting better at it. Especially after the experience she'd had with renovating this place. Naveen, Louis, Lisette, and Charlotte had been by her side every single evening, polishing light fixtures and refinishing the tables. Even Maddy, Georgia, and Eugene had come by a few times, sweeping and mopping and sanding down the floors.

Tiana started her rounds at their table. Georgia and the gang had a standing invitation to dine whenever they wanted to, no reservation needed.

"How're y'all doing tonight?" Tiana asked.

"This place is hopping," Maddy said. "I know Donald will be sorry he missed this."

"From what I hear, he's found good luck up there in Detroit. I'm guessing it won't be long before you join him up there," Tiana said. She winked at Maddy, who blushed like a schoolgirl. "I'll see you all a bit later. Don't leave without trying my newest creation, Mardi Gras beignets. They're covered with praline sauce!"

She left her old schoolmates and went over to Mr. LaBouff, who was holding court, as usual.

"Hey there, Mr. LaBouff. Addie Mae said to tell you that your oysters will be right out. Although I really think you should try on one of the other dishes for size. Addie Mae makes a mean muffuletta."

"Nope." He shook his head and cradled his ample belly. "Bring on the oysters Rockefeller. Or oysters LaBouff, as I like to call them."

Tiana laughed. "Coming right up."

She stopped by Mr. Salvaggio's table to check in on him and his wife, then went over to Roselande, who had joined Lisette that evening.

The girl had really come into her own since she'd moved to New Orleans that past year. Maison Blanche had dedicated an entire display case to her products. People around town claimed that Lisette's skin cream was the perfect balm for skin burned by the hot Louisiana sun.

"Tia! Tia!" Tiana turned at Charlotte's call. Her friend ran up to her and enveloped her in a hug. "Oh, Tia, it all looks wonderful in here. I'm so happy I made it back from Baton Rouge in time for your big Mardi Gras celebration. What a perfect way to end this perfect day!"

"Based on that smile, I take it your speech at the State Capitol went well," Tiana said. "I hope you gave them hell, Lottie."

"You know I did!" Charlotte said.

Tiana's heart swelled with pride as she listened to her friend recount her impassioned speech to the state legislators on behalf of the Federation of Civic Leagues. Lottie had joined the group last year after organizing a campaign to bring better conditions to the schools in communities like Tremé and the Ninth Ward. But she no longer limited herself to New Orleans. Charlotte had begun to travel around the entire state of Louisiana, fighting for those less fortunate.

But she hadn't given up on finding herself a duke. She'd booked a passage on a luxury cruise liner to England leaving after the Easter holiday.

It took Tiana another half hour to visit the rest of the tables in the dining room, but she made it a point to drop in on each one of them. She was convinced that the key to her restaurant's success—besides the food—was the hospitality. Each patron at Tiana's Palace knew they were appreciated.

She returned to the kitchen to get started on desserts. A few minutes later, Eudora walked through the door.

"Do you need a rest, Mama?" Tiana said as she drizzled praline syrup on the order of beignets she'd just made.

"No, baby. You know I stopped sewing to embrace the excitement of the restaurant business."

"Well, that's not the only reason you're here," Tiana said with a laugh. She rounded the cooking station and enveloped her mother in a hug.

"No, it isn't," Eudora said. She and Tiana stared up at the portrait of her daddy that hung on the wall, looking down over the entire kitchen. "I'm here because this is exactly where he would want me to be."

"And it's exactly where I want you to be, too. What did that man from the paper call you? The queen of Tiana's Palace?"

"Well, he's right," her mother replied with no small amount of sass.

Then she and Tiana burst out laughing.

"Ah, what has my two favorite ladies in New Orleans in such a good mood?" Naveen greeted as he came upon them.

Tiana turned around. "The band taking a break?"

"Only because I insisted," Naveen said. "If it were up to Louis, he would have us playing nonstop all night long."

"That's because he's doing what he loves," Tiana said.

After much soul-searching, Louis had decided to remain in New Orleans instead of petitioning Mama Odie to help him change back into a gator. But he still took his boat out to the swamp every so often, just to be closer to the place where he'd grown up.

Naveen put an arm around Tiana's shoulders and pulled her in to his side.

"I only have ten minutes, so I want to make the most of

it. Mother," he said to Eudora. "If you do not mind, I am going to steal my wife away for a bit."

"As long as you bring her back before the second dinner rush," Eudora said.

"I promise."

"Where are you taking me?" Tiana asked.

"To the best view in all of New Orleans," he said.

Five minutes later, she and Naveen were standing at the railing of the restaurant's outside balcony. She stood with her back to his chest, his arms wrapped around her. Tiana rested her head back, listening contently to the beat of his heart as she watched boats of all kinds floating along the river, their lights twinkling among the waves.

"This really is beautiful," she said.

"Very, very beautiful," Naveen replied. She looked up to find him looking at her, not the river.

He dipped his head and placed a gentle kiss upon her lips.

"Tell me. Are you happy, my love?"

"I am," she answered. "So much happier than I ever imagined I could be."

Not too long before, she would have maintained that no matter how well things were going, she would never be truly happy again, because her father was no longer with her.

But he *was* here. She felt him every time she walked into the kitchen at this restaurant. She felt him whenever she walked into her mother's house in the Ninth Ward, or when she was in the house she and Naveen shared uptown.

She felt him everywhere.

And because she knew his spirit would always be with her, no matter how far she traveled or how long they were apart, Tiana now knew true happiness.

She took Naveen's hand and squeezed it, taking in the view.

She'd learned a lot about letting go that past year. About not holding on to the past and embracing what fate had in store. About taking pride in a hard day's work, but also taking time to rest and find peace in the quiet moments of the day.

Most of all, she'd learned the importance of spending time with those she loved. She now understood just how precious time was, and that it wasn't promised.

Another Mardi Gras, and once more she was forever changed. It was just as Roselande had said: symmetry was the universe's way. And Tiana looked forward to what new transformations the future—and she—would bring.